No Cure Required

New City Series, Book 5

By Stefanie Simpson

Contents

Since I suffer with pleasure, why should I complain,
Or grieve at my fate, when I know it's in vain?
Yet so pleasing the pain is so soft as the dart,
That at once it both wounds and tickles my heart

~ HENRY PURCELL, LOVE IS A SWEET PASSION

Thank you, sweet love, for I am yours.

We are seen.

ACKNOWLEDGEMENTS

Thank you to everyone for the support in creating this book, in particular, Sarah Smith who is a joy, and Heather Lynn who is a champion. Brooke Winters, Anne Pyle, and Christopher Jacob for beta-ing. And Elisa Winthers whose insight and hard truths helped me enormously.

I am deeply humbled and thankful for all the support I've received.

Thank you as ever to the Writers of Twitter, and the Witlings.

By Stefanie Simpson

FOREWORD

I've been chronically ill for many years, but a few years ago my health deteriorated, and though I'll not go into the details, I was afraid. I'd been writing for a while, but I constantly wrote to deal with my fear. I wanted to finish something, to have something of myself in the world before it was too late.

This book was a long time coming, and in it is a disabled heroine with fibromyalgia. Writing this was hard, but worth it because I see myself in a book.

However, my experience of fibro is not a universal indicator of everyone's experience with chronic illness, it is different for everyone who lives with it. I would never claim to speak for others, but I do claim to speak for myself and my experiences, and that is valid.

My struggle, my pain, my acceptance, for good and ill are mine, and I choose to share them with you. It is not easy to do.

I hope anyone who reads this takes away some form of universal understanding and reality. You'll not find an abled point of view about disability. There's no inspiration porn, tragi-masturbation fodder for ableds to feel better about themselves, if you're looking for that, this isn't the book for you.

I will not apologise for my honesty because putting myself in this position is a risk. To be vulnerable fills me with unease yet it was something I had to do, so be kind.

By Stefanie Simpson

Please note, this book contains graphic adult sexual content, including BDSM. Strong language. Adult themes, including references to coercive relationships, depictions of suffering, toxic family members, familial death, grief, and physical suffering. Please be assured, it'll be okay.

HOPES

Willow drove out of Harringly West like she was on fire. Finally. It had taken more than a year to get to this point, but it was necessary.

She said goodbye to her parents, goodbye to her life, and hoped for the best. Not that she had any idea what she was doing. For all her bravado, she was terrified. Oh well. Willow zipped up the motorway and sat-nav'ed her way to Chadford New City.

A huge risk, but the payoff would be worth it.

As she pulled into the ARC Foundation's carpark three hours later, exhausted and dizzy, she closed her eyes and rested her head on the steering wheel.

Tapping woke her. She blearily squinted into the light and wound the window down of her old red hatchback, making the glass screech.

"Miss, can I help you?" The security guard had a pleasant face, but he was the size of a bulldozer.

"I'm Willow Morris. I'm here to see Danni."

The bulldozer smiled. "She's been waiting for you. Come on."

Willow drank some tepid water from the bottle next to her and rubbed her face. Her legs seized, and she eased out of the car with difficulty. This was why she didn't often drive; the pain after all that concentrating and tension in her legs was a bitch. Grabbing her sleek black cane, she managed to stand, stretching her back and hobbled along after the security guard.

"I'm Dave."

"Nice to meet you, Dave."

The world warped, her vision spun, and she focused on walking in a straight line, which she managed, more or less.

By Stefanie Simpson

The ARC foundation was an old rundown building near the industrial side of Chadford, north of the river. Not being a residential area had its advantages, it was easy to spot people lurking, and being remote gave a lot of the people that came to ARC some peace of mind.

Willow didn't class herself as strictly a woman fleeing from abuse, but she wasn't far from it.

Danni, who greeted her, was a short solid woman with a bowl haircut and glasses Willow was sure were from the eighties. The manager of ARC had a reassuring presence; a pillar that you could lean on.

"We were starting to worry," she said, shaking Willow's hand.

"I was tired, sorry."

"No, no, I understand. You must be exhausted." Danni peered over her glasses.

"I am."

"Well, we won't keep you too long. Your temporary accommodation is ready, and I've set you an appointment to view a house match in two weeks. The paperwork needs to be gone through, but it should be fine."

Willow nodded, already struggling to keep up. The driving took more out of her than she thought.

Danni guided her to a comfortable chair in her office, and Willow sank into it.

She doubted herself; maybe she was foolish upending her life.

"Willow?"

"Hmm?" She blinked and paid attention. "I'm sorry."

"I think we should get someone to drive you to the bed and breakfast." Danni frowned. Her motherly look reassured Willow, and she wanted to go to sleep. Her legs were aching, and the dead pain ran through her nerves, up the back of her legs and caught her breath.

"No, it'll be fine."

"It's not safe for you to drive, is it? I'd put you in the secure residential hostel, but there are no beds. Don't worry, I know the person, he'll get you safely to where you need to go."

Danni smiled, and Willow closed her eyes.

She woke a while later, confused. She wasn't in bed, and this wasn't home.

Blinking, she let her vision focus and felt like absolute crap. Tasting her mouth, she stretched, and as her blurry, warped vision sharpened, a man was standing in front of her. Her breath caught, eyes wide, and fear crept up her throat.

He put his hands up with a gentle look on his face. He was tall, broad, and dark haired. He wore a polo shirt that barely contained his muscles. She wondered how much time he spent in the gym for a body like that. Light golden skin, dark eyes, stubble, slightly pointy face, but gorgeous. He really was.

Willow's mouth flapped, and she cleared her throat. "Hi."

"Hello," he said with a scowl.

She shivered.

"I'm Matthew Denbridge. We do security for ARC. Danni said you needed some help."

"Oh, I'm sure I can manage."

"I'm sure you can, but she doesn't ask personal favours from me often. I frighten most people here." He shrugged a shoulder. "But there's nobody about today. I'll drive you to the B&B." He put his hand out, and she looked at it.

When she didn't take it, he let his hand drop and stepped back with a frown. "You're not one of those are you?"

"Excuse me?"

"Unnecessarily independent."

Willow went cold. "I'm not a fan of strange men offering to drive me places, to be perfectly honest."

"You think Danni would let just anyone in here?"

"I suppose not."

She struggled to get up from the low chair until Matthew leant down, took her shoulders, and lifted her like she weighed nothing, and helped her stand.

Her ears rushed, and she lost her footing.

He held her upright.

"Let go," her words slurred, "I don't like being manhandled."

"My apologies." He let her go, and she fell back into the chair.

They looked at each other for a moment, and she burst out laughing. Matthew stared at her. Willow picked up her cane and rocked forward.

"May I please assist you?"

"Fine."

Helping her out of the chair made her head spin, and all the blood fell out of her head. Matthew put his arm around her and held her. Her face pressed into his chest. Laundry, deodorant, steady heartbeat.

She did something odd then; she relaxed. The only thought that came to mind was safety. He was a sturdy comfort. Some random stranger. She must have been beyond tired.

"Ready?" He gave her a minute, and when he spoke, the sound reverberated through his massive chest. What was wrong with her?

"Ready," she mumbled, and letting her go, he steadied her by the shoulders. Taking her free arm, he looped it through his, and she hobbled along, pain shooting through her.

"Are you okay?"

"My pain's bad, it's hard to walk." She took a few deep breaths.

"I can carry you."

"Huh?" She looked up at him. Willow wasn't short, five-foot-six, but he was ridiculous. "I'm far too heavy." Willow was curved, all hips and tits. Containing them was always a challenge.

"Nonsense. I can carry you."

"Really? I doubt it, pal."

He grinned with knowing smug arrogance. "Want to bet?"

Willow narrowed her eyes. There were never going to be many times in her life when a big sexy wall of muscle would carry her about. Might as well make the most of it. "What do I win?"

With a laugh, he shook his head. "I don't know, what would you like?"

Willow clung onto his arm staring, she felt the heat in her cheeks, knowing how red she'd be. She lifted her chin. "Go on. Try it."

Leaning closer, he turned slightly, and his face came close to hers. "Brace yourself." He bent low, put one arm under her knees and the other around her back and under one arm, and hoisted her up.

She yelped.

He straightened and raised his eyebrows. "See."

"Fine. Can you walk all the way to my car, though?" She clutched her stick and handbag on her lap while she was squished into his hold. It was nice, actually.

He strode out like he was carrying a delicate little kitten. Willow, torn between totally impressed, turned on, and mortified, couldn't take her eyes off him.

"Which one is yours?" Not an ounce of strain in his voice.

"Who are you?"

With an open face, he glanced down at her. "Just your average security guy. Which one is your car?"

Willow laughed with ease. It was a lifetime since she'd done that. "The hatchback that looks like it should be scrapped. Used to be red."

"Ah, I see it."

Matthew set her down, and she leant against the car as she ferreted out her keys and he unlocked it. The door opened with a loud crack.

"It always does that, ever since it fell off."

"Does it have its MOT?"

"Yes. Though when the next one is due in two months, it won't. I only needed it to get here. I don't often drive."

He nodded, and she got in the passenger side. Matthew squeezed into the driver's seat and spent several minutes trying to move the seat back and adjusted the mirrors. "At least I'm fully comp. Do you have insurance for this thing?"

"I think so. It's not my car."

"Whose car is it?" Every question he asked went higher in tone.

Willow bit the inside of her cheek. "My dad's, actually. It's the run around for the estate."

"What do you mean, estate?" Matthew managed to start the car.

Her humour evaporated, and Willow didn't answer at first, unwilling to share so much. "It's complicated."

"Are you okay?" They turned out onto the main road, and Willow took in her new home as they wound along the ring-road and out again into Downly, part of the Greater Chadford area.

The winding roads and old buildings were nice as they made their way.

"Hopefully."

"Danni's a great person and if she can help someone, she will. ARC is a wonderful charity."

"They are. How long have you worked for them?"

"Oh, I don't. Denbridge Security volunteer time. They had some problems in the past. I know Danni from way back, always kept in touch. I offered to help her out."

"It's your company?"

"I'm the boss."

"Wow. Thank you, for helping me. You must be busy."

"Never too busy for Danni."

The double-fronted dark brick building was covered in ivy with an arch at the front gate.

"It's pretty," she said as Matthew pulled into the car park. "Wait, how will you get back?"

"Someone's picking me up. Let's get you settled."

"I can manage."

He stared at her with a blank face.

"Okay," she drew it out as she said it.

He rewarded her with a grin. Willow inwardly sighed. Oh dear.

Recovered enough to walk into the B&B, Willow sorted out her check-in while Matthew brought her two suitcases, one storage box, and a holdall.

Her room, on the ground floor annexe at the back of the building, was a small self-contained bedsit. At least she had her own shower and toilet. It was enough until her house match was sorted out.

When Matthew put all the things in the room, they looked at each other.

"Right. Will you be okay?"

"Yes. Thank you for all your help. I appreciate it."

"You're welcome. Here," he fished his wallet out and handed her a business card. "My friends call me Matt. I don't know your story, or why you've come to ARC, but people do for a reason. If you ever need any help, you're in trouble, or too tired to drive, give me a call. If I can't help, there'll be someone who can."

"That's very kind of you, but–"

"No, promise me."

She looked up at him, the golden tone of his skin and straight black thick hair was cast in shadow. He looked somewhere between dangerous and reassuring. She'd never met anyone like that. He was beautiful in a very masculine way.

"I promise. Thank you, Matt." She offered a small smile. She wished she was prettier and less like a loser. Willow shrugged off her doubt, the very real voice that held her back and kept her a virtual prisoner for the past ten years, but she wasn't that Willow anymore. For a moment, he kept still, eyes narrowed, assessing. She wanted to shrivel away, but stood straight instead, meeting his stare. He cleared his throat and turned about, examining the room.

She repeated the words that had sustained her for the past few months: Fuck pity. Nor was she too proud to accept the help that she needed when she needed it. It was why she was in Chadford. If Matt's pity got her something she needed, so what, she'd use what she could in any way. Being disabled didn't give her many advantages, so she might as well take any help that was offered.

"Well then, I'll leave you in peace."

"Thank you for this."

"You're very welcome, and remember if you need anything, please call." He tilted his head, and he made Willow's heart beat harder. Or that could be exhaustion, she couldn't be sure.

With a smile, Matt left her, and stripping her clothes off, she crawled into bed and went to sleep.

Matt reluctantly let the woman go, he had a compelling desire to stay with her and make sure she was okay. He wasn't sure it was even a sexual impulse, he merely wanted to help her. He thought of his mother, he thought of ARC, and perhaps she reminded him of the past.

Willow was vulnerable and raw. He saw it in her huge brown eyes. She was beautiful with quiet, understated beauty. The way she held her ground was tremulous, but that made him want to chase her, he smiled to himself as he waited in the warm sun.

His lift arrived, and Josh, face hidden by a cap and long blond hair under it, turned the car and eased out into traffic. "What's up?"

Matt turned to him as he drove. Josh barely spoke, his fire-hoarse voice grated in his throat whenever he used it.

"A woman."

Josh nodded.

With a sigh, Matt rested his head back. "I don't know her story, but there's something."

Josh's silence was his reply.

"I should stay away from her."

"Hmm."

Matt laughed. "Yeah, yeah. I know."

Matt should stay away from her. He decided to do that, after all, it's not like she was staying at ARC, and the odds of meeting her again were pretty small. Right?

SOCIAL

The first two weeks of Willow's new life were mostly spent recovering from the past few months. Allowing herself time to process everything and rest. Physically and mentally.

By the time she'd pulled herself out of her funk, she was moderately recovered.

Willow had been in touch with Danni several times, and with everything in motion, she went to meet her potential housemates.

The house match programme was designed to match people new to Chadford via ARC with appropriate homes.

It sounded like a cat rescue to Willow when she first came across it, but the more she read, the more it seemed like the thing that would help her the most.

ARC wasn't only a women's refuge; they were a place for vulnerable people to go. Trans, gay, homeless, disabled; anyone who found themselves in a vulnerable position. Willow never thought of herself as vulnerable, but the last years had shown her that she was. People could not be trusted.

Willow poured out the whole sordid history to Danni on the phone, unable to reach out to anyone in her family who wasn't on her side. She was Willow, the disappointment and disabled failure. Danni set everything into motion along with a few people to whom Willow reached out, and they'd helped her. More than she ever hoped for.

It took ten minutes to start her car, and she drove out further out of Chadford.

The winding roads and old houses thinned out into farmland, and off a main road, sitting back in long-established gardens was a large Edwardian house.

Blackthorn Villa was beautiful. With large windows, and a huge front door in a porch.

She parked on the drive, secretly pleased. It was lovely, private, and quiet. Pub and shop at the end of the road with a bus stop into town.

This might be her new home. A place where she would be safe.

Taking a deep breath, she eased out of the car, grabbing her cane and handbag, and made her slow way to the front door. She pressed the old bell, feeling a pit of nerves in her stomach.

"You must be Willow," a tall, beautiful woman said when the door opened, and Willow found herself stretching her back upright to meet her eye. "I'm Darby." She stepped back, and Willow hobbled in and took in the hallway. Minton tiles, ornately carved staircase, and immaculate mouldings.

"This is beautiful."

"Thanks."

Willow looked at Darby again. She had a perfect figure, full wide mouth, and large eyes. Her skin was a rich umber, and her hair meticulously and finely braided, coiled on her head and wrapped in a red scarf that matched her lipstick.

She should have been on a magazine cover.

Willow, with her shorter body, dull mid-brown hair, boring face, and oh yes, the disability. Willow shrivelled in on herself, but Darby grinned warmly.

"Come on, Jane is in the kitchen."

She followed behind and caught sight of the stair lift. This might be okay.

The kitchen at the back of the house was warm and bright. Patio doors were open, and a grey long-haired cat lounged in a sunbeam, tail swishing lazily. Plants were scattered about, and the smell of fresh bread grew strong.

Jane was tidying up and looked over at them.

"Willow!" She took her apron off and enveloped Willow in a warm hug, which made Willow go still. "Tea?"

"Yes please." Willow took her in. Jane was a little taller than her, pale with lilac-grey hair, large framed glasses and a tattoo sleeve.

"We're so glad you're here."

Willow cleared her throat and laughed. "Me too. Can I sit down?"

"Of course, you don't have to ask."

Willow flopped into a dining chair and rested her arms on the table.

"Are you all right?"

"I've been driving, and I'm tired."

"Here, have some cake. Sugar and gluten-free. That's right, isn't it?"

"Yes. That's so kind, you didn't need to do that."

The two women joined her at the table. Jane poured the tea, and Darby dished up the cake. The cat got up and jumped on the table, and Darby shooed her off. "Princess, you pest."

Princess purred and found a new spot to bask in, watching the intruder.

"Here's the thing," said Darby, "this is Jane's house, and we've been friends for years. We need a third person for the living costs."

Jane slid over the cup and plate to Willow. "I was made redundant a few months ago, and my grandmother died a few months before that. She lived here, and I worked and took care of her for years."

"I'm sorry."

"Thanks." She picked at her cake. "I don't want to lose this house, it's important to me, so we thought of having a lodger. We thought this charity house match idea would be perfect. We have a stair lift, and the bedroom is at the back, nice and quiet. You have your own adapted bathroom. I mean they told us about your needs for having fibro, so I think we have what you need. We've been worried though. About what you think of us."

"Are you a couple?"

"No, actually. I mean, we're both gay, but we're best friends."

Darby laughed. "We've known each other for years. We're not talking about that. We have a specific circle of friends, and we're unconventional."

"Like a women's group?"

Jane hesitated and sipped her tea. "No. There are men and other genders in the group, but we don't all associate with each other. It's that sometimes we hang out together. Often here, because of the space."

"Okay. I mean, it's your house. I'm not that social, so I'm quite happy to be in my room."

"Some of our friends are weirdos. In a good way."

"Most people think I'm pretty weird, to be honest."

"Good." Jane grinned. "Well, I have my own business, it was a pastime I did before when I could, but now I'm making it my business, so I'm about a lot."

Willow picked at her cake. "I start work soon. It's only two days a week at ARC. I couldn't manage more right now."

Jane showed Willow the house. It was beautiful. A large 'drawing room' with nice settees and piles of books was the most comfortable room Willow had ever seen. It reminded her of home, but more welcoming.

She shook it off as she tested out the stair lift.

The bedroom was bright and airy, with wooden shutters at the large window. It was dotted with wooden furniture.

"I love it." Willow relaxed. She could live here, independently, alone but with people. She hoped they were as nice as they seemed.

The small but perfectly laid out wet room, complete with a fold-out seat made Willow happy, and she eyed the big bath, looking forward to sinking into it. It would be physically easier to live here.

"Well?"

"When can I bring my stuff?"

Jane grinned, rolling her tongue piercing through her teeth. "What do you think of Darby?"

"I think she's the most beautiful woman I have ever met, both of you are. I'm very dull in comparison."

"You think I'm beautiful?" Jane laughed.

"Yeah."

"Smoke and Mirrors. And whenever you want."

The three women sat in the garden later. Willow sat in a comfy lounger, resting her legs before driving back to her temporary housing, Jane sprawled out on the lawn, and Darby gracefully sat in a wicker chair that she dragged outside.

"You want to ask about the fibro?" Willow thought it was best to get it out the way.

"No, it's not our business."

"If I live here then you should know. I fall over a lot. My balance isn't always great. I have a fair amount of pain. Sometimes I throw up or get headaches. My vision is okay. I went through a bad patch a few years ago, and it debilitated me. Everything was hard. But with some medication and therapies, I regained a bit."

"Why move to Chadford then?"

"A man. So, um what did you mean about your friends?"

Jane and Darby looked at each other, and Darby took off her sunglasses. In the sun, her eyes were flecked with amber.

"We're in this group, sort of. It's a small community."

Jane fidgeted. "What she's trying to say is, it's a lifestyle. Of sexual preferences. You know. Kinky stuff."

"Oh. Oh. Okay. Like, um... oh."

"Yeah. I mean, one of the reasons Jane and I are best friends is that we have the same predilections. Is this a problem for you?"

Willow thought for a moment. "Do you have sex parties here? Is that a thing?"

"They are, but not here. But now and again we like to hang out with like-minded people. We don't flaunt it about, but you might see things now and again that are out of the norm."

"Okay. That's fine by me."

"Good." Jane relaxed.

Less than a week later, with the paperwork signed, Willow moved in.

Jane opened the front door, exclaiming, and Willow got out of her car relieved at last to be home.

"There you are! I was going to text you and offer to come and help."

"No, it's fine. I don't have much with me."

"Well I didn't know, so I asked our friend in case you had a van full. He should be here soon to give us a hand, seeing as Darby is out."

"Oh no, there's no need, I can manage." With that, a small sporty car revved up the drive, and a tall man unfolded himself from it. "Oh my god," Willow whispered.

"I know," Jane shook her head, "he has this effect on those so inclined."

"Willow?" he shouted, taking off his sunglasses.

"Matt." She flushed and didn't quite know what to do with herself.

"You two know each other?"

"Matt helped me out at ARC when I first arrived."

"Oh, I see." Jane raised a perfectly manicured arched brow and rolled her tongue bar through her teeth.

Willow's instinct was to flail, but she didn't. "Oh god, no, it's not-"

"Not what, exactly?" he asked. That deep voice made Willow quiver inside. Quiver? She'd never quivered. She'd thought about that day too much, and although some nice fantasies followed, she wouldn't let herself like a man. They were gross and entirely unnecessary.

Willow set her mouth in a line and glared. "Thanks for coming to help me, but I can manage, really."

"Well, I'm here now, so I might as well take your things in." His jaw flexed, and tone was curt.

"There's no need." She met his face.

"Just let me take them." Matt sounded strained, and Willow was bright red and furious.

Jane went from one to the other, amused. "Okay." She drew the word out.

Matt glared in the tension, but took a deep breath and with a grin took her two cases from the open boot and went in.

Jane took Willow's arm.

"Not a word," Willow murmured.

"Oh, bitch, no, I need to hear everything."

"Wait, why is he in your group?"

"There are all sorts of sexualities in our group. You'll have to ask Matt, but he's definitely Mr A-type." Jane winked as she took the storage box.

Willow stared after Jane, clutching her holdall and handbag not knowing what to think. She tried to hold onto everything as she closed the boot of the car, but dropped her bag, then her cane, and then her holdall. She'd make the worst juggler ever.

"Need help?"

No, no, she didn't need any help. "I'm fine." She didn't look at him. What did Jane mean, A-type? If he was controlling and... shit, kinky stuff? It spoke of fantasies in the dark, things to only think of while she saw to her own needs.

"Are you all right?" He bent down and picked up her cane, handing it to her, and took her holdall and handbag.

Her eyes darted about as she hobbled in, and he watched her as she went. The stair lift was slow, excruciatingly so, and the loud whirring of it sat in the quiet as he waited for her to go up. She glanced at him, and his scowl melted, replaced with a small smile. Willow reddened and focused on the stairs with his eyes fixed on her, and he took each stair as the lift crawled up.

He pulled his lips into his mouth fighting a grin. "So, Willow, ARC matched you here?" Even the way he said her name did something to her.

"They did." She fussed the hem of her top.

"How serendipitous."

"Why?"

"I get the pleasure of seeing you again."

Willow blinked at him. "Hardly."

"There's no pleasure in our meeting again? You didn't call me."

"I didn't need to."

"I'm almost offended." By his smirk, Willow guessed he was teasing, but she wasn't sure.

Willow nearly replied, but the chair halted.

Jane stood at the top of the stairs. "Right, do you want a tea, Matt?"

"Sure, we need to talk about Saturday."

"Excellent, Willow?"

"Um, no thank you. I'm fine."

"Okay then."

After Matt put her things on the bed, he left, and Willow lay down. She wondered about him. He was attractive, but a man and they were dangerous, and she was not going that way again. No way. This group were so different though. There was an open realness she'd not known before that reminded her of uni. The staid awkwardness of her own life felt stark. This was a chance, and she should take it, and she would.

Willow rested for a bit and began unpacking. As she hung up her clothes and settled in, she kept thinking. These people were exciting and interesting, and she was boring, ordinary, white, straight and privileged. Yes, she was disabled, but that didn't mean she fit in with them. That's what she wanted, to be wanted by nice people.

She'd do her best. It would be an adjustment from the reserved family she'd come from. Suck it up Willow, she thought and made her way downstairs.

Matt and Jane were talking quietly when she joined them.

"I've set up a cupboard for your food. I'll do you a dinner when I cook if you like." Jane nursed her tea.

Matt stared at his mug, and Willow felt bad, she must have offended him.

"That's very kind, thank you."

"Not at all. So, this Friday, there'll be some people here, and then we'll all be away Saturday."

"Going anywhere nice?"

"Working a small convention, doing demos."

"Demos?" Willow had to ask, why couldn't she say okay, and then shut up?

"Bondage."

"Oh." Willow smiled and hesitated. "Well, I hope it goes well. Um, Matt?"

He looked up, his dark eyes could only be described as broody. She'd never been attracted to broody, and damn it, she wasn't attracted to him either. "Yes?"

"Thank you for helping."

"You're welcome." All the kindness he'd shown her evaporated and his cold voice filled her with disappointment.

Willow hobbled off and went upstairs. She'd gone and fucked that right up.

Matt wouldn't look at Jane after Willow went upstairs, and he turned his mug. "Say it."

"You should."

"No."

"Why not?"

He finally held her eye. "You tell her?"

"Of course not, you should though because living here, she can't not know. You're disappointed she's not falling all over you or is intrigued? I see it, she's attractive, your type too."

"Stop it. I don't have a type. I'm pan, which is the very definition of not having a type."

Jane gave him that disbelieving look and her eyes almost rolled back into her head. "Oh, come on. When was the last time you were with anyone other than Tabbie? There's something sweet about Willow, I just get this feeling that you'd be good for her and she'd be good for you."

"Thanks for the tea." Matt left.

He was disappointed. His life wasn't for everyone, but it wasn't what most people thought, well, mostly. All he wanted was someone to care for, to love. A great big hole in his life.

When his phone pinged with a message from his ex, he knew it was ridiculous to reply, but he did. Maybe it wouldn't be that bad this time. Maybe.

By Stefanie Simpson

YOU'RE NOT SUPPOSED TO BE HERE

W illow took a taxi to her new job. Her first job. She wondered how she'd cope, even if it was only two days a week, Tuesdays and Thursdays. Plenty of time to rest and recover.

Eight until five was a long day, but she knew how lucky she was to get the job and finally make her own way in the world.

Danni met her outside, arriving herself. "Come on then, let's get you settled in." She waddled in with her heavy bags and Willow trundled in behind her.

A few minutes later, a tall, pale, beautiful woman in thick-framed glasses waltzed in.

"You must be Willow, I'm Suzy. I believe you'll be working with me, finally, someone to give me a hand. I'm swamped." Breathless, she dropped her things in an office as Willow struggled to keep up with her.

Danni popped her head through the door. "Sorry, Tuesdays are a bit hectic, I'll leave you with Suzy, she'll take care of you. Any problems, give me a shout, but I'm with social services all morning." With that, she vanished, and Willow turned back to Suzy.

"Are you ready for exciting office work?"

"Very."

"Excellent." Suzy's warm, wide smile made Willow think that this would be okay.

Suzy showed her where everything was, and the systems they used. Willow had done some online IT courses on the sly in the last six months as part of operation 'Get Out of Prison', and though she knew what she was doing, she was overwhelmed at first, trying to take it all in, but by lunch, she was in the swing of it with the two of them working in silence until Suzy yawned.

"Right, I'm starved, coffee?"

"Yes please."

Suzy made them a drink, and they settled down to lunch. "The only thing I don't like about working here is the only place to get any food is the dirty burger van up the road. I used to work up by Berkley House. Really posh. Good food."

"What made you come here?"

"A boy." She smiled. "Really, I wanted a change, and this is a challenge, but a good one."

"ARC is great."

Suzy put her sandwich down and wiped her hands. "How's the house?"

"How do you know?"

"I suggested to Jane that she try the house match programme. ARC can't keep expanding beds, and not everyone is in danger, so they don't need the secure accommodation. They've been doing it for a while."

"You're friends with Jane?" Willow, leery of telling Suzy too much, wondered if she was in that crowd.

"We're good friends. In fact, Jane told me about this job." Suzy sat back, considering Willow. "They told you?"

"A little. It's not my thing though. I feel a bit of an outsider. Can I ask you a question?"

"Of course."

"About Matt? I think I offended him when he was nice to me, I just... I don't know, feel bad."

"Matt? Wow." Suzy shifted, excitement on her face.

"Oh, it's not like that, I mean look at him, and look at me. It's ridiculous."

"Why?"

Willow blinked. "Being disabled, and him being a contender for the world's strongest man; there's no way he'd be interested in someone like me, and I'm, what's the word, vanilla?"

"Matt's a good guy, he's a bit intimidating at first. I've seen him get shit occasionally, but he doesn't talk about it much. He can't stand seeing hate around him. A few years ago, I was hassled in a club, he didn't think, just stepped in. That's the kind of man he is. He sees anyone in distress who needs help, he will help them. He's a proper alpha, not an arse. Not that many men understand the difference. For all that, he has the worst luck with relationships. Honestly." Suzy pulled a face and shook her head in disbelief.

"Why?"

"Mmm, it's not my story to tell, but basically one of his exes won't let him go."

"Sounds complicated." Willow wanted to ask more questions, but held it back, she didn't want to look too keen.

Suzy shrugged. "I'll be at the party on Friday."

"Can I ask something personal?"

Suzy narrowed her eyes. "Go on."

"Jane said there were all sorts of sexualities in the group, I'm curious."

"Generally, we don't talk about each other's sexualities. It's rude. If you want to know about Matt, you should ask him. He's open about it."

"I'm more wondering if I'm the only straight and boring person."

"Not the only straight, I am, and there's a few others on the fringes. Not sure about the boring part."

Willow smiled tightly and finished her salad.

Willow slept most of Friday day and felt like crap as usual, but she was rested and ready to face having to be social.

She leant against the window, taking in the bright, warm August day, and watched Jane set up the barbeque as Darby organised.

Willow went with a red maxi dress, which sat off the shoulder. It barely contained her boobs, but the dress was panelled around the bust, and she hoped for the best. She didn't own many dressy clothes and thought it was the nicest smart-casual thing she had for a barbeque with people she didn't know. It had nothing to with impressing Matt.

Shoving her hair on her head in a messy bun, and a touch of mascara, she was ready. Willow nearly put a gold necklace with a small heart on it. She didn't know why she brought it with her. It was the past and a painful reminder. Maybe that was why she kept it. To keep her focused.

It made her think of Matt. Thinking of him in that way did no good. He wasn't for her, and she wasn't for him.

She had no room for that shit.

When Willow made it to the kitchen, she was already regretting her dress, her boobs were not as contained as she liked. People filtered in, a few looked twice at her watching her limp slightly, their eyes on her cane.

Jane came in, wearing jeans and a vest, her tattoo sleeve wound around her arm with bright patterns in a sea of blue. "Wow, look at you, hot damn, Willow."

Willow shrugged. "I'm overdressed."

"Not at all, you should see some of the crowd. Matt's here."

"Is he?"

"Don't play coy with me, you care."

"I don't think he does, not that I'm bothered. I feel bad if I upset him that's all."

Jane leant in. "You know for a big macho guy, he's kinda sensitive underneath."

"Really?"

Jane was distracted, and Willow perched on a stool nursing a wine and people-watched. Matt came in from the garden, putting his sunglasses on his head. At his side was a woman with pink hair, tattoos, fake tan, and an impressive body. She was contrived and overdone but beautiful. Willow blinked at her perfection.

"Hi."

Willow smiled. "Matt."

"This is Tabbie." Ah, so that was her.

Tabbie looked Willow up and down with 'that' look. The pitying one. The one that Willow loathed with every fibre of her being and made her want to use her cane like a deadly weapon. She let it go, she always let it go.

"Hello."

Tabbie smiled and clung onto Matt, who was staring, and his eyes dipped to her cleavage.

"Matt, are you getting the drinks?" Tabbie's tone was sharp, and Matt dragged his eyes away from Willow.

He cleared his throat. "I'll have a beer please."

Tabbie gave him a sour look and fetched two beers from the ice bin.

"Settling in?"

"Yes, thank you. Work is nice. I work with Suzy."

"I haven't seen her for a while. How is she?"

"Fine. She should be here soon."

After a moment of awkwardness that allowed Willow to admire Matt's body in his t-shirt, he left with Tabbie pinned to his side.

Willow slumped.

"Well, hello, red." Suzy looked luminous and attached to her hand was a handsome blond man, all open warmth, introduced to her as Nathan.

"Hey." Willow passed the time with the couple until they greeted other people. Willow made her way outside, needing to escape the crowded kitchen.

The cool breeze in the bright, warm day was lovely, and she found an empty beanbag under the dappled shade of a tree and flopped down into it with the grace of a slug.

Not spilling her wine counted as a win as she fidgeted into it.

Across the lawn, sitting so close that she was virtually on her lap, were Matt and Tabbie. She fawned and purred all over him.

They looked good together, but she wondered at what Suzy had said about them. She tried not to watch and was grateful at Darby for coming over with some food.

"Thank you."

"What's up?"

"Nothing. Tell me about everyone that is if you're not busy."

"Of course." Darby smiled and joined her on the beanbag. She smoothed out the bright yellow and black patterned sundress, her hair perfect in a matching yellow scarf. "Right, the person in the blue shorts and check short sleeve shirt is Max. Quiet but nice, he's a comic artist, he does little cartoons of us for fun, and adorable. Mel with the quiff is next to him. They or them. Also, a complete flirt. Next to Max on the other side is Sara in the green jeans. She's a mechanic and Jane's ex, but they're friends now. Hmmm. Who else is interesting? Tabbie, I take it you've met her."

"She's..."

"Obsessed with Matt. She's dicked him about for years. On and off. She reels him back in, and then drops him."

"Why, what does that mean?"

"She gets what she wants, they get into it, and when he doesn't give her what she demands, she drops him, leaving him high and dry, and actually, it's fucking cold. There's this thing that we do," Darby spoke slowly, "and it's difficult to explain, but important, to do with communication and reassurance on both sides. It's emotional and psychological. It's also open to abuse. It's mean when people use it to manipulate the other person. Anyway, she won't let him go. The last time, I thought he'd finally moved on. Matt needs someone to care for, he needs that on a fundamental level; it's part of who he is. Tabbie's good at drama and being needy. It gives him what he thinks he wants. You'd be perfect."

Willow choked on her coleslaw. Darby patted her back. "Don't be fucking silly."

Darby laughed. "I'm serious. You're not dramatic or overly needy. But you need someone, you need support, and someone to love you. I see it."

Willow stared at her.

"I see things, well, I'm good at reading people. And, you're his type, a bit pasty, but you have the body. The exception to Matt's type was Kai. They're a sweetie. Total twink, adorably pretty and everyone loves them. Neither were old enough or secure enough. Anyway, Kai moved to London for a job, but that was about five, six years ago now." Darby gave Willow her perfect smile, and Suzy and Nathan joined them before Willow had a chance to ask anything else.

Darby's words stayed with Willow, and she began to tire in the heat and chatter.

"I think I'm going in."

Saying goodbye, Nathan helped her up, and she tottered back to the house. Cool inside, she breathed deep, grabbed some snacks and another wine and went up.

Curiosity pulled her back to Matt. She might as well have not existed to him, he was so engrossed with Tabbie. No one had ever looked at her like that. No, Darby was very wrong on that front.

There was no chance that he would be interested in her. Maybe if she had been nicer to him.

She fell on her bed, door locked, and relaxed. Her legs tingled, pain in her calves and back, and knew she wouldn't sleep.

Music drifted up. The sound of people having fun. She let it wash over her, and her mind wandered back.

Giving up the expectations other people had of her was liberating, and setting her own terms based on what she needed was a necessity. Regret nipped, and she shut it down.

Not quite asleep, she lay still, awareness of her physical body pulsed in her mind with her slow breathing. She blinked awake as the door went.

"Huh?"

"Willow?"

She slowly sat up and fell over when she tried to stand.

Jane shouted through the door. "Are you all right?"

"Yeah, I was meditating. Kinda spaced." She crawled to the door and unlocked it, remaining on her knees with it open.

"Sorry, I wanted to check if you were okay."

Willow's closed her eyes and sank back down.

"Do you want some help?"

"No. I'm fine." Although, she couldn't move.

"Shall I get Matt?"

That woke her up. "No, god no." She made a face and crawled away.

Jane helped her back into bed.

"You don't need to help me, it's not part of the deal," she said, her voice croaky and slow.

"It is, I like to mother. I looked after my gran for years."

"Thank you. It's nice to have help without strings."

"Strings?"

Jane sat on the bed next to Willow, all propped up with pillows.

"People expected a lot of me. There was pressure to get back to it, or they'd want something from me, so they pretended to care until they realised that it wasn't going to happen. People drop off. Their love or friendship is conditional. Or they patronised and pitied me."

"That sounds shit."

"It was."

"Fresh start then? Clean slate."

"Something like that."

A beat of quiet. "Matt makes you think of the past."

Willow pulled a face and stared at Jane. "Are all lesbians mind readers?"

Jane laughed. "Has Darby been on at you too?"

"Yes. She said — never mind." Willow focused on her wine instead.

"I read people. It's part of what I do." Jane nudged her shoulder.

"What do you do?"

"I do all the admin and organisation from home but have to go out for a feminist, sex-positive kink events company. I organise displays, events, all as risk managed as possible and consensual. Mostly fem-dom stuff."

Willow slow blinked. "Are the others involved?"

"Some."

"Is Matt?"

"Kinda. He's more the security and in charge of safety. Well, he's managed scenes in the past."

"I don't know what to do with that." Willow nearly dropped her glass, and Jane righted it for her.

"For most of us, it's like a part-time gig to scratch an itch. Tabbie is our main attraction. She also runs an adult shop. Darby is good with ropes, it's her thing. She works in an office." Jane shrugged.

Willow spent a minute processing the information. "I didn't know it was a thing."

"It's not common, and we're quite protective of ourselves, but you live here. You should know."

"That's fair. Thank you for telling me."

Jane had left the door open, and Darby appeared with a bottle of wine and glasses.

"What you doing up here?"

"Hiding," said Willow.

"From Matt," whispered Jane, and Willow nudged her.

Darby raised a brow and set the bottle down, pouring them each a glass. Willow took it.

"I thought so." She lounged across the end of the bed. "It looks like those two are back on."

Jane sighed.

"Do you like him?" Darby asked Willow, picking up their earlier conversation.

"I don't know him."

"If he asked you out would you say yes?"

"No."

"That's a shame. Why not?" Darby pinned her gaze.

Willow formed her thoughts carefully. "I'm used to boring and average. It's easier, but even that is... the expectations a partner has of me aren't always things I can give. I don't want someone who would demand of me. Besides, I don't want and am not looking for a relationship." She pulled a grossed-out face.

"But you said you don't know him, so how do you know he would be demanding?"

"Are you going to tell me he wouldn't be? Anyway, isn't this a moot subject? He's with Tabbie again."

"It'll be over by ten o'clock." Darby raised one brow, and Jane laughed in reply.

It was nice, the three of them, and then because nothing stays that way, the party moved into Willow's room.

Matt watched Willow out of the corner of his eye, finding her restrained and quiet. She watched people. Her soft full figure, those huge keen eyes. She was gorgeous, and her body was lovely. Her quiet dignity was so unlike the brashness he was used to.

Tabbie laughed at something, and she moved closer. They did this dance far too often. Back and forth. She'd get her rocks off, want and demand more of him, and then screw him over.

He loathed it. They'd build up a few scenes, and he'd feel it — the joy and fulfilment of that power, and when he wouldn't do what she wanted, she'd take it away.

The games were tedious, and though he liked Tabbie, there was no way this was happening again. For a moment when they started talking, he wondered if it'd be different. A simple question, *are you going to the party?* He'd bitten on the lure, but he wouldn't be snagged. He turned, and Willow had gone.

A glance was all he'd had of her, under the tree in that dress, her hair lifting in the breeze. The sweet innocence in her face.

He wanted to see her again.

"Are you listening?" Tabbie asked.

"No, sorry."

"What's the matter? Matt, please." She knelt before him, and a few people looked at them.

Matt set his jaw. "Do not do this here."

Her practised deference fell off her. "What is it? The new girl?"

Matt squinted and tried to move away.

"Look, you don't expect her to do what I can do for you. There are things we can give each other."

"And a lot more that we can't. I do not want to perform, I do not do this shit in public. I'm not right for you. You know this."

"But it's us."

"It's really not."

Matt unfurled and went into the kitchen with Tabbie on his heels as ever, he wanted to find Willow and keep her near. Catching himself, realising he was thinking of her as his, no, no he couldn't do that.

Too late. They moved through the party, Tabbie hanging on like a limpet. Darby headed upstairs with wine, and waiting a few minutes, he followed.

By Stefanie Simpson

WRONG PLACE

M att's voice froze Willow. "Where are our hosts?"

She hoped he wouldn't come upstairs. His heavy feet on the stairs made her expel her breath.

"Well, well," he said with a dirty grin on his face. A second set of lighter feet followed him.

Tabbie appeared in the doorway. "What are you guys doing up here?"

"Chilling out with Willow."

For the first time, Tabbie faced her and smiled, but it wasn't particularly genuine. "Oh, you're the girl from the charity."

"Yep. That's me." Wow, the girl from the charity. Twenty-bloody-nine, thank you very much, but no, she was the pitiable girl.

Tabbie went on, and Willow wondered if she was a cat on purpose. "Jane's a good person. Heart of gold."

"Tabbie, watch your step," Jane spoke in a hard tone, and Willow raised her brows at it.

"What? People take advantage of you, just because-"

"Shut your fucking mouth." Jane sat forward. Darby winked at Willow, who wanted to curl up, and everyone else to fuck off.

"I'm sorry, Jane." Tabbie smiled contritely.

"Thank you. Don't be a bitch in my house, it doesn't suit you. Matt?"

He was fighting laughter, and Willow wondered if it was over what Tabbie said, or Jane's reaction.

"Yes, Jane?"

"If she's your sub again, keep her in line, or leave."

He sobered up. Matt shifted in his perch at the end of the bed behind Darby with his legs sprawled in front of him. Tabbie was in front of Darby next to Jane, so Willow had a good view of her.

Sitting forward, Matt's tone was dour and serious. "She's not mine. So don't put her behaviour on me."

Tabbie's face dropped, but she kept her composure. "Willow, how do you fit into our group. We're all pretty queer and kinky." Tabbie preened.

Darby laughed. "Tabbie, you sub, but you're straight. Fucking queer people doesn't make you queer."

"I wouldn't presume to know people's sexualities unless they tell me." Willow made sure her voice was even.

"I think I'm the only pan here," Matt said, eyes locked onto Willow.

Willow's lips parted. Something was alluring about him, and if she were weak, she'd be tempted by him. She returned his gaze, making him smirk.

"Yes, yes, you're so special." Darby kicked him, and he laughed, breaking the moment.

"I am, thank you, I'm also Persian, so there." His glance returned to Willow. She was sure he was showing off for her, then dismissed it as ridiculous. She wondered about who he was, his life, all the things that made him but didn't ask.

"Partly Persian." Darby rolled her eyes in a dramatic turn, making Matt grin and wink at her.

There were things here Willow didn't understand and wasn't sure she wanted to. "Right, out." She barked. Everyone looked at her. "I'm not sure why there's a party in my room, but it's not why I came to bed."

"Shame." Darby made herself more comfortable.

Instead of arguing, she tilted her head, annoyed. Tabbie shook off any disappointment and was talking to Darby with Matt joining in now and again, but Willow didn't heed the conversation.

"You okay?" Jane nudged Willow.

"Yes, bit... overwhelmed right now. Big changes. New job. Lots of people I'm not sure of."

Jane nudged her. "Do you want us to go?"

"Partly, it's nice sometimes to-"

Willow didn't finish as two more people came upstairs. A gorgeous tattooed man — whose name Willow didn't catch — and a lanky, handsome pale man with a shaved head, Filip.

The conversation came from everyone and Willow couldn't keep up. She did notice that Tabbie focused her attention on Filip, and Matt seemed relieved.

Willow didn't think she had the energy to devote to knowing the dynamics of this group of people. She scowled into her wine. Was life like this for other people?

"I think new girl has had enough."

Matt's voice made her look up. "I prefer Willow."

He looked surprised for a second at her sharpness with him, but he bowed his head in apology. "Willow."

"Anyway," Jane said in a drawn-out voice. "We'll leave you in peace."

"Oh come on, it's a shame for you to be sat up here, alone, while we party downstairs." The concern in Tabbie's voice was unconvincing. A light kept flashing Willow's head in pink that said fake, fake.

"I'm tired, and I don't feel like justifying my need for quiet," Willow said kindly.

Jane ushered people out, Matt was last to leave and looked back at her. She hoped Jane was wrong because she did not have time for it.

Two glasses of wine. That was all Willow had, but at ten-past-six in the morning, when she woke after a bad night's sleep, she felt like she downed a bottle of vodka.

Stretching, she would have slothed out like a motherfucker, but she needed the bathroom. With a sigh, she unfolded her body, assessing the pain level and stumbled along, managing not to fall over. She reached her bathroom door and realised the water was running. Without thinking, she opened the door to her bathroom full of steam, and as she processed the scene, she saw Matt, happily wanking away, one hand on the tile, in her walk-in shower.

"What the actual fuck?" Not meaning to shout it, the words came out, and her stomach dropped as she took in what she was seeing.

He was perfect. Strong and muscular body, perfect bum, impressive but not scary cock in hand, his head leaning forward, water pouring through his hair.

Matt stopped and turned, and then what happened next would be etched onto her caffeine deprived retinas for all time. It only occurred to her then that she wore nothing.

"Fuck!" His voice was strained, body taut, eyes locked onto her, and he came.

He turned from her as he did, cum disappearing into the shower. Neither said anything, embarrassment finally kicking in, and she grabbed her robe from behind the door and put in on.

"What are you doing in my bathroom?" She barely got the words out.

"Your bathroom?" he shouted with his back to her, though it meant she really got to look at his bottom, and back, and legs. She'd never seen a more masculine display, his skin golden all over, the dark but groomed hair on his body slick in the water.

"Yes. My bathroom. It should have been locked."

The second door of the bathroom to the landing was always kept locked, and then she remembered Jane asked her to unlock it because of the number of people at the party. She had forgotten all about it.

"Get out, I need a piss."

"I'm naked, get out and let me-"

"I think we might be past that stage, pal, I've just seen you ejaculate."

Matt started laughing.

"It's not funny, I need to wee."

"Well let me get out then."

"I'm not stopping you."

"I think you've seen enough."

"Fine." She plonked down on the loo. "Do what you fucking want, you will anyway."

Matt waited until she flushed and washed her hands before turning off the shower. She couldn't take her eyes off him as she backed out the bathroom and back into her room.

Willow hid under the sheet, leaving him to it. A hot sleepless night, coupled with wine, and lack of coffee, made for poor decision-making skills. What was wrong with her?

Nothing would shift that image from her mind. She laughed once, then her heart turned, and the pulse between her legs was inevitable.

The knock on her door made her yelp.

"What?"

"I'm done, you should come lock the other door."

"I don't think I can."

Her bathroom door opened a few seconds later, and Matt edged in the bedroom. "I cleaned the shower. I'm deeply sorry. I've locked the door to the hallway, and I'll go out yours."

His tone was apologetic, embarrassed, and she felt bad. At least he cleaned the shower. Then she started giggling and couldn't stop.

An hour later, when she made herself almost presentable, she went downstairs.

People were dotted about, one still out cold on the small couch in the kitchen diner. Willow ignored the party fallout and started making herself a thermos of coffee, and cereal.

"Hey!"

Tabbie was far too bright. Willow slow blinked. Tabbie was freshly showered. Even makeup free with ruffled wet pink hair and casual clothes, she was gorgeous.

"Morning."

Tabbie leant on the counter as Willow poured the water.

"Look, I get you're not keen on me. I'm sorry if I came across like a bitch."

Willow put the kettle down. "You lot are very different from what I'm used to. I don't know you, any of you, and your all, 'how do you feel?' It's weird."

"We're all pretty open."

"I got that."

"Communication is a big deal for us because of what we do. Not everyone is."

"No one talks about how they feel at home."

Tabbie watched Willow stir her coffee with a concerned look. "Be careful of Matt."

Willow was getting beyond exasperated. "I'm not interested in him, really, I'm no threat to you, I mean, look at me, I'm not a threat to anything. Maybe the cat, I can out nap even that creature."

Tabbie grinned. "I get it. Most people are hesitant when they find us, give it time, you'll be as open and dirty as us."

"Oh, no, it's not my thing. I'm dull with everything. I'm not interested in sex. Or relationships."

"How come?" Tabbie tilted her head in a frown.

She wasn't the person Willow expected, but Tabbie wanted Matt. Being territorial was understandable, and she was the interloper after all.

"People are crap."

"Fair enough. He likes you."

Willow threw her arms up in the air. "I don't care. And on that note, I'm going back to bed." She picked up the bowl, thermos, and mug and walked out of the kitchen, clipping every piece of furniture on the way.

"Shit, wait." Tabbie took the bowl.

"Thank you."

"Must be hard."

"It's annoying, I adapted, not much else to do."

Tabbie left Willow at her door, looking as if she wanted to say something else.

"Say it."

"It's addictive. Once you start. He's addictive. What he can give, what he can do, is special. He makes you feel like a goddess, and you would happily do anything he asks. I've never felt that way when subbing, not for anyone. It's hard to let go of that, even when you know he's over it. That's why I said be careful."

Tabbie left, and Willow shivered. The image of Matt wanking came back in glorious colour, and she poured herself a coffee.

Maybe she would spend some time thinking about that very thing with the door locked.

An hour and two orgasms later, Willow was soaked and panting, and Matt fixed in her mind. In her fantasy, she had joined him in the shower, and they fucked.

Not made love, not gentle, but fucking. She'd never do it. Ever. It was nice to think of though.

The house was clean by the time Willow emerged, and Jane was pottering in the garden while Darby lounged back reading a book.

"You could help." Jane huffed at Darby.

"I mowed. Again. Day before yesterday. I hate gardening, and yet you always make me do it."

"You live here too, you can't expect me to do it all by myself."

"Get a gardener." Darby shot Jane a look.

"I don't want some blokey perv rooting through the veg."

"Can't we find lady gardeners?"

Jane threw her head back and laughed. "Lady fucking gardeners. That's the aim in life, yes."

Darby threw one of the pillows at Jane. "Anyway, I washed your clothes and vacuumed. I even mopped. So shut the fuck up, and let me read." She looked up as Willow stepped onto the patio. "There you are!"

"Just about."

"What's up?" Jane said, ditching her gloves and putting the cushions right on the lounger while Darby still sat on it.

Willow opted for the wicker chair, tucking her feet under herself. "You're far too perceptive."

"I'm sitting here, you cock," Darby said, shooing Jane off.

Huffing, Jane lay on the grass. "Do tell." Jane closed her eyes.

"Tabbie and I had a chat, she was nice, I think. Also caught Matt wanking in my fucking wet room because I forgot to lock the landing door last night."

Darby dropped her book and took off her sunglasses.

Jane sat up. "Get the fuck out."

"That's what I said."

Jane and Darby erupted in laughter, and Willow couldn't help joining in as she told them.

"That's... I can't even." Jane lay back down.

"Oh god, don't tell him. Shit, I shouldn't have said anything."

"It's fine. We've seen Matt enough times, it's not new to us. But I'm surprised at him."

"So, he performs then?" Willow picked at the side of her nail as she asked, not looking at them.

"Once or twice in the past. He's not that much of an exhibitionist. He didn't get into it. Tabbie is, loves it."

"That became an issue?"

"Yep, one of them."

"She warned me about Matt. Said I should be careful."

"Not an unwise thing. There's always risk, right?"

"I guess."

Yep, there was always a risk. Though, she wasn't sure how she'd ever look at him again after what happened earlier.

Oh well.

Matt didn't say goodbye to anyone but left. Horrified didn't cover it. The drive to work let him think as he shuffled through motorway traffic.

He'd slept like crap after staying up until the early hours. The couch was too uncomfortable, and his back ached. He kept thinking of Willow, how easy it would be to get to her tits in that dress. Her big innocent eyes, her wry cautious manner, there was so much mystery to her, and he wanted all of it. He liked how she was unsure but wouldn't cower. The graceful lift of her chin and stubborn look of those doe eyes followed him. She screamed for help in silence. The need to figure out if her vulnerability was separate from his interest.

A quick shower to wake him up seemed like a good idea at the time. He'd thought about her too much and needed to be somewhere. He had his work gear in the car, and it'd save him time. He'd done it before. He knew it was her bathroom, and the thought of her being in the shower, fuck, he couldn't help it, he was so hard.

How long had it been, exactly? Six months? Seven? Work consumed most of his time, and relationships — or the idea of one — wasn't a priority.

He wanted to ask Willow out, date her, find out if there might be anything. The fact that she was the first person that he was attracted to in the last few years said something. He didn't want to throw that opportunity away, but god he'd messed that up, hadn't he? She didn't seem phased when he said he was pan, or Persian, interested maybe — there was interest in those pretty brown eyes — but that part of the night might have been overwhelming for her.

The incident in the bathroom made the whole thing a moot subject, and she'd never look at him again. The image of her, naked in front of him as he was getting close. Matt wanted to crawl up his own arse and never see daylight again.

He pulled into the carpark and got his shit together and made the twenty phone calls he needed to before even setting foot inside.

RIGHT TIME

Willow rang her mother, it was time. They'd barely spoken since Willow told her parents she was leaving home.

You'd think she was a child. Willow understood her parents to a degree, it wasn't a question of right or wrong, but they kept her insulated from the world. To Willow, it was isolating and did more harm than good.

"Hello, mother."

"Willow," the strained sound of her mother's voice, and clipped tone made her heart sink. "How are you, dear, we were getting worried. Not hearing from you for nearly a month."

"Actually, it's nice. I like my job and the people there. My housemates are lovely."

"Who are they?"

"Jane and Darby." Willow knew her mother, and what kind of reaction she would have. Anyone living together out of wedlock scandalised her, never mind anything else.

"And your health?"

"It's not too bad, I'm tired but resting. Eating properly."

"Well."

There didn't seem to be much else to say, and the awkward silence between them.

"Would you like to speak to your father?"

"Yes." Her father was even more remote than her mother. He'd had hopes for his only child, but she'd disappointed him long ago, and it didn't matter what she did anymore as far as he was concerned.

"Hello, how's Chadford?"

She had the same conversation with him as she had with her mother.

"We do worry, especially your mother. You should call more."

"Sorry, dad."

"We've seen Oliver. He's asked after you."

"I don't care, and don't bring him up."

"Willow." His tone, derisive and firm, made Willow's eyes roll back into her head.

"Dad." She returned the favour.

"You won't do better than Oliver."

"You mean, you won't do better than Oliver. This is why I don't call, this is why I left. I'm not here for you to use to save the estate. It's tough. Bye, father."

She gave him no time to reply and hung up. The divide between her and her family and all the bullshit that filled the distance weighed on her. Though there was nothing she could do to change it.

The lack of control in her life was the past. She had control, she was in charge of her choices, and would never go back to that way of living.

Willow was quieter that week, got on with her work, and hid in her room, reading. She barely saw Jane or Darby. When Willow decided to join Jane for dinner, she raised her brows at Willow as she made risotto.

"I thought you'd ghosted out on us."

Willow didn't answer at first. "Need some help?"

"What's going on?" Jane's smile faded.

"My parents. I made the mistake of talking to them. It's a long story, but I know I've done the right thing."

"Do you want to talk about it?" Jane kept adding stock and stirring.

"No."

"Well, you can set the table, if you're able to."

Willow left her cane and set out three places.

"Darby is on a date."

"Oh? Who?"

"Althea, Alie, she was in our group for a while, but she works a lot, she's a solicitor. Anyway, early in the year Althea and Darby got back in touch. There's a lot of history there, much to work through. Alie came to the demo." Jane grinned, still stirring.

"How'd the demo go?" Willow laid out the cutlery, feigning nonchalance.

"Really well, we had a great crowd. Tabbie sold a lot of things from the shop."

"That's great."

"Matt's stepping back from managing the demos. He wants to concentrate on his business."

"How come?"

Jane served up, dropping a few flakes of parmesan on the top, along with olive bread and salad. "Do you know why we all hang out?"

Willow shook her head.

"Because we're queer and kinky. There aren't that many of us. We flock. We need each other. But, and this is the thing in the club scene, a lot of it is all bonking and flings, exploring who we are, and perving in public where we validate each other and ourselves. There comes a point when you want more than others like you, parties and wild nights.

"I want a wife. I want kids. The works, but finding someone like that, considering my life, isn't that easy, though I'm only twenty-seven. Matt's wanted to settle down forever. He's not a scene guy and doesn't swap partners. He wants love. When he's had partners, it's a relationship, and that's not always what it was. He needs it. Tabbie wants to share him publicly and show him off, like the perfect dom trophy, but he doesn't share. It's not his thing."

"I see."

They ate companionably with a glass of white wine.

"I'm not looking to date." Willow had to say it.

"I know."

"Then why do I feel like I'm under scrutiny about Matt?"

"You're not."

"Uh-huh." Willow levelled a dry look at Jane who ignored her and ate her dinner.

Feeling better the next day, Willow went into Chadford. Taking advantage of when she was feeling okay had risks, she'd be tired and in pain, but if she wanted to live a fuller life, it was the price she had to pay.

Jane dropped her off, and Willow did some clothes shopping and went for lunch, nothing exciting, but things she rarely got to do on her own as her choice.

By Stefanie Simpson

Sitting in an independent café, complete with bunting and quirky tables, eating her gluten-free lunch, she people-watched.

Crowds milled past, and she thought of the first weeks of university.

Keen, bright, a bit of a party girl, Willow had high hopes for her classical singing. She was going to travel the world. See every theatre, stand on every stage. Do the Proms, and every classical music festival going. She was going to work with the best.

None of it happened, and she never made it through the first term.

Something shook her out of her thoughts, and blinking, she watched the people carry on past, but across the wide pedestrianised street, someone was watching her. Willow squinted into the distance, heads of people blocking her view.

Then he was gone. Couldn't have been him. Impossible. She stared, searching for him with cold calm. When she found no sign of him, she looked back at her half-eaten lunch no longer hungry.

Easing to her feet, she let the dizziness pass before she picked up her handbag and went out. Her back crept, and she focused on each step. The ground undulated beneath her, and her harsh breath came short as all movement blurred.

Willow had exactly twelve contacts in her phone. Jane sat above Matt and being shaky, not concentrating, and of course, the inevitable brain fog, Willow called Matt and not Jane.

"Hello?" His deep voice made her shiver.

"Matt? How do you have Jane's phone?" She struggled to get the words out.

"Willow? I don't, you called me."

"Oh, crap, I'm so sorry, I'll let you go." The heat in Willow's face burnt and she wanted to fall down a drain.

"It's okay, what's up? You don't sound good."

"No, Jane was going to pick me up, sorry."

He cleared his throat. "No, don't be. I wanted to talk to you."

"What about?"

"What happened–"

"No need."

"Yes there is, where are you? I can pick you up."

"Matt, really."

"Tell me where you are, right now."

The tone of his voice made her swallow. He was getting impatient. In truth, him picking her up made her feel safer. She focused on where she was, her eye catching the street signs, and she blinked it into focus.

"Okay, I'm at the top of Old Market Street. By the roundabout."

"I know it, I'll be five minutes." He hung up.

Willow leant against a wall and kept her eye on the street behind her clutching her bags. The familiar face didn't materialise, and by the time Matt reached her, she was sure that she'd imagined it.

A car beeped, and Matt opened the door to a huge shiny black SUV. It was ridiculous. She nearly laughed. Parking in a loading zone, he hopped out and went to her, holding his hand out for her bags. With his free arm, he held out his elbow, and she walked with him, taking one last look behind her.

"What is it?" he asked as he helped her into the car. Willow missed her footing on the step up and stumbled a little. Matt held her and lifted her up and set her in.

"Nothing." She settled and breathed again when he walked around the car.

"Tell me." The engine idled as he put his seatbelt on.

"I told you, nothing. Thank you for this, I appreciate it."

"You're full of shit Willow Morris, do you know that?" He smiled as he spoke and raised his brows at her as she gawped.

"Fine, I'll ring Jane."

"No." He indicated and drove off. "Tell me exactly what's got you spooked, and don't bullshit me, it's my job to know this shit."

Willow took a slow breath. Fuck it. "My parents are okay people. Remote, but they don't understand or care to. I'm not who they hoped. As if I had a choice in being disabled. My father wanted me to get married to this guy, Oliver."

"Like an arranged marriage?"

"Yep. But not of my choice and it was about money."

"Like cattle? Like it's 1850?" Matt almost sounded hysterical.

"Pretty much."

"Why?"

"That's not something I'm prepared to share with you. There was another guy, not a good person. I thought I could trust him. But I was wrong. I thought I saw him just now and panicked." Willow spoke quietly, her gaze fixed out the window, but she didn't see any of it. She felt old and angry.

"What did he do? Do you need help?"

Willow turned to Matt, his face set and mean.

She smiled. "No. It's unlikely he'd know where I was, never mind come here. Sometimes your friends are your enemies. But that's too dramatic. I left a toxic life where no one was on my side, and I couldn't advocate for myself. That's all."

"I don't think that's all at all. I think something happened to you."

"What? No, nothing happened to me." That was a lie, an easy automatic one. "I walked away before it did. It's more that tension and manipulation dictated who I was over my disability, over who I am. Before I became ill, I was a classical singer. I rode a horse. Gerwin. She was beautiful. I did a host of things, and it was taken from me. I gave up my life."

"I'm sorry."

"Don't be. I know myself in a way I would never have done had I never become ill. My privilege has been challenged. It's eye-opening."

Matt didn't answer, and they drove in silence.

He helped her out of the car when they reached home and carried her bags inside. Jane was tinkering in the garage on her motorbike. A sleek black Vincent Shadow. She had her hair up in a scarf and a smudge of grease on her face.

"Hey!" She beamed and followed them inside, careful not to touch anything. Her eyes darted between Matt and Willow.

"I accidentally called him instead."

Jane said nothing, and Willow put the kettle on.

"I'll get off then." Matt cleared his throat.

Jane pulled her lips into her mouth. "I've got to finish up, see you later Matt." She turned and left.

Matt hovered, eyes on her. Willow concentrated, pain and sluggishness creeping in as she made the tea, making her clumsy.

"I'm sorry, about the other day. I'm not that guy. Usually. I apologise unreservedly."

Willow tried to suppress her laughter, forgetting about her family and trying to coordinate herself for a moment. "It's fine."

"I'd like to make it up to you."

"Why?"

"Because I like you, and I'm interested in you. Would you like to go out?"

Willow spilt the milk and tried to mop it up. Matt approached with caution, cleaned up for her, and finished making the tea.

"Sit, I'll bring them over."

She sat at the table. Her body flagging, yet her brain scrambled at his words, and she slumped down into a dining chair. She'd rather be in bed.

Matt set the cups down. "Are you okay?"

"I'm tired and in pain."

"Sorry, I should go."

"No, it's fine. I can sit here for a bit before I go to bed. You might as well say what's on your mind." Willow clenched everything and looked up.

He sat next to her. "Would you like to go out to dinner?"

Willow turned the cup and held it, relishing the heat that burnt into her hands. Her skin tingled. "No. And it's not because I don't like you. I think, not that I know you very well, but you're an impressive guy."

"If it's about what happened–"

"No. Not at all, though it's not an image I'll forget anytime soon. I should thank you, it's the closest I'm likely to get to anything so," Willow laughed and looked up. He was grinning with his brows raised. She cleared her throat in a giggle. "Anyway, I'm not the girl for you. I would never be able to give you what you want."

"What do I want?" All amusement left him, and he sipped his tea.

"A sub, right? It's not me. It's not who I am. I spent years being controlled by other people, and I'm sorry, but I'll be damned if that's going to happen again. I need to make my own life. Find my own path, one that isn't defined by other people, especially men."

"I see."

"It's got nothing to do with you as a person, not anything to do with anything about who you are. Perhaps if I weren't disabled, I wouldn't be so vulnerable, and things might be different."

"What's disability got to do with it?"

"I'm physically weak. I have no stamina. I couldn't do what you'd expect of me."

"Slow down. I'm not asking for anything. I'm asking you out to dinner. That's it. We could get to know each other, and honestly, you don't know anything about what I want."

"No, you're right. I don't."

They looked at each other.

"If I were straight or white?" He narrowed his eyes, almost in challenge.

She shrugged and considered the question. "I'd have the same answer. I don't want anyone." She shuddered, thinking of the past.

"Ever or not yet?"

"I don't know."

Matt drank some tea and stood. "Can you manage?"

"Yes, thank you."

Matt looked sad, and she thought he might say something else, but he didn't and left.

Sitting in the company car, her light perfume lingered as Matt started it but didn't drive off and stared for a minute, not thinking.

Tapping on the window made him jump. He opened it, and Jane leant on the frame.

"How's the bike?" he asked.

"Not doing what she's told. I'll fix it. What's going on?"

"Is it weird I like her?"

"No. She's adorable and sweet. Innocent. She needs support and someone to love and care for her. Not that she understands that yet. She will."

"She said no."

"Don't rush her, she's not ready. Something happened."

"I got that too. She was afraid when I picked her up. Thought she saw someone. I got the feeling he's a 'needs my fist in his face' kind of someone."

Jane scowled. "Noted. I'll keep my eye on her. Gently does it, Matt."

"Yeah, I got that."

Matt went back to the office with Willow on his mind. He wanted to respect her privacy, but something gnawed at him, more than she wasn't interested. He was fairly sure she was, and her reluctance meant he wasn't a fetish for her.

He should stay out of it. Should. He should leave her be. He sat at his desk, fidgety yet pensive.

"Matt?" Meera, his assistant brought him a coffee and his messages. "What's up your arse?"

"You are the most delightful woman." He looked flatly at her as she shrugged. Short and round, she was supposed to be fifty-two, but she could have been any age. Her soft light brown skin and brown eyes knew all.

With long dark hair piled onto her head and thick glasses, the woman grinned. "Fucking hell, Matt, you going to tell me or what?" And a sailor's mouth, Meera managed to be professional when it mattered, but she swore a lot.

"Can you contact Josh for me?"

"I can." She sat down. "Who is she?"

"Oh fuck off, Meera."

She cackled.

"Please, phone Josh, get him in."

"I'll message him, he won't answer the phone."

"Don't be pedantic, get him in the office, or I'll find a better assistant."

"There is no better assistant, dickhead. I'm the dog's bollocks. I'll get him in, even if I have to go and pick him up myself."

"Fine." He made a shooing gesture and got back to work.

Josh was one of the best investigators he had, and Matt hoped he wasn't doing the wrong thing, but the disconcertion about Willow's situation prickled. He knew he wouldn't be able to relax until he knew.

Still, it didn't feel good.

By Stefanie Simpson

SHE'S IN PARTIES

Willow sat in the front room surrounded by twenty people she didn't know. Nearly all the group were there for Darby's birthday. When Jane told her they were having a party, she had no idea this was what she meant.

Tabbie and her newly bright red hair stood in front of everyone with her latest products. There was everything anyone could possibly desire on display, and Willow didn't move. She stared straight ahead, clutching her glass of wine like a buoy.

Next to her, Suzy laughed with Mel, and across the room, Jane sat with people who Willow didn't know. The only person missing was Matt.

Even Filip was there, eyes on Tabbie.

Tabbie started talking again, and Willow blinked.

"This is the OmUlit2. This version, as opposed to the first model, has four vibration settings." She held out the bright pink vibrator, curved in shape, the small end was for the clit, and the length with a bulbous end was for the g-spot. Willow was drawn to the bright silicon toy; it could be nice. Her fantasies of Matt were getting out of hand, and she'd never been particularly sexual, but thinking of him did things to her.

It was probably curiosity more than anything else. He was forbidden, and the things he did and desired, weren't hers. That was all it was. Definitely.

Yep.

The thing was handed around, and when it reached her last, she turned it over and held it out to Tabbie.

The woman took it back with a smile. The look in her eye made Willow think she was laughing at her, but that wasn't it. She had the feeling they were all laughing at her. Just as her discomfort got the better of her, the door went, and Jane answered it. Matt waltzed in.

His presence took up the whole room, and the atmosphere shifted. Filip became quieter, and Mel looked longingly at Matt. He smiled at them, and then his eyes darted to Willow.

His smile dimmed, and she looked down. The dynamics in the group were alien to her, she was so bad with groups of people. Unused to them for nearly ten years, her self-awareness made her hyper-cautious of doing and saying the wrong thing.

Her awkward frustration grew, and she wanted to go to bed. But if she did, they'd all think it was because of Matt.

Suzy nudged her.

Willow shook her head slightly as the group got rowdier. Matt settled where Mel had been sitting, and they sat on the floor, turned back up to Matt. Willow half-listened to them flirting, and Matt's rich laughter made her stomach dip.

"Willow, was there anything you wanted to buy?" Tabbie asked, and the room went quiet.

"No, thank you."

"Why not?"

Willow stared at a loss.

"Tabbie, that's unnecessary." Suzy sighed at her. Tabbie shrugged and turned back to some of the others.

"Ignore her."

Willow looked upward. "I don't get why she thinks I'm a threat. They're not together, he's not even speaking to me, so what's the big deal?"

"It's complicated."

"I get that, this whole group is weird. I'm going to bed." Willow stood up and left the room. She felt eyes follow her as she went up. In the cooler hall, she took a deep breath as she sat on the stair lift.

Matt appeared.

"What?" she snapped.

"Nothing. What's wrong?" He leant on the newel post.

"Nothing."

"Well, between us, that's a lot of fuck all." His eyes sparkled with warmth.

She relaxed. His casual tone reassuring. "Seems so."

He waited, eyes on her as she went upstairs, his presence burning in her cheeks. She wouldn't look at him. He followed her up as she reached the top, struggling to get up.

"Let me help you."

She inwardly sneered at his concern and ignored him.

A flash of hurt passed his face. As she stood, instantly sorry, she tripped over her own feet and landed with a sharp thump, flat on her face, waiting for the world to devour her from mortification.

She expected him to laugh, but he crouched down and put his sure and warm hand on her back, and Willow wanted to cry.

"Are you all right?"

"Fine," she said into the carpet.

"Come on. Let's get you up." He helped her turn and sit.

She saw the light touch of pity, and she wanted to hit him. With a deep breath, she let it pass. "I'm fine."

"You're not. You're grumpy and upset and need some help. Let me help you. It's allowed."

"Matt, that's kind, but I don't want your pity."

"I don't pity you. I want to help you get to your room because I can't leave you here, okay?"

Her eyes fluttered closed in place of a scream, and she nodded.

Matt moved to a kneel and hauled her up. Carrying her into her room, he lay her on the bed gently. "There, not so terrible. Now tell me what's wrong." Matt shut the door.

Willow didn't move. With a neutral expression, he slipped off her ballet pumps and placed them under her chair. She watched him line them up.

He was always so careful and neat. His hair was perfect, clothes immaculate. She wondered if he ever slobbed out. She glanced around her slightly messy room and wondered if it bothered him at all.

Sitting on the edge of the bed, he faced her, sitting too close for comfort. "Well?"

She didn't speak. She didn't know what to say to him.

"I think Tabbie makes you uncomfortable. I think that me not coming over to talk to you made you unhappy."

Willow glanced down.

"Why?"

"Look at me. Look. I'm a disabled nobody. People can be comfortable in feeling superior. I have to defer to others. I didn't want you to pick me up. Yet I had to. I have to give my power to other people all the time. I hate it."

He tilted his head in question.

"You don't understand it, how could you? You don't think I'm furious because I don't rage at the moon. Well, Matt, you can shove it because I'm livid. Anger takes energy that I don't have. Letting shit go is an art form, but it takes a lot to do it. I'll let her bitchiness go, but I don't have to like her and be the good saintly inspo-porn disabled person." Willow's face was red, and her eyes burnt with anger.

"I like you angry. I see it, I understand." The enigmatic look on his face only annoyed her more. "You were jealous."

"No. I'm — excuse me — we are under scrutiny from everyone, and I loathe it."

"Why?"

"Because they think we should be together."

"We should, but I won't push you."

Silence sat thickly between them, and she wanted him to kiss her. He wanted to; the look on his face was perfectly clear.

He leant forward, eyes on her mouth, and Willow's heart almost hurt, it pounded so hard.

"People will think something is going on between us if you don't go back downstairs."

Matt smirked. "I'd rather be here getting to know you."

"I don't care."

"You're pushing against this. I won't hurt you."

"Liar. That's what you do."

Matt went cold and sat back. "No. I like control, and you don't know the first thing about what I want. That's why I'd like to get to know you, and you get to know me. Aren't you even a bit curious to find out, don't you like me at all?"

Willow picked at the duvet. "Yes."

"I can tell you about it."

She flushed and looked up.

"I'm sexually attracted to people who suit my sexual appetite more than their bodies or gender. I've joked I'll fuck any willing sub. I like to dominate, be obeyed, I like restraints, and yes pain, and fucking. But this is how that works; I discuss with any partner wants and desires. We set the boundaries, and anything that happens is completely consensual and desperately wanted."

Her mouth went lax, and she breathed harder. The tone of his voice made her skin hot, and her clit pulsed.

"Not so bad, is it?"

She managed to shake her head. His lips parted, and he leant forward.

"Good. I won't push, but I'm not your enemy. I like you Willow, and whether you admit it or not, you need people who can support you. I think in the past, you haven't had much choice in that, but it doesn't mean you don't need it."

That little spear of truth went right through her.

She looked up and blinked back the pain.

"Shit, I'm sorry." Matt took her hand, and she shook her head. "I promise that you're safe with me. I swear it."

"I want to go to sleep. I'm so tired." It had been a long week, and Willow hadn't been in the mood for a party or people at all.

She sat forward and tried to get up, but her legs were unsteady. Matt helped her to the bathroom and was there when she came out and helped her back to bed.

"Trust me, okay?"

Matt picked up her nightie, and Willow nodded. He slid her top up carefully, without leering or even looking at her. Pulling it over her head, Willow held her breath, but Matt only looked into her eyes. She swayed, almost hypnotised by him. His fingers brushed her skin as he reached around her, leaning close and unclasped her bra. She swallowed hard as she let it slip down.

He took it without looking at her breasts and eased the nightie over her head.

"Thank you." Her whisper was close to his face as he straightened the fabric. "I can do the rest."

Matt held her face with his hand and ran his thumb across her bottom lip. "I like you Willow. I'd like to know you better."

She smiled softly, he kissed the top of her head and left. She took off her jeans and got into bed, imagining him coming back into her room. She hated being manipulated, and as much as he was doing just that, part of her didn't care. Chadford so far had been mostly kindness and friendship, and she wanted to trust that he might be one of the good people.

Waking in the dark, she checked her phone. It wasn't even four.

She moaned and rolled over. The sound of laughter drifted up. Bloody hell, didn't these people ever sleep?

Once out of the bathroom, she pulled on a pair of leggings and went downstairs. She hoped she'd avoid everyone while she fetched a drink. She needed to remember to get some bottled water to keep in her room, seeing as the bathroom water was undrinkable. A group was sat in the kitchen, and Willow went cautiously, debating going back to bed, but her dry mouth was annoying.

Hearing the people talking, she halted, thankful the hall light was off.

Tabbie's voice carried, "I mean come on, you've got to admit she doesn't fit in with us."

"Who said she has to?" Jane snapped.

"No one, but she's weird. She's not like us. Vanilla custard."

"I like vanilla custard, thank you." Matt's voice made her stomach dip, and she leant against the wall.

"Just because you fancy her, doesn't make her part of the group."

"Enough Tabbie." Darby's authority carried. "Why does it matter to you what or who she is? If Matt and her get together, that doesn't affect any of us. She's a good person, but if you have a problem with her, I suggest you fuck off."

"And if I did that who'd be your performer?"

"Do you think finding someone to get paid to do demos is that hard? Get over yourself, you're not that fucking special, I think most of us can vouch for that."

The music pulsed as the conversation grounded to a halt. Willow waited a minute until chatter got up again and she hobbled into the kitchen with a thick atmosphere.

"Did we wake you?" Jane asked.

"It's fine." Willow grabbed a glass of filtered water and went out without looking at anyone and then hobbled off back to bed.

She did not need overcomplicated people. Willow needed stress free and simple. For that, she guessed she should back off. As she got back into bed, she thought that might be easier said than done.

REFLECTION

Willow managed to get some sleep but felt terrible all Saturday. There was no sign of anyone else until after lunch. Darby appeared, hair in a scarf, sunglasses on, and refusing to speak.

Willow sat in the front room watching a film. Darby grunted as she joined her, sipping her giant mug of coffee.

"I heard what was said about me last night," Willow said.

Darby nodded. "She's a bitch sometimes."

"It's fine. I've been thinking about what she said. I think she had a point. I'm not part of the group, and I'm okay with that. I'm not used to having friends. Besides, I'm not included so it won't affect much."

Darby drank her coffee for a few minutes. "Don't you like us?"

"I like you and Jane, and fine, I like Matt. I don't know anyone else. I think they probably feel like Tabbie. I don't want to make anyone uncomfortable."

"No."

"What?"

"No. We're not a secret club, where we have to have criteria to enter. Jane has adopted you, you're hers now, like it or not. Deal with it."

"Yes, but-"

"But nothing. Can I give you some advice? And I promise it's the last time I'll bring it up. Go out with Matt."

Willow blinked and turned back to the film, not that she watched any of it but thought about what Darby said.

"Right, I have to go to the hairdressers, I'll see you this evening."

"Evening?"

"I'm having my hair redone, do you think this shit takes an hour? All day. All bloody day." Darby went back upstairs, and Willow listened to the film, her mind wandering back to Matt.

The credits had rolled, and the title screen flashed over on a loop. She paid it no heed, and making her mind up, took the risk.

Just a date, that's all he'd wanted. She could do that. One date.

Willow picked up her phone and composed a message. Then deleted it. Then composed another one. For twenty minutes, she typed and deleted.

In the end, she sent, *Hi. Can I change my mind about dinner?*

Why?

She looked at that single word and wanted to take it back. What a nob, thinking he still would.

She didn't reply. Instead, she turned off the telly and went to read in bed instead. Not that she managed to concentrate on any of the words.

Why have you changed your mind?

What was she doing? So out of her depth with someone like him, she'd only get hurt.

Willow threw her book down and got up. Restless, she put on her sandals and went into the garden. The late summer was cooler, but the day fine. She meandered around the established beds, and down the path, thick with lavender, her fingers brushing it, the scent in the air as bees and butterflies pattered around her.

It was lovely. The path wound to the back of the garden and the small veg path that Jane was cultivating. Most of the peas had been picked, and Willow took a remaining pod and ate the sweet, warm peas out of it.

Turning from the sweet, earthy smell of compost, she wandered back and crossed the lawn.

Two missed calls, and another text was waiting for her. *Willow, I don't like being ignored, darling, please answer my question.*

She didn't know what to do with that. Though she did start it. Her reply was as neutral as she could manage. *I'm not your darling. My name is Willow. I shouldn't have changed my mind. Sorry.*

His reply was immediate. *Apologies, I'll attempt to remember that. Perhaps I can take you out as a peace offering?*

Willow laughed, how could she not. There was a charm about him when she wasn't being unsettled by his presence. The allure of him; the danger and dip in her stomach was too irresistible. This was such a bad idea, but Willow couldn't help herself. Games like this were out of her league. Look at what happened with Peter. Fucking Peter. The evil piece of shit. Fuck him. Fuck pity and manipulation and everything that happened.

I'll take it under consideration.

Are you going to play coy with me? Saturday, I'll pick you up at six.

No, I'm busy.

Liar. Wear that dress. Winky face, he ended that with a winky face. She shouldn't analyse emojis. It was banter. Only banter. Willow's hands started to sweat, and she put her phone down.

She jumped when her phone went again. *I'm waiting to hear you say yes.*

Willow choked a laugh and felt unnaturally brave. *I hope that's the norm with you.*

Yes, always, yes is important to me.

Good to know. Willow took a deep breath. *Yes.*

Perfect, see you Saturday.

She was convinced he usually got what he wanted. But then, she'd said no at first, and he'd backed right off.

She contacted him. It would be fine. She could handle it.

Sweat broke out afresh, and she wiped her top lip and went to bed for a bit.

Willow had been twitchy all week. Nervous. On Thursday, Suzy sat opposite her at lunch.

"What's going on?"

"I'm going out with Matt on Saturday," Willow said quietly and with absolute seriousness.

Suzy's eyes lit up, and Willow shook her head.

"Don't, I did an impulsive silly thing, and I wish I hadn't, but now I can't back out, and I'm scared, and please help me."

"It's okay."

"It's not, I tried to back out and he was all... intense and 'no, you started this, let's go out.' I know it's only dinner, but what if he turns out to be a creep, or I like him, and he doesn't like me, and honestly I'm so shit at this."

"Okay, slow down." Suzy put her hands over Willow's, cold and clammy again. "Breathe with me."

They took some slow breaths.

"Matt will be a gentleman and take care of you. If you're not interested, he will respect that. If you can't do this, then that's okay, but tell him now."

"The thing is I do want to go, and at the same time, I don't. There are bad things in my life, in the past, and I don't understand why he'd be interested. Him interested in me? It's bizarre."

"No, it's not. Now, what are you wearing?"

"He asked me to wear the dress from the barbeque."

Suzy laughed. "Nice." After a moment, she picked up her coffee and sipped. "Can I ask you a question?"

Willow nodded.

"Have you had much experience? You don't seem to have much confidence."

"Some, and I don't. Part of being here is to become independent, put my mistakes behind me, and removing toxic people from my life is helping me." Her hand went to her neck, the little heart not there, and instead, pressed her hand into her skin. "I was naïve and foolish and trusted the wrong people. I'm afraid I'll do it again."

"Willow, you hit fucking gold." Suzy grinned.

After work, Willow went into town with Suzy, she got her hair cut, and she bought some new makeup, with Suzy helping her.

"Thank you," she said as they were testing lipsticks on Willow's wrist.

"You're welcome." Suzy had pinched out her contacts before leaving and put her glasses on. She peered over them, and her warm grin made Willow happy. "It must be hard, having to adapt. Bravery isn't big things, it's the little continual things of life. I went through something as a girl, everyone said how brave I was, but I wasn't. It's all the years since, living with consequences. I can't understand your life, but I know how that feels. You're very sweet and pretty. Matt likes you, and that makes you lucky because people throw themselves at him all the time. He has no interest in them. But that doesn't mean you're obliged. It doesn't mean you have to do things you're uncomfortable with."

"Thank you, Suzy."

Willow spent the next day in bed, sleep evading her. She tried reading but couldn't concentrate. Lying in a not really asleep but definitely not awake state, she let her mind wander about, thinking of Matt. Matt's perfectly lovely back. His bottom. His very lovely cock. She put her hand between her legs to stay the pulse, but she wanted him.

With a frustrated sigh, she sat up, realising the pain in her stomach was probably hunger. She got up and shuffled out. Not paying attention to where she was going, Willow tripped over her foot that rarely co-operated, missed the newel post as she reached for it, and went head first down the stairs.

She didn't even have time to think 'not again' before tumbling all the way down and smacking her body as she went.

Willow was cold, and blinking open her eyes, she realised that she was not under a duvet. Huh. Her head throbbed, and vision wobbled as she tried to look around. Information filtered into her brain and sluggishly began processing.

Lying on the floor — nothing unusual there, so she fell. Her back and legs hurt, and one leg was elevated. Ah, stairs. She was good at throwing herself down them.

Willow didn't move. She let the pain build and settle. She listened to it, trying not to feel it. Moving in waves, it was mostly on her previously injured leg, but these stairs weren't like her parents' house, and Willow wasn't injured but bruised and shocked. She hoped.

At least she had pyjama bottoms on and wasn't flashing her minge to anyone in the house. When the scratchy carpet and being cold got too much, she attempted to stand, only for her vertigo to kick in, and invisible hands pushed her down to the floor as everything spun.

She blinked rapidly, unable to keep her eyes closed or open.

The thought of needing to get help flittered in, but before she could figure out how, the thought went again, and in the distorted blank space it left, she tried to remember what she was thinking.

Her heart beat faster, and pain radiated through her chest. She couldn't take a deep breath.

The first time it happened at university, she thought she was having a heart attack. It was unlike any pain. The memory of that sensation and the fear it garnered always faded until it returned.

Willow attempted to relax and wait for the worst to pass. The floor moved like water, and reaching up, she felt for the button to bring the lift down, but she couldn't reach it, and her arm flopped down.

Frustration built but it did no good. Shivering, she wondered where her mum was, but then she wasn't at home.

There wasn't carpet in the hall at home. Where was she? Why was she on the floor? Her leg throbbed, and a stab of pain shot through her nerves. Oh yeah, she fell down the stairs.

She tried to recall a name, the woman who lived in the house — what was her name? The word sat on her tongue, and she opened her mouth, but only a croak came out.

Willow wanted to get up and struggled until she was pushed back down. She slurred something, but the meaning of what she wanted to say escaped her as soon as he tried to speak. Panic edged at the back of her skull, filtering down her to meet the pins and needles in her arms and legs. Her hands trembled, and the pain intensified.

Willow kept blinking, but slower, listlessly, in time with her breath.

Somewhere, far away, was a noise, loud and alien, and only the volume registered. No articulate thought formed in response. As the synapses and transmitters of her brain — and all the bullshit she didn't understand — tried to process information and what she needed to do like an infected PC, more information assaulted her.

A change in the light, more noise. She kept blinking. She was supposed to do something. On instinct, she opened her mouth and tried to form words. Hands on her, there were hands on her. She wanted to fight, make them get off her, what were they doing? She wanted to scream and make them stop touching her, but she couldn't speak.

Her breath hitched, and a tear fell from one eye.

A fuzzy face appeared in front of her. It cleared as she blinked and they unfocused again as it split in two.

Words. Someone was speaking to her. A flash of lilac. Jane. It came back to her; Jane.

Then she was gone. Willow made a noise. Her muscles seized, and she couldn't stay her tears. Her body twitched hard, sending another round of needles stabbing through her body and her breath stuttered. She wanted to push the thing sitting on her off.

Only nothing was sitting on her, why couldn't she get up? More noise, more hands on her body. This time she put her hands up to fight, but a warm, sure hand rested on her forehead, and Matt appeared in front of her.

"Hey." That even deep tone made her lip wobble, and she cried. "Shh, sweetheart, it's all right now. I've got you. I'm going to pick you up. Willow, look at me."

He spoke clearly, and the words registered. She took a breath, pain lacing her, and grunted.

"I'm picking you up." He did, and the sensation of rising and falling at the same time overwhelmed her, and she went lax. Vision spinning and spots dancing, she wanted to vomit.

"All right, it's all right."

Willow didn't realise she was sobbing. Pain overcame her, her strength to fight it left.

There was nothing to hold onto, only Matt. He moved and carried her upstairs. The cool calm of her bed, the soft comfort and dim light was a balm to her senses.

"Hey, can you look at me?"

Willow took a second to absorb the relief and opened her eyes. Matt's face was cast in shadow, full of worry.

"If I'd have known you go that far to get out of a date with me–"

Willow closed her eyes, turning her head away.

"I'm sorry, come on, look at me."

Willow wanted to sleep. Blinking tears away, she looked back at him, and even that took effort. Someone else was with them, Jane came and sat on the bed, pressing a cool cloth to Willow's brow.

She wiped the tears from Willow's face, and Matt lifted her head to put some water to her lips.

"Did you hit your head?"

Willow made a 'no' noise, her head didn't hurt, but she didn't know. Matt seemed to understand. Jane left them, and he took his shoes off and lay down next to her.

He smoothed wisps of hair stuck to her damp skin and took a deep breath. Willow's body relaxed, her eyes so heavy as everything continued to spin.

She felt her blood pump, she felt the Earth move under her, she felt everything in a hyper-sense of unreality and wanted nothing other than oblivion. Yet for the first time, she wasn't so afraid, and Matt's presence gave her comfort.

With her eyes closed, she focused on her breathing, and Matt's fell into sync with hers. His hand smoothing her hair as she breathed in, and Willow found an anchor. The scent of him, clean and masculine was new and exciting, yet familiar as if once forgotten.

Strange, disjointed thoughts of them together distracted her enough from the pain until exhaustion took over and she fell asleep.

Matt watched Willow. Her eyes relaxed, breath calm and her body gave, as though she stopped fighting herself. Jane had sounded terrified in the phone, and he came as quick as he could. Jane was unflappable. She'd dealt with more shit than most people and cared for her gran for more than six years. She also ruled any demos with absolute control. Jane panicking was not good. At all.

Seeing Willow like that scared him, and he understood her fear and reticence. Matt needed to have a long, hard think about his feelings for her, and what would be best for them both.

As Willow slept, he smiled with a clench in his stomach. He'd not had the thrill of that feeling for years. Not since Kai.

Pulling out his phone, he searched fibromyalgia and read up on it, all the while, staying close to her, wanting to hold her, but resisting the urge.

TOE IN THE WATER

W illow opened her eyes to warmth and a dark room. She hummed and nestled further into her duvet. Something was different. She wiggled her hips and found that she wasn't surrounded by only her duvet. A hot thing, solid, and oh shit another person was behind her. Willow swallowed as her heart skipped, and she realised it was Matt. All her breath left her.

She blinked and came up blank about how he got there. She remembered getting up yesterday. Then nothing. Not a single thing. She didn't know if she'd gone out drinking or what.

By that realisation, she knew that she had in fact been unwell. Her life was riddled with pockets of missing memories. A fact often used against her. She did what she always did and went with it.

"Hey."

Willow shivered at Matt's voice. He was right behind her and spoke softly in her ear.

"Morning," she whispered, a little stunned.

"Evening actually, it's six in the evening."

"Oh. Which day?"

"Friday."

"What happened?"

"You don't seem particularly alarmed I'm in your bed." Matt propped himself up behind her and straightened her messy hair out. She wanted to hum, it felt so nice.

"If I don't remember things, it probably means that I've been unwell. Did I collapse?"

Matt took a deep breath. "All the way down the stairs. Jane rang me. We debated taking you to hospital, but Jane said that it's usually more traumatic and you'd rather go to bed when you collapse. I was worried you hit your head."

"Thank you, for coming to my aid. I appreciate it. You didn't have to stay."

"I wanted to see that you were all right. I couldn't leave you."

Her body ached as the bruises deepened, and she nodded, her throat closing with emotion.

"How about I get us some food?"

"Yes please, I'm starved."

The bed dipped, and she shifted to see him. His polo shirt was rumpled. He straightened it and patted down his hair before going. Willow sighed when he'd gone and assessed the damage before closing her eyes again. Everything hurt, and her sore ribs when she took a deep breath brought tears to her eyes.

Sounds startled her, and Matt set a tray down on the dresser.

"Okay, loo?"

She smiled. He was sweet and caring. Odd that this man who barely knew her was so kind. It was more than she'd received from any man.

"You're very good at this," she croaked as he helped sit her up.

"Jane and I have a lot in common. My mum was sick a few years ago, and I cared for her."

"I'm sorry."

He smiled, it was gentle and sweet. "Thanks. She's fine now. Anyway, it means I know what I'm doing. Right, let's get you standing."

Willow let herself be taken care of, ignoring the voice that questioned the cost and strings attached.

Willow leant against the sink, washing her hands and patted her face with cold water. A swathe of bruises ran up one arm, and she tentatively lifted her t-shirt, a black livid bruise crossed her ribs to her back.

"You okay?" Matt called through the door.

"I'm covered in bruises. You can come in."

Matt sucked his teeth in a wince. "Looks painful."

"They are. I think I might have bruised a rib too." Willow took a deep breath, sharp, and it made her head spin.

"Well, I think you get a valid pass on standing me up tomorrow."

"I'm sorry."

"It's okay." He helped her back to bed and settled the tray over her lap.

She tucked into her sandwich, and Matt tucked into his. "I can't cook. At all. A sandwich or something out of a freezer is all you'll get out of me."

"Sandwiches are good, thank you." Food was wonderful right then, anything shoved her way remotely like food, she'd have eaten.

"Shit. You can't eat that," he said, almost lunging for her plate.

She clutched it closer. "Well. It bloats me and makes me tired. I'm already tired." She shrugged and took another bite.

After a drink of water, she looked him over. "You've been here all day, right?"

He nodded with a mouthful of food.

"Don't you need to be at work or something?"

Matt took a moment and wiped his mouth with a paper napkin. "I'm the boss, I can do what I want. Rotas are assigned, jobs are covered, my amazing assistant Meera has everyone in their boxes," he smiled at Willow's frown, "she's basically the work-mom, we all do what she says." He grinned, but it fell. "I was supposed to go and visit mum and nana tonight, but I'm officially cancelling our date until you're better, and I'll go and see them tomorrow."

"I'm sorry."

"Don't be."

"Maybe we shouldn't. I mean, I'm a mess, it's not fair to you."

"Bullshit. I can take it easy with you, and there's no rush. When you're better, we're going on that date. If you didn't want to, you wouldn't have taken the risk and texted me."

"Why?"

"I like you. I want to get to know you. You're also very lovely to look at, which is a bonus, but you're a good person. Stop asking questions so I'll compliment you." He winked and took a large bite of his sandwich.

Willow's heart fluttered, and she remembered him in the shower again. Blinking rapidly, she picked up her sandwich.

"Are you thinking about the shower?" He narrowed his eyes.

She dropped it, and he laughed. "Fine, yes, I think about it."

"How often?"

"Most of the time my eyes are closed, to be honest."

Matt laughed. It was full and deep, and she watched him throw his head back, the back of his hand over his mouth. His Adam's apple bobbed up and down, the light stubble on his neck of him not shaving that day looked rough. She wondered how it would feel against her skin. Between her thighs.

She'd never had a man there. She wasn't a virgin, by any means, but she'd never been eaten out.

"Not hungry?" he asked, a teasing twinkle in his eye.

He had no idea. She was starved.

While Matt took their plates down, Willow nestled back into the pillows, feeling wretched.

Matt came back and sat next to her again. "What do you want to do?"

"About?" Willow took a slow blink.

"I can go, I can hang out with you, whatever you want."

Stay, ideally, but she wasn't fit company. "I'm too tired to do anything. I'm sure there are things you could be doing."

"Yes, but I can work on my phone. Or read. Hey, I could read to you."

"That sounds nice."

"Are you reading anything?"

Willow went red.

"Oh, now really?" Matt teased.

With a sigh, Willow nodded to the bedside table, and in the drawer, Matt found a book. He chuckled.

"I did not see you reading EE Queen. Have you read the others?"

"Yes."

"Hmm." He glanced sideways at her with that twinkle in his eye. Willow really liked that twinkle.

Matt settled in and opened the book after fetching his reading glasses from his jacket.

"Susan let the music wash over her as every set of eyes devoured her body, one man at the front especially, he'd been at the club three times that week, always front and centre, always for her. She was a goddess for him, making him hard, making him desire her.

"She usually took twenty-pound notes but took his desire for her as payment. What little she wore fell from her body, exposing her truth as she danced. She never switched off, she was always alive and vital for sex, for the need to consume the lust offered to her. She wanted it more than food."

Matt's deep even tone was so soothing, Willow floated. Susan's exploits in his voice made her body ache for sex beneath her pain. The two sensations mixed. It nearly felt as though Matt were caressing her body.

She shivered and fell asleep.

Matt shifted, his erection digging in. He glanced down at Willow to see her asleep, lips parted and breath steady. She was lovely.

Putting down the book, he eased up and adjusted himself. He didn't want to leave her, but he should let her sleep.

The sweetness to her, the bubble he wanted to form around them both was the most tempting idea, but he was afraid. For her, and for what he could offer. With a frown, he picked up his jacket and shoved his reading glasses on his head and went down.

Darby and Jane were in the front room.

"How is she?"

"Asleep. Covered in bruises."

"Are you all right?"

Matt frowned. "I um, I'll see you." He left before they said anything else. Taking a drive, skirting the ring road back to the south riverside block of flats where he lived, he took the narrow winding B-roads. He loved driving, and though he should get back to the office and catch up, or go see his mum, as the late summer sun cast an orange light, he wanted to empty his mind and think.

He thought about Kai, how they'd not been ready. He knew they were happy now, all loved up. He felt a twinge, not for the past, but for the same thing. He wanted love.

Maybe wanting it wasn't enough, but he always had hope. The idea of hope came with Willow's face, but with it, sadness. He wanted to make her better, not that he could.

Matt swallowed his emotion and fear. The sight of her at the bottom of the stairs wouldn't leave him.

He couldn't take it away, but maybe he could make her happy. Right then, he decided, if she'd let him, he'd give her that.

A settled feeling came over him. He was going to take Willow out when she was better, he was going to introduce her to his wants, and see where they could compromise.

Willow worried. She couldn't help it. She woke at four am and wanted to throw up. Alone in the dim predawn, she managed to stand. Testing her legs for their weight-bearing abilities, she found they were all right. After achieving going to the bathroom without crawling, she faced the stairs.

Slowly, with her cane, she made it to the stair lift and clung on as she whirred down. In the kitchen, Princess lay in her cat bed. Her long fluffy grey fur was all mushed up and squiffy as she raised her head in disdain.

"Wow," Willow said, crouching down and scratching under her ear, "you look like me." Willow made a coffee, knowing she'd had too much sleep, and felt like she'd been kicked repeatedly by an entire rugby team.

Willow found the ibuprofen and sat gingerly at the table. Princess sauntered out of her cat hut and hopped onto the table and sat in front of Willow, purring.

"Hey little cutie," Willow whispered and petted her fur until she was tidy and princess-looking again. "Maybe I'll come back as a cat in my next life. That would be nice."

Princess yawned with a mew, and Willow took a deep breath before making her way back upstairs. Princess followed, waiting at the top of the stairs after zooming past her on the way up. She pattered in with Willow and jumped up on the bed, promptly curling up and going back to sleep.

Willow got back under the now cool covers and snuggled in. She eyed the book Matt left out. 'Susan Strips' was a guilty pleasure, one that Willow revisited far too often. She picked it up, clicked on the lamp and started reading, only now she heard Matt, and her skin goosed. She put the book back down.

Was it too early to text him?

She picked her phone up and saw a message waiting for her. *Thought I'd let you rest, I want you to let me know you're okay when you can.* Two kisses at the end. That was good, right? If he felt sorry for her, he wouldn't put kisses.

Maybe.

She tapped out a text after staring at her screen while her coffee cooled. She wisely drank it before sending it. *Thank you for yesterday. As horrible as it was, you made it bearable, and I'm grateful.*

She debated a kiss at the end, one or two? Two. He set the tone, she should mirror it.

Her heart thudded as she laughed at herself. It was a fucking text message, and she was nearly thirty.

Willow ran a bath and snacked before sinking into the water and read her book. She heard Matt's voice in her mind and had to put it down and put her hand between her legs to either relieve the ache or stay the need. She went with relief, which didn't work.

Willow was not a horny soul, in fact, she rarely experienced sexual impulse for anyone. Never Oliver, and only a little with Peter Cloughton.

She shuddered at the thought and wondered if it was him she saw in town, or it was the nagging insecurity over what happened.

Perhaps if she talked about it, and for a minute she wanted to talk to Jane, but she wanted to tell Matt. Maybe he'd know to what to do. Those thoughts ended any lingering sexual desire, and Willow went back to bed.

In the morning Matt took a call on his private work phone. The only person working on any investigation was Josh, and Matt answered on the second ring as he got into the office. He liked going in on a Saturday. No one about to bother him. He wanted to check all the job rotas.

He watched the computer screen boot up as he waited for Josh to speak. He knew how difficult it was. Most people didn't give him the chance, but Matt had the patience of a saint. Or a really good dom.

"Found him." Josh didn't mess about with words. Economy was necessary to save the pain in his voice.

"Where are you?"

"Harringly. You should come here."

Matt closed his eyes for a minute and opened the calendar on his desktop when he signed in.

"There's nothing I can't rearrange. Do you really need me there?"

"Yes. In person."

Matt felt an uneasy creep of fear. Ending the call, he buzzed Meera. She said nothing when he told her, his tone said it all.

It was a particular tone, dry and quiet. Everyone who knew him understood that voice.

"I'll see to everything."

Matt took a company car, not his own, and drove down straight away. He had a holdall in the office — he always kept a bag for emergencies — and he picked up some food for the drive down.

By the time he reached the outskirts of Harringly West, he was amazed that Willow had driven all the way by herself.

He drove through the village. Pretty grey stone cottages, a green with a pond. Boutique shops and a thatched pub. Idyllic. Beyond that was a sprawling estate and farmland. He drove through it, practically able to smell the privilege and he thought about his mother, their tiny flat when he was a kid where he didn't have his own room and nothing new.

The rolling land gave to higher ground, and he found the small old market town beyond.

Matt pulled into the pub and inn car park and sat in his car for a minute before getting out and stretching. He made his way inside and found Josh in a dim corner, cap low on his face.

"Wearing that gets you noticed."

He looked up, burn scars marred his face and neck. He took his cap off and, long dark blond hair flopped forward.

"Why am I here?"

Josh said nothing but tapped his empty cup. Matt muttered to himself and ordered them coffee and some food. The server looked at Josh with curiosity and him with fear from the bar. He hated when people tried to work out who he was. Matt returned a bored stare before focusing on the matter in hand.

Josh ate and picked up a folder from the chair beside him and slid it over.

Matt looked at the photos and read over the police reports and Josh's meticulous notes. He pushed his lunch away. "Where is he now?"

Josh took a sip of tea. "Gone."

Matt restrained his anger. "Find him. He might have gone to Chadford."

"You should protect the woman. They want her back. Stillwell furious. Cloughton dangerous. Lots of money. Big stakes." Josh coughed and sipped his tea.

Matt let his heart pound and blood rush. With a single deep breath, he nodded.

It seemed that he'd managed to develop a crush on a woman who desperately needed his help. He wondered if she had any notion of the trouble she was in.

By Stefanie Simpson

THIS IS WHAT YOU CAME FOR

Once, when Willow was seven, she ran away. She'd been in the kitchens with Mrs Dorel helping with the cooking. The scent of chicken and roast potatoes always made Willow think of her. Willow's help consisted of pretending to do the washing up while standing on a chair. Mrs Dorel, a grey-haired woman with a warm, kind heart, was the nanny, housekeeper, cook, and all-around estate organiser.

Willow's parents were absent much of the time, and she more-or-less thought of Mrs Dorel as family. Willow knocked a plate, and it fell on the floor as her mother came in.

The woman wasn't maternal or affectionate, but neither was she cruel, merely distant.

Except for that day. That day, she'd been in a temper about something, and took it out on Willow. As she looked back, she understood and forgave her, but at the time, Willow was devastated. The sharp, loud voice cut through her and after being told off, she packed a blue backpack with her favourite toys and books and ran away.

She crossed the length of the estate in her wellies and brown duffle coat, and tramped through the piles of autumn leaves, through the browning long grasses of the fallow field, and past the pasture where the horses grazed.

Her favourite horse came her way, and she rubbed his muzzle, reaching up to the enormous creature, and went on. She skirted the hedges with one purpose in mind. Mr Cloughton's house.

Old Cloughton was the estate manager, and the family had been there for three generations. His son, Peter was set to be the fourth.

Peter and Willow were thick as thieves. He was also five years older than she was. At eight, Willow was bright and happy. She could ride, she read a lot, she was the hope and future of the estate.

With all the worldly arrogance of her age, she marched to the Cloughton's and found Peter riding his bike on the way.

Willow loved Peter. Not that she knew what love was, or understood it, but looking back, she did.

Peter took her to his dad, who wiped the tears from her frozen face, and took her home in his old Landrover. She giggled as they bumped along the wet, muddy lanes with Peter next to her, holding her hand.

It was nearly dark when they got home, and the house was mid panic in their search for Willow. Her father shouted at her, her mother cried — a thing that Willow had never seen — and Willow was sent to her room.

Mrs Dorel hugged her. The warm softness of that embrace made her feel safe again.

Willow, staring at the ceiling of Blackthorn Villa during a Sunday of baking late summer sun, shivered.

That memory always stayed with her. She didn't know why, but it never left her. Something about that day, about her mother, and how everyone behaved irked her.

Mrs Dorel left the estate not long after, and Willow didn't know where she was, or if she was alive. Peter's face, as she saw him on his bike, was a wide innocent grin. What happened to him that changed him into such a dickhead?

Her phone pinged. *Can I call you?*

Willow's heart dipped at Matt's message.

She shook off the past, feeling out of sorts, and rang him.

"What's wrong?"

She'd only said hello, and he knew. It made her smile. "Just thinking about the past."

"How are you?" There was hesitation in his voice, and emotion clogged her throat. Maybe she was due on. That would explain the state of her.

She wished she could do something about it. Perhaps she could now.

"I'm," she couldn't think of any words to say.

"Willow, do you want me to come over? Do you need anything?"

"No, I'm okay."

"Liar."

"It's a girl thing."

She practically heard him sweating in the silence. "Do you want me to bring you anything?"

"So brave."

He chuckled. "Come on, what do you need?"

"Nothing."

He sighed down the phone. "I'm going to say something, and it's either going to scare you away, or make you understand, okay?"

"Go on."

"We've not gotten into this, we've not even had dinner yet, but I'm drawn to you. Very drawn. There's something about you, about being around you."

"I feel it too."

He sounded relieved when he answered. "Good. I'm glad it's not just me. But some things might get in the way. Hence caution. I need to know your story, it's bugging me. I want to help. I also want to explain about me, my sexuality is an important part of my identity, and we should discuss it."

"That's fair." She forced the words out.

"Good. It's not only physical; for me, it's psychological too. I hate the notion of secrets, if I want to know something, I expect a straight and honest answer. Some people don't like it, but for me it's communication. I'm the same in return. Does that make sense?"

"Yes. I'm not sure how comfortable I am with it, there are reasons that I'm cautious."

"And I need to know those reasons if I'm going to accept that. So, when you're not in as much pain and feel up to it, I want to have our date. Maybe you in those cute pink pyjamas with a takeaway, but I want it to happen, and soon."

Willow swallowed. "A takeaway sounds nice, I could do with a curry."

"How about tonight? We can hang out at yours again. I'll bring whatever you want."

"Okay."

Willow's heart pounded, though she wanted to be better so that they could go out. Still, he'd not run away from her, so that must mean something. Maybe. He wasn't Oliver nor Peter.

She sent Jane a text, and she came rushing up the stairs. "Hey," she said, breathless, still wiping her hands on a tea towel. "What's up?" Her newly re-dyed lilac hair was bright as it caught the sun.

"Matt's bringing our date here. Tonight."

Jane beamed. "Don't have loud sex."

"I'm, we're not, I can't," Willow stuttered, and Jane laughed.

"I know, come on treacle, let's at least change the sheets."

Willow giggled.

They changed the bed, cleaned her room, well, Willow did a bit, but Jane went like a whirlwind. Willow went with comfortable yet shaping leggings and a light green linen shirt. It had a nice knack of hanging off a shoulder. She wore a strappy yoga bra underneath, supportive, a little sexy, but comfortable.

She made it downstairs in time, and Darby looked her over in approval.

"Nice. I wish I weren't going on this date now."

"How's it going?"

"It's okay. I'm cautious. So far." Darby's full hair natural formed tight curls through it, and it parted in the middle. It suited her. "Right. I'll see you later. Enjoy Matt." Darby smiled and winked before heading out.

"Well, I should get ready too." Jane stretched before getting up.

"You're not leaving me?"

"I'm not bloody-well chaperoning you. I'm meeting up with friends and going out on the pull. Maybe, well, I can live in hope."

She beamed and went upstairs, and not a minute later, the doorbell went. Willow, holding her cane so tight her knuckles went white, opened it. Matt, in a faded black t-shirt and jeans, looked so good. Willow tried not to ogle. By the look of him, she failed in concealing the fact.

She was distracted by the delicious smell of food. He held the bag up, and she stepped aside.

Leaning forward, he kissed her cheek. His aftershave, nearness, soft lips, and rough of stubble pinched through her nerves, ending with a frisson of expectation and dip of her stomach.

When she looked up at him, his look darkened, though it was probably the light, and eyes dipped to her shoulder and the black straps on show. Matt looked almost predatory and she the gazelle, and what was weirder, she liked it.

"Let's get you comfortable."

She managed a nod, and he led her into the lounge. "You can lie down upstairs if you like?"

"No, this is fine."

"You're nervous."

"Bit."

His jaw flexed as he went into the kitchen and dished out the food. They sat near each other, quiet at first while they ate, Matt brought some beers and even gluten-free ones for her.

"This is nice," she said, desperate to break the tension.

Matt took a bite of naan bread and raised his brows as he chewed. "Best curry place I've ever found. And the company's not bad either."

"Thank you." She ate some chicken and took a drink, and glancing at him, took another. "So you know I was more or less set up for a socially engineered marriage?"

Matt paused mid-chew and nodded.

"It's oh so much worse than that." Willow took a few more bites, feeling Matt watch her. She didn't know where to start. "I thought Oliver was okay. I've known him forever. They have a small holding, it was part of the estate once, but when we ran out of money, my family started selling the land. Bear in mind that I mean like a century ago. Anyway, they've had it for about thirty or forty years I think. It's a way of not paying inheritance tax. You own a certain amount of acreage, and you don't pay tax on the value of the land."

Matt dancing his head about in understanding.

"Our family have nothing really. I'm the last one. My last name is Morris-DeWorthy. DeWorthy is the family name. The Morris bit comes from my father. You see his mother was the last DeWorthy and she married a rich man, by the name of Morris. They lived it up, so I understand. She had money and kept the estate. I was ten when she died. Grandma was glamorous and aloof, but kind to me.

"Anyway. When she died, my parents — or so I think — expected to get her money. She didn't like my mother. No one does. Grandmother put all the money in trust for me and left my parents destitute. I get the money when I'm thirty or marry."

"Fucking hell." Matt put his plate down and wiped his mouth.

"When I went to uni, my parents told me that I was allowed to go, as long as I agree to marry Oliver."

"Why?"

"The Stillwell family have a lot of money and want status. Our family have titles and the estate. It's meaningless, but they value it. Oliver and I marry, then we get cash, my parents get the money from the trust, and the Stillwell's get the family status. That they're morally corrupt is irrelevant, apparently."

"Did you agree?"

Willow looked at him, her head high. "Yes. I had little choice. I never planned to go through with it. I was never going to go home after uni. I don't care about land and status. I fucking hate tweed."

Matt laughed without mirth. "So, what happened?"

"I collapsed during a concert I was singing in, I was a classical singer by the way. I had ten thousand tests, but they couldn't find anything. My parents took me home, and there were days I couldn't stand up. They paid for me to see doctors, so many hospitals. Took four years to diagnosis. I lucked out on a decent doctor.

"My family, needless to say, were disappointed. Oliver was so attentive. He'd visit me all the time."

Willow trailed off and swallowed hard. She put her plate down and drank her beer.

"Tell me about Peter Cloughton."

That name sent shivers through Willow, and an unsettled feeling tingled in her mind. "What do you know?"

"When I picked you up from town, something scared you. I wanted to know what was happening. It's my job."

"I'm not your job." Her breath came quick.

"No." Taking a sip of beer, he took the plates in, clearing the leftovers and came back. Willow's heart dipped as she wondered what he knew, and if she could trust him.

Matt sat back down, facing her and spoke directly. "Peter Cloughton is an interesting character, and I'm surprised he's mixed up in your life."

"What would a nice good girl like me have in common with him?" She shook her head. "Peter was a good kid. I was in love with him when I was young. He was the bee's knees. His dad was the estate manager, so we grew up together. Whenever things were rubbish, I'd go to him. We'd play all over the estate. He'd take me out on his quad bike, and we'd be out all day. Play in the woods.

"Then I went to boarding school." Willow stared off, remembering how afraid she was, how she didn't want things to change. He'd hugged her, and she'd cried when they sat in their favourite place in the woods, leaves not yet turning.

Objectively, she knew he'd humoured her when there was nothing else to occupy him. It must have been flattering to have a starry-eyed fan who loved him.

"I didn't see him for years. Then a year after I came home, I heard he was back on the estate. He came to visit me. My parents were away all the time, and I was usually alone. Considering they had no cash, they managed to live well. Peter spent a lot of time with me, but he'd changed. Rougher. He looked old. He was..." she frowned, "meaner. Nothing overt, but little things I couldn't place, but he made me feel horrible, though not outwardly. I can't explain it."

"I know what happened."

She spoke quietly, still lost in her thoughts. "Did you know Oliver and Peter were in on it together?"

Matt's face changed colour, and his eye twitched.

"I'm not proud of it. Oliver and my family suffocated me. Mother controlled everything. I wasn't allowed to have a phone, I had no internet access, and the only people who came to see me were Oliver, his family, and Peter. Peter seemed like hope when I had none. He was so opposite to them. Over months, and then years, he tormented me with the idea of leaving, like a dangled carrot. Then he'd disappear, only to return again when I got over it. He'd go silent and then pay me attention. He played with my emotions, he manipulated me when I was alone, and I was so isolated that I couldn't see it. I loved him. Well, I thought I did, but I loved a version of reality that he offered. Hope." Willow licked her lips and blinked it all back. "How do you know?" she managed to ask.

"I sent a guy down to Harringly. I trust him implicitly."

Her face filled with heat, unable to quite grasp it. "And?"

"Cloughton vanished."

Willow went cold, and his words stole her breath.

"My investigator is looking for him."

"How long have you known this? How dare you do this and not tell me. If you know what happened, how could you not tell me?" She virtually screeched at him as her panic rose. Maybe it was him she saw, maybe Peter wouldn't let it go.

Matt moved smoothly and sat next to her, sitting on one leg. He leant forward slowly and caged her, one arm on the armrest. She pushed back into the settee, wide-eyed, and for the first time, apprehensive.

The show of dominance caught her breath, and surrounded by him, she had nowhere else to focus.

"I'm not Peter. I don't know the whole story, all I know is that you were virtually kept prisoner for nearly a decade. I know that you and Cloughton had a relationship and that there was an incident where you fell down the stairs and broke your leg. I know that less than a year later, you leave. You cut Peter out of your life, and there were a lot of rumours about you when everybody learnt of you and Peter."

"My parents were livid about him. Oliver too, said how betrayed he was. Oliver never gave a shit about me. It was a business transaction. There were times when he was kind to me, but then he'd show his true colours underneath. So patronising and pitying. It would be easy for him to have me as a wife. The invalid," Willow spat the word, "fuck pity."

Matt smiled, but his eyes glittered.

Willow spoke in a rushed voice. "I had to leave. I told them I was going. We argued for months. Peter had given me a secret phone that he used to keep in touch with me. Just a crappy one, it didn't even have internet, and he controlled the credit he put on it, but it was a way of keeping me connected, and I clung to it. I'd made sure not to spend all the credit on it. There was this girl from uni that I kept in touch with. She wanted to help me. When I fell, she wanted to come to the hospital and take me home. In the end, she helped me make a plan. I got stronger. I resisted.

"If someone said eat this, go to bed, I used to do it, it was easier than arguing about it. I didn't have the energy for it. But I started. I refused to see Oliver. Before the fall, there were times I could manage, I'd try to leave the estate, Peter would always turn up then pull me back in. It took me a long time to see that Oliver and Peter had an understanding. When I was restless, he returned, and get me to stay.

"Then after the fall and it all came out, Oliver laid that shit on so thick, how I'd been unfaithful, how I'd ruined my chances for anything better," her mouth turned down in disgust, "but he'd forgive me, and take me back. Like I should be grateful to him. I gave Oliver nothing, we weren't a couple. We'd never kissed never mind had sex, and he was having it off with Fiona in the village. Everyone knew it, not that she had any money. But I'm disabled, so I've got to be some meek fucking saint and put up with it for the sake of people who couldn't care less about me. No way."

"You were expected to still marry him?"

"Oh yes. I kept putting them off. I was too ill. It wasn't a lie. Oliver thought that using Peter against me would work."

Matt sat back. "And it was for money?"

"What else? I think Peter was promised a cut of my inheritance."

"I can tell you about him if you want."

The slow understanding of what Matt had done sank in, and she wasn't sure how she felt about it.

"He went to prison for assault, three more arrests for drug offences resulting in fines. Three other assault charges never went anywhere. Cloughton beat up a girlfriend so bad she had to have reconstructive surgery on her face."

Willow made a noise, trying to force back her revulsion.

"Are you sure he didn't push you down the stairs?"

Willow shook her head, her mouth watering, and she swallowed back her bile. "I don't remember, there are so many things that are fuzzy. They used my brain fog against me, I have patches of memory missing, I know that.

There's so much I'm not sure if they made me think I remember, and things I think I do, but was told..." Willow took a deep breath. "Matt, I can't do this."

He leant forward again and caught a tear that fell. "Nothing will happen between us if you don't want. I understand now. You were abused by everyone you should have trusted. Do you know why you're so brilliant?"

She frowned.

"You endured. You survived. Because you changed it. You removed yourself, you resisted when you were vulnerable. You're not weak. You're strong and resilient. I'm sorry I went behind your back."

Willow took a deep breath. When composed, she looked at him. There was so much strength. He was like Danni; a solid hope. She had the urge to cling to him, to hold onto someone better. Clinging to others wouldn't help her.

"What are you thinking?"

She lowered her head, and Matt leant forward, touching his forehead to hers.

"Matt, you make me want things that aren't mine to have."

"Why aren't they yours?"

"Because of what's wrong with me. Because of the past. I can't submit to another."

Matt smiled. "You do know that all that power is with a sub. A sub gives consent, they desire it, it's not enforced. It's a want. I love pain, and all the good, dirty stuff, but it's so much more than that for me. It's all in the mind. I will never hurt you. I will never do what you don't want. Do you understand?" Matt kissed the tip of her nose and leant back. "If you need me, I want you to come to me. For anything."

"You sent an investigator to my home?"

"Yes."

Willow kept blinking at him.

"I want to make sure you're safe."

"Why?"

His twinkle — that was the only way she could describe his look — dimmed. "I know what it means to be vulnerable. I will always try to protect those I care about."

Matt looked so vulnerable himself then, and she wanted to lean forward and kiss him. So odd. The room spun. She'd never even been kissed by anyone who really cared about her. Kissing Matt would be a bad idea, no matter how tempting he was.

He read her desire, and that twinkle returned. He held her face, brushing his thumb over her bottom lip. "You're so lovely."

She tried to shake her head.

"You'll never believe it, will you? All the lies, all that manipulation. God, you must hate what I am, be afraid of it. I wouldn't change, I can't."

"Nor should you." She held his hand. "It's part of you, of who you are. I'd never ask anyone to suppress their identity."

Matt smiled. "That's a fucking nice thing to hear."

She giggled, breaking the tension. Then she said it. Said the words that were at the back of her throat. Willow wasn't a pitiable survivor to be sheltered. She was more than that. People saw her illness and mistook it for weakness. People did take advantage, she was manipulated, and she had to give over control of her life. But some of it was a choice, and she always knew who she was. In front of her was something new. Her stomach fluttered, and heart pounded. "I want to find out."

"Find out what?" Matt held his breath and moved closer.

Willow's eyes dipped to his lips, the bottom one fuller. "What it would be like to be with you, to submit."

"No. It wouldn't be right."

"Then why are you looking at me like that, virtually pinning me to the settee?"

Matt blinked as if coming around from a dream. He stood up.

"I didn't mean-" She reached for him, but he stepped back.

His face contorted for a second. "This isn't right for you, I'm sorry. I'm so drawn to you, it's hard not to want."

Willow's face hardened. "I'm not broken. Don't you dare feel sorry for me."

"I don't, but I'm wary of this kind of relationship will mean for you." Matt softened.

"Maybe it'll help me."

Matt chuckled. "Help you?"

"No one has made me feel like you do. No one has respected me or liked me like this, and you like me, right?"

"I do. Okay." He sat back down.

"How would this work?" Her face flushed.

That almost dangerous and delicious smile ran across Matt's face, and her stomach dipped. "Submitting can be non-physical."

"How?" She could barely breathe at the look on his face; it spoke to a primal want, something forbidden she had no words for.

Matt leant forward, bracing his arms either side of her with his mouth lingered close to hers. "What do you want?"

"You to kiss me," Matt demanded truth from her, it was implicit in everything he did, and she wanted to give it to him. She tilted her head. Understanding flashed into her brain, intangible and difficult, and Willow needed time to work it out.

"No. I like watching you, all your thoughts and emotions are clear."

She frowned. "I've kept so many secrets."

"Covered yourself to remain safe. You've protected yourself for years, and now you're beginning to see you don't have to. You can be you."

Willow tried not to breathe, but her heart was so loud, she was sure he could hear it. His warm breath against hers, Willow was hot and cold, and the too familiar ache in her gut and between her legs made her shiver. Matt only smiled.

Her eyes fluttered closed at the heat from his lips on hers, and her mouth opened.

"I'm not going to kiss you."

She couldn't stop the whimper that she made, and he laughed, sitting back.

"You're perfect."

"I'm not."

"Your response to me is, and you're everything I've looked for, but I'm not therapy for you. I want a relationship, I'm not looking to scene. You're not ready for that."

"I want to be, not with anyone but you. It's weird."

"That's why you need time."

Matt took her hand in his and kissed the inside of her wrist. "I should go."

Willow slumped back as he left. In his wake, she felt bruised and exhausted. Then she remembered she was bruised and exhausted.

WE HAVE TIME

Matt's heart was thudding, and his dick ached. He had to leave. Not that he wanted to. Matt had infamous discipline, but he kept it in check and order. Caging it, shaping it into control, but Willow tested it.

All he wanted to do was kiss her, strip her and fuck her. The images in his mind weren't loving or what she deserved, but deeply fierce.

He wanted her so much it hurt. It was too much, too soon. Experience taught him that.

No, he'd get a handle on it, and when they knew each other better, and she was used to him, rather than excited the idea, then they might move forward.

It was torture. He grinned and adjusted himself as he got into his car. Looking back at the house, he felt bad for leaving her there. He worried, and taking out his phone, texted her.

Are you okay, do you need help? Sorry I just left.

I'm fine.

He tapped the steering wheel. Fine wasn't okay. *I'm coming back in.*

No.

He raised his brows at her denial. *Do not argue with me.*

For a moment, he questioned being dictatorial with her, but fuck it, he wasn't in the mood for her independence, though he loved the pushback. He'd always preferred it to complete and practised obedience.

She took a while in getting to the door, her eyes were heavy, and she looked in pain.

Matt cupped her face gently, making her look at him.

She crumpled and cried, and he held her close.

"I'm sorry." He rocked her as she slumped in his arms. Afraid to hold tight because of her bruises, he soothed her back.

Willow's legs gave, and needing to protect her, he picked her up, she muffled cry of pain, and he kissed her head as she leant on his shoulder. Matt carried her upstairs, hating her suffering, loving her closeness.

He set her down in the bedroom. Her big watery eyes set on him, her vulnerability was a delicateness he had no right to. But Matt wasn't ashamed of who he was and knew he could give her so much.

When she was ready.

"You must be exhausted."

She nodded.

"Let me help you, sweetheart."

"I'm not your sweetheart," she slurred.

"You are."

"No, Peter used to call me that, I hate it."

Matt went cold. The same rage he'd been ignoring bubbled up. Every time she mentioned it, every time he thought about it, he wanted to kill him.

"Then I'll never call you that." Matt undid the buttons on her blouse, the hair on his arms stood up, and he concentrated on the ample delicious form of her body instead. "But I like pet names."

"I don't."

"Will doesn't suit you. Do you have a middle name?"

"Rose."

"Rose, yes, that suits you. My Rose, how about that?"

Willow swallowed. "What are we doing Matt?" She slow-blinked and swayed.

Matt sat her on the bed. "Right now, I'm trying not to touch you the way I want to while I help you to bed, and you're vulnerable."

He slipped the blouse off, and her bruises made him wince.

She looked at him, and he was utterly lost.

"I need a wee," she whispered and smiled.

Matt giggled and tried to straighten his face but couldn't.

"Really, really, right now."

He hoisted her up again, carrying her into the bathroom.

"Well, there you go, Rose."

When he heard her moving about in the bathroom, he helped her to bed. She swayed and stumbled, her eyes heavy, and movements tentative.

She inched up her bra and managed to get stuck in it, she wobbled and struggled, and fell over.

Matt was stunned for a moment as the sight of her luscious body filled his vision.

"Willow?"

She mumbled as she struggled. Matt took the thing off her, messing her hair up. She flopped down on the bed and watched him as he undressed her.

"Fuck." Reaching over her, he grabbed the nightie by her pillow and helped her on with it. Her hands grabbed at him, trying to pull him down to her.

He resisted, and she let go, arms limp at her sides.

Wriggling the covers from under her, he tucked her in and kissed her forehead.

"Stay."

"I shouldn't."

"I don't want to be alone." She was already half-asleep.

Matt took everything but his underwear off and got into bed. Her t-shirt nightie made its way up to her waist as she shifted, and he spooned her.

His arms went across her, and he held her in a way he'd not held anyone for years. It was almost brutal. He buried his face in her hair.

They'd not even kissed, but she'd seen him come, and he'd seen her naked, and that bottom that pressed into his crotch was perfect.

Lust peaked, and his dick throbbed hard. Pre-come leaked, and he gritted his teeth. Matt wrestled with it, and finally, it ebbed.

Willow nestled closer, the rhythmic rise of her breath lulled Matt, and he went to sleep.

Willow stretched and shifted. Her ribs were killing her. She took a breath, feeling herself being crushed and wondered what horror the day had in store for her.

As she blinked out of that place somewhere between dreaming and reality, she knew that it wasn't her own body crushing her for a change.

A weighty arm hung over her. She shifted, finding herself pinned in place. Forcing a deep breath, her heart turned, but she wasn't sure if it was because she was finally getting oxygen, or that it was Matt's very nice arm that was holding her.

"Matt." Her voice had the strength of a wisp.

She wiggled, and he moaned. Willow pressed her face into the pillow to stifle a laugh. The conversation from the previous night returned, stealing her mirth.

He squeezed her, and she made a high noise and turned into a groan and wheeze. As much as she needed air, it was nice to be held. Actually, it was wonderful.

Matt took a deep breath in that ended with a snore, and she grinned. His hot breath on her hair and the press of his chest against her back was comforting and a turn on.

It'd be even more pleasurable if she could shift his arm. Seriously, how did a limb weight so much? She put her hand over his, and his fingers spread, hers fell into holding his hand automatically. Urging his arm down, he went, and his palm pressed against her belly. With the pressure off her ribs, she took a deep, steady breath. Yes, air was nice.

Her nightie had rolled up, and his hand on her bare skin made her clench her thighs.

Matt moaned. She wanted to moan with him.

"Willow?" he mumbled.

"Yes?"

"Good morning." He pressed his hand into her. "Your skin is lovely."

"Thank you." Willow licked her lips at the feel of him touching her.

His mouth brushed her neck, and her breathing kicked up. "Are you turned on?"

"Yes." Willow gripped the duvet, trying to retain composure.

He laughed. "Me too."

His erection pressed into her, and she shifted against him.

"Are you thinking of it?"

"Yes. It's hard not to."

Matt went still. "Do you think about me? Do you touch yourself?"

"Yes."

Matt hissed in a breath and swore. "I can't. We can't." Letting her go, he got out of bed. She wanted him to come back, to hold her again and tease her.

She turned in time to see him side on, cock straining at his moulded boxers, strong thighs, perfect bum. She wanted to bite it. Good grief, what was wrong with her?

"Matt, I want this." She blinked, the world unfocused, but she did, she wanted it.

He paused with one leg in his jeans. They looked at each other for a minute before Matt shook his head and finished getting dressed.

His perfect black hair was messy, the stubble on his face darker, and in the dim summer morning light that crept through the shutters, he looked perfectly sexy.

"You're a real challenge to me. More than anyone I've liked. I'm so tempted to see what happens, but it's not good for you, and you might not believe me, but I don't want to get hurt. I'm the big strong alpha, right? Always in charge. But I have feelings, I'm not a stoic toxic masculinity bullshit type. I say how I feel and what I want, and that makes me vulnerable."

Willow sat up. She didn't care what she looked like, she didn't care about anything right then, but him. "Someone being so open and honest is unknown to me. It sounds so nice. I want to try."

Matt tugged his t-shirt over his head and checked the time. "I need to get home and ready for work." He sat on the edge of the bed and put his boots on. He turned and leant forward. "I enjoyed spending last night with you."

"Me too."

"Good. Have a think, but space might be a good idea right now for both of us."

He kissed her forehead and left. Space? The quiet room, normally so comforting was cold and empty. Good grief, how could the slightest attention from someone like him have such an effect? Because he was lovely, and she'd never had anything like it that's why.

Willow lay there debating if he'd given her the brush off or not. She went with yes. He'd been nice and attentive, and he though left it in her hands, she got the feeling he didn't want to pursue it.

Not that she could blame him with her past. Space. He said it was good for them both. She sighed with a wince.

When she eventually made it downstairs and made coffee. Darby, perfectly ready for work, and Jane, in her dressing gown, sunglasses, and her hair worse than Willow's sat there in silence.

"Have fun last night?" she asked as Jane, and Darby stared at her.

"The question is, did you?" Jane said in a low husky voice.

"It was fine."

"Sex with Matt isn't merely fine, or so we understand." Darby shrugged.

"We didn't have sex, nor is it likely. He stayed because I wasn't feeling well and gave me the brush off."

"Really?"

"It was a 'nice but see ya' vibe. We both need space right now were his actual fucking words. It's probably for the best. I'm a fucking liability."

Darby frowned and stood, after finishing her tea. "Right, I need to get going, but tonight, we're going to watch telly, and talk shit. Okay?"

Willow nodded.

When Darby left, Willow sat with Jane. "Good night?"

Jane looked over her sunglasses and winced. Princess hopped onto the table and sniffed Jane and then got down again.

"Says it all. Remind me not to do shots, I'm too old." She put her head on the table.

"There, there." Willow patted Jane's head.

"I met a girl. She's pretty, but then she went home with someone else."

"What a twat."

"Wanna hang out with me and slob? I'm not getting anything done this morning."

"Sure."

Under blankets in the living room, they slobbed out watching films or napping, but by lunch, Jane got her shit together and had things to do.

Willow got around to registering with a GP and got herself a nurse's appointment but didn't have high hopes as she sat in the overly bright room in the late afternoon.

The middle-aged woman with bronze skin, pink glasses, and short bleached hair smiled at Willow when she finished typing her notes into the computer.

"You seem to be doing okay, I'll chase your notes, but otherwise is there anything we can be doing for you?" She smiled expectantly at Willow.

"I want to look at ways of dealing with my periods. I wasn't allowed to before."

The nurse pursed her lips, and a look of understanding passed between them. "Of course. You can go on the pill, which might regulate some of your symptoms."

"My memory is terrible, I always forget medication."

"In that case, you could try the implant, but there's also the option of the coil. It's more invasive, but it's localised. It is painful and can take time to settle, but there are fewer side-effects. Some women stop having periods and find it helps with PMS. Let's schedule you an exam with the lady doctor and go from there."

Reassured, but dreading having someone up her vagina, she left the surgery with a prescription for painkillers that the nurse had a doctor sign and filled it. The look she gave Willow when looking at her bruises made her feel bad, and though tempted to emphasise that no one did this to her, she didn't want to make a thing of it.

Her back and ribs were killing her when she left and called a taxi. When she got home, she looked at her car. She should get that shit scrapped. Or send it back to her parents somehow, there was no way she was going to drive it. Willow was astonished she managed to get to Chadford in it.

She wondered at a lot of things. How desperation drove her and gave her strength. But that energy was finite and spent. She was recovering, and the weary disassociation of the past befuddled her memory. It was only weeks ago, but Willow then was another person in another world.

Willow often floated around in her head, unanchored to her body. A sense of unreality coupled with her fragmented memory and thinking made for a weird take on the world. She wasn't sure anymore how else she could live. A decade was a long time.

A week. A whole fucking week and nothing. Matt had left it in her hands. When she was better and ready. For his own peace of mind, he needed to hold back, afraid he'd devour her. But he itched. Finally, on Saturday, even though they had a huge contract and he was busy and distracted, he messaged her.

Hope you're feeling better.

The contract was so big, he managed it in person, not a thing he'd done for the past year. He loathed corralling people, crowds, the potential outcomes and risks that he juggled.

This job was a big deal and would send Denbridge Security in the right direction. Having Liana, the popstar in his portfolio of clients would open doors.

She'd been having some difficulties with her team. Denbridge would manage her arena tours personal security after a public incident when a fan assaulted her.

She was beautiful with a model-perfect face that matched her talent and fame. Her bleached hair was set into an artful ponytail, and her makeup was immaculate. He shook hands with her and her manager, Trent, who made Matt's skin crawl, though he couldn't figure why. Her assistant went through the schedule, all the while Liana stared off in silence. Focusing on work was better, and he managed to put Willow out of mind because something was going on.

A day of media spots, rehearsal and then opening night was exhausting, and once she was ensconced in her hotel suite, Matt left the personal security team to it, trusting them implicitly.

It was after midnight when he got back to Chadford. Expecting a text or two from Willow, he saw nothing, and the disappointment cut him.

Not good. Not good at all.

YEAH, BUT NOT THAT MUCH

Willow typed away. She sat in her comfy chair with her feet up. Relieved that she was allowed to work from home, she didn't feel so bad. She made it into work, only to be sent home again. The bonus of her job was that she didn't need to be in the office.

Suzy could call or email her, and Willow could get on with it.

Working in her pyjamas was the best. The 'cute but tired' slogan summed her up perfectly. Sometimes. She didn't, not at all, think of Matt.

Nope.

She'd looked at the one text message over and over again. She'd nearly answered a hundred times, yet something held her back.

She kept thinking of him checking into her past. How would he react if she had done it, anyone else to her? He'd do his nut probably.

An investigator looking into her past, her relationships, all of it. He'd know all the ugly things that were said about her. Things Peter had done.

The more she thought about it, the more space Matt gave her, the more pissed off she was. How dare he?

Men were weird and unpredictable, and more often than not, full of absolute shit. Matt wasn't like any man she'd experienced before. He was sweet and caring. Kind and sexy. He was gorgeous and could carry her about.

Willow sighed, pushed it to the back of her mind and finished her work.

At two, she'd finished everything and stretched. Finding her way downstairs, she ate some cereal and looked out to the first signs of autumn. Rain pattered, and there was a chill in the kitchen that was new.

Time began to slip away. Willow worked, sometimes from home, but Suzy and Danni were happy. Suzy would look at her sideways sometimes, the question in her eyes, but Willow wouldn't face it.

There were no more parties, Jane and Darby went out, but no one came to the house. The weather cooled. Summer was over.

It had been more than three weeks. Three. Sometimes she wanted to call him, but the longer it stretched on, the harder it was to bridge the gap. Examining the why of it consumed her, and she understood that it was only fear. He was too much, too big, and a great unknown before her.

Regret over her choice weighed in, the hurt she might have caused him crushed her. Perhaps it was for the best to spare him and herself.

One Friday, on a bright early autumn afternoon, Jane came back from the shops, and Willow helped her.

Jane slipped off her blue coat and shivered. "The air's turned now, starting to get chilly."

"Yes."

"Willow, enough, come on. Moping doesn't suit you."

Willow put the bag of apples down. "Am I moping? Did you know Matt sent an investigator to my home to check out my past?"

"He fucking did what?"

"I like him really like him, but that part of him, the alpha in charge and take control of everything, worries me and if you knew about my past, you'd understand. I need to be me without anyone else in the way. Turns out I'm miserable. Who knew?" She shrugged as she put the apples in a bowl.

"Well, you should talk to him. It's not fair to string him along."

Willow looked up. "Am I? Shit, I didn't think. You're right." Nodding, she texted him.

Hi. Sorry I've not been in touch, been thinking about everything. Maybe we should talk.

Good. I'll come over.

Willow put her hands to her cheeks to stem the heat, but it didn't work.

An hour later, he arrived. Jane made herself scarce, and they sat in the kitchen. All the tension between them had changed from sexy to frigid.

"I'm sorry, I didn't mean to not reply."

"You did, otherwise you'd have replied. Don't bullshit me, I'm not in the mood."

Willow swallowed, feeling like she was being told off at school. She straightened her back and held her head up. "I am sorry. I'm not experienced with this, and I don't know how to do it right. I don't like that you dug into my past. It was presumptive and rude. The more I think about this, the more I realise my first inclination was correct and that what you want isn't right for me." She made herself look him in the eye.

"Okay." He shrugged, stood, and left.

Willow put her head on the table and failed at not crying.

Matt had known it. He'd known it an hour after he'd sent her the text message she didn't reply to. He'd thought she been ill, but when he'd asked Jane — like a schoolboy — if she was okay, she said that Willow was fine.

At least she dared to say it to his face. He regained respect for her in that. Matt wasn't heartless, he did understand, and the dominant in him wanted to fight her on it, claw her back to him. He wasn't that wanker. She was wrong about what she thought she needed, but he couldn't tell her that.

Best to walk away before he got hurt.

He drove back to the office realising that was too late. She'd given him hope and took it away again.

A week later, he was still feeling miserable and irritable and thought about her far too much. He couldn't shake it. Part of him knew it was best to back off and let her come to him if she chose, but another part wondered if she was too insecure to do it, and he'd fucked it up.

A text from Jane brought him out of his thoughts and diverted him from insurance renewal. *Party on Saturday. Be there and stop being a miserable shit.*

Fair enough. He didn't want to lose his friends over it. Fine, he'd go.

Willow fretted. She wore a wine-coloured long-sleeved shirtdress, with a tan belt and black leggings. Not trying too hard. Not trying at all actually.

She sighed before putting on some lipstick, at least with a bit of makeup, she looked more human.

Darby told her that Matt would be there. For all she knew, he already was.

Willow went down and undid a button on the dress to show more cleavage. It was ridiculous, but she didn't care. Maybe she could try again with him. Maybe.

The kitchen was full, and front and centre was Tabbie. There were new faces there, a short redhead head covered in freckles in the arms of a tall dark-haired guy in glasses.

"Hi! I'm Effie, this is Stuart." The tiny woman stuck her hand out, and Willow shook it.

"Willow."

"Darby told me about you. We work together in the place that Suzy used to work." She beamed.

Willow grinned too. Stuart was stoic and quiet and only seemed to want to be near Effie as she and Willow chatted. She liked her very much and found her to be a happy distraction.

They were laughing as they talked about growing up in the country. Stuart occasionally speaking, and Willow wondered if they were into the scene like the others.

Stuart's fingers wound around Effie's tiny hand and turned the sparkling rock on her finger with her sitting on his lap like a doll.

Willow thought they probably were part of the group, and she desperately wanted to ask her.

Stuart excused himself and Willow looked Effie in the eye. "Can I ask you a question?"

Effie's grin took up her face and her nose crinkled before she ran her hand through her thick deep red waves. "You're wondering if we're among the scene of pervs and weirdos?"

"Bit."

Her feet swung with nothing to perch on. "Yes. Weird though, I bumped into Darby one time at Kink, and I nearly died of embarrassment because we work together. Seriously. But, we're all the same weirdos. I'm a sub. Are you?"

Dodging, she asked, "Do you know Matt?"

"Oh my god. I love Stuart, he's fucking perfect for me. Matt makes pretty much anyone fall in love with him. It's hard not to go gooey-eyed. It makes Stuart go all serious and moody. It's fun to tease him." She winked. "You and Matt..."

"No. I messed it up. I'm not into it. Well, I don't know, we never got that far."

"Ah. Stuart and I danced about for a long time. He's an introvert, seriously and such an arse but the best dom. I'm outgoing but like to sub. It's different for everyone. I like to push his buttons, he likes to punish me. It's a whole thing we've developed." Effie wiggled her eyebrows and took a sip of her drink. "Though, from what I understand about Matt, he's fully into the whole package, not just sex," Effie said quietly.

"Yeah."

"That scares you?"

"Yes."

"That's fair. There's nothing wrong with not wanting something."

"You're right. He's a great guy though."

"He is."

Both sighed as Stuart came back. He picked her up and set her back on his lap. They were cute.

Matt arrived later, and Willow retreated in on herself. She watched him covertly, the kitchen getting louder, a few people moving into the lounge. Mel stuck at Matt's side as they laughed and flirted. Willow knew her mistake and seeing him happy was bittersweet.

She wanted him to be happy, and in a single bolt of understanding, she wanted him to be happy with her. Too late. His light tawny skin caught the late afternoon sun as he laughed, shaking his head and he was so beautiful. Magnificent. A cliched thought, but he was. So much power, balanced with a gentle heart.

Suzy and Nathan joined her, Effie and Stuart, and the four talked happily, but Willow pulled back. It was warm in the kitchen, yet she was cold and slipped away. No one would notice her absence.

In the quiet of the hallway, Jane caught her.

"Running away?"

Willow managed a nod.

"Will?"

She cleared her throat. "You know that thing when you understand something too late." She shrugged. "He seems happy. He should be. I'm sorry." She didn't say anything else and went upstairs. Jane pressed her lips together and shook her head, as if she would say something, but didn't. Tabbie's laughter cut the air.

By Stefanie Simpson

In her room Willow watched the leaves fall outside from her chair by the window, the wind tumbled them through the air, and it reminded her of home. She heard the party downstairs.

The opportunity for a better life slipping away, Mel fawning all over Matt, Tabbie laughing, her eyes darting to Willow all made her uncomfortable.

She tucked her legs underneath her. It was her own fault, but she couldn't help but feel bitter.

Her phone rang, the high shrill noise making her jump. It took a moment for her to recognise the number, and she ended the call. No, not answering that call ever. Oliver could go fuck himself. Though she wasn't surprised, it was only a matter of time before he had her number.

It rang again.

She knew his patterns. He'd never ring her two times in a row. He'd be cryptic, and she'd stew until she called him, too curious not to, but she didn't play that game anymore.

She ended the call.

He sent a text. *It's urgent.* Well, there it was.

When the phone rang, she answered it.

"Willow, finally."

She loathed the petulant tone he used when he was annoyed with her.

"What do you want?" her cold, bored air that she'd perfected over the years came back too easily.

"I'm sorry Willow. I don't like your choices, but I'm not calling about us. It's your mother. I'm sorry Willow, she died this morning."

Willow didn't move or speak, she couldn't even think. Shock closed her throat and stopped her lungs from working.

"My parents are with your father, he's distraught obviously. She had a heart attack. It was quick. You have to come home. I can come and get you."

"Okay."

He was gone. Just like that.

Slowly, her senses returned coupled with a loud screaming in her ears.

Blinking, she stood and on wobbly legs, slid out her suitcase from under the bed. She wondered when he was going to come, about work, and a hundred different things. It was sudden and quick. Quick. She shook her head as her hands trembled. She fumbled the zip on the suitcase.

She heard laughter from downstairs, and Willow closed her eyes to it, sitting on the bed. Tears of frustration fell down her face. Not grief, she couldn't feel that. She couldn't even open her suitcase. Swallowing it down, Willow tried to make herself cold and pretend like she used to. Pretend and play a part.

Cold fish. She could be a cold fish again.

She opened and closed her fists and opened the case and started filling it. Someone knocked her door. Blinking out of it she answered, "Come in."

Jane appeared. "What's this?" She put the plate of food down. "Where are you going?"

Willow looked at her unable to say it. She didn't have the words. She carried on packing.

"You're leaving? Just fucking off? What about the rent? You can't go. Where are you going?" Jane raised her voice.

Willow opened and closed her mouth. Her face distorted and she doubled over.

"Shit, Willow, I'm sorry, what's the matter?" Jane approached, urging Willow to sit on the bed.

"My, my, mother." Willow's eyes widened and said everything.

"Oh god, I'm sorry."

"Oliver is coming."

Jane leant back and shook her head before peeling out of the room. Willow kept packing. The thought of going back hit her. She didn't want to, she knew what would happen. Old behaviour, old routines. She wasn't strong enough to leave twice.

Jane came back with Matt in tow.

"Hey."

His voice made her take a sharp breath, but she didn't look at him. Matt approached and lifted her chin up.

A tear fell, and she fought it. The angry, acidic pain in her belly growing every second as the news began to sink in.

"Jane," he said without looking away from Willow. "Help Willow pack everything she needs. Hey, Rose."

Willow looked up.

"I'm taking you to Harringly, I'm coming with you."

She began to shake her head.

"Listen to me. You may not want me, but that doesn't mean I do not care about you. You need an advocate because you're walking back into a toxic life. I will not let you be pulled back into it when you worked so hard to escape. Do you understand me? How could I allow you to be in such danger?"

Willow came out of her haze. His voice cut through it like a knife.

"You're allowed to have someone on your side to help you."

"I don't know how long I'll need to be there."

"It's okay. I'm going home to pack, I'll be an hour, when I get back here, I want you ready to go. Understand?"

"Yes." Her heart remembered to beat again, and she wasn't alone. It was weak of her, but she didn't care, she didn't want to go alone. Jane took her by the arms as Matt left.

"Now. What will you want to wear?"

Matt's heart was in his throat. She was petrified and in shock. Letting her go alone would be devastating for her, besides, Matt had a bad feeling about what was in store, and it was time to put Oliver and Peter in the past. Willow might not want him, but he'd be damned if he allowed her to be manipulated again. She wasn't weak, but she was vulnerable.

Downstairs, he whispered into Mel's ear and told them. Mel had lost their father recently, and tears welled up. Matt's good friend hugged him and went to tell Darby as Matt left.

"What's going on?" Tabbie called. Her eyes always out for his business, and it was getting on Matt's nerves.

"Tabbie, I'm not in the mood right now."

"She's playing you."

"Is she? Fuck, not everyone is like you."

Tabbie narrowed her eyes. "You're making a mistake pining after her."

"You're only bitter because it's not you I'm pining after. Go back to Filip, he wants you Tabbie, but won't put up with your bullshit forever."

Matt slammed the front door behind him. Once packing in his flat, he rang Meera and asked her to sort everything out with the promise of a week off when he returned, and then Josh.

The low rasp that greeted him let him know Josh was working.

"I'm going to Harringly, Willow's mother died. I have a feeling your prey will head that way too. Call me later."

Josh grunted and ended the call. Matt scrubbed his face before grabbing his bags and headed back out opting to take the SUV over the sports car.

The house had emptied out, he saw Effie wave from the kitchen as she helped Darby tidy up. Stuart scowled at him, but he nodded in respect and waved before taking the stairs two at a time up to Willow.

He heard her on the stairs before he was halfway up, and his heart clenched. He'd never heard a sob like it.

Jane was trying to comfort her, but Willow was inconsolable.

"What's the matter?"

Jane answered, tears streaming down her face too. "She doesn't have a black dress."

"Huh?" He took Willow into his arms. "My Rose, tell me." He nestled her into his chest, aching for her.

"I'll have to wear a dress, my old one got thrown because it was too small, and Jane doesn't have one I can borrow, I'll be expected to wear the right dress for the funeral." Her voice was thick and strangled.

He closed his eyes and held her tighter. "We'll buy you a dress on the way. You can rest in the car. It's comfortable. Are you packed?"

Jane, wiping her eyes spoke. "All ready."

"Give me your phone." Matt took it when she handed it over and found the message from Oliver. *I'm getting a lift, on way now.* "Right, let's go."

Willow put her Chelsea boots on as Matt took her bags. Darby gave Willow a tight hug, and they left.

Matt adjusted the seat, so she lay back, and they headed out of Chadford. Driving was always centring, and he relaxed, Willow's blotchy face fixed on nothing. Knowing it was the right thing to do for her, didn't make it particularly easy. This was going to be awkward as hell.

By Stefanie Simpson

THE UNLOOKED FOR

M att's voice made Willow blink as they parked near a high-end outlet shop at a shopping complex on the way out of Chadford.

"This place okay?"

"Um, yes."

"Come on." He held his arm out to her, and she took it, clinging on. Even in her numbness, it was wonderful to feel him near and not so daunting.

The warehouse-sized shop was too bright, and Willow winced. He led her to the dresses and picked out a handful in her size, and then led her to the changing rooms.

She stumbled into one, the assistant watching them both, and she struggled to change.

The first was too small and too dressy, the second was a plainer one, sleeves to the elbows, skirt to the knee, high-necked.

Matt pushed off the wall. "Very elegant."

"It's got pockets." Willow put her hands in them.

"That's good, right?"

She fell back into the changing room. Opening the curtain, she slumped down on the stool. Matt followed her in, helped her up and undid the zip, helping her change in silence. She didn't have the words.

He passed the assistant the unwanted dresses and Willow clung on to him.

"Nearly done. You can rest in the car."

They paid, and when she got to the car, he helped her in, and she slumped down.

At some point, Willow fell asleep. The smooth, quiet ride and heated seat helped her drift off. She woke with a sick feeling and a thick head.

"Ugh." She wasn't sure why she was moving for a moment, and then horrible unwanted clarity shuffled into her brain, prising her thinking apart.

"Hey, how you doing?"

She blinked and let nausea come. She didn't have the strength to fight it. "Matt, can we stop I need some food, and maybe throw up."

"Sure, can you hold on, there's a service station in less than ten miles."

"Okay."

"There are some travel sweets and maybe mints in the glove box."

"I didn't think you'd be the type for travel sweets."

"It's a weakness." He smirked.

Willow smiled and ferreted out the tin of sweets. She took one and picked one out for Matt. He opened his mouth, and she popped it in. The feel of his lips brushing her finger made her flush, and then reality came back to her.

"Talk to me," he said, lodging the boiled sweet in his cheek.

The taste of sweet artificial fruit confused her, the sweet was pink, but she wasn't sure what flavour it was, raspberry? She looked at the tin.

"Willow?"

"Sorry. Rose was my grandmother's name. I remember the smell of her perfume, her clothes, the way she walked, but I was little when she died. Odd that I don't even remember my mother's perfume. Isn't it?"

Matt didn't say anything.

"I couldn't tell you her favourite jewellery. I don't know her face in a smile or the sound of her laughter. I know her shrill annoyed voice, and I know the look she'd give me when she was disappointed or exasperated. I know that very well. I know that she drank too much vodka and was frail and small. She was a petty woman who didn't love her child."

"I'm sorry."

Willow crunched the sweet. Definitely raspberry. "I'm being unfair. She wasn't that bad. Just cold. I understand her frustration, all the pressure of the estate and not having access to the funds. You know the problem? It's not tied to the estate, and it's nowhere near enough to shore it up. The marriage is though."

"This is going to be about more than your mother."

"Yes. It's now about the future of the estate and how that's my responsibility to step up and marry Oliver. Push out a baby and hole up there to die. I don't even care. They should sell the fucking thing. It's a burden that eats money."

"I'm going to help you through this. I'll be here fighting for you."

"Why?"

Matt didn't answer.

"Don't get me wrong, I'm glad you're here with me. Truly, I'm so grateful. This has got to be a serious inconvenience, but I feel so much better with you."

"I want to help you. I couldn't let you walk back into that alone not when I can be there."

They turned off the motorway for the services. Matt filled the car up while Willow got out and wandered off inside. She took deep breaths of damp, petrol scented air, the sound of traffic muffled by a line of trees. In the ladies, she looked in the mirror, her face swollen from crying and she washed it in cold water, the sick in her throat rising with every breath and retched.

She gave herself a few minutes to sit afterwards, her head spinning.

"Willow?"

She unlocked the stall and saw Matt. He put his arm around her and helped her get back to the car. He went back and bought a pile of food for them both, and they sat and ate. She wasn't hungry but needed to eat.

"Better?"

"Much, thank you."

"Come on. Let's get on."

The next hour was silent. Dread and worry filling her up as they neared the one place she never wanted to see again.

Willow directed him to the estate once they left the A-roads and wound their way through farmland the to the driveway. They crunched up the gravel, surrounded by tall pines, once immaculately kept, but now sadly overgrown, and in the falling darkness, creepy.

The drive opened out into the formal gardens, and Matt braked.

"Shit me." He leant forward.

The huge manor house was early Georgian, the stucco cracked but complete. Grand and ornate, lichen covered the pillars, and the stone steps were worn.

"Yep."

Matt looked at her. "I had no idea."

"The house earns nothing. Too small and unimportant for the national trust. No interesting ancestors, no one important. A few of the lower nobility but nothing special. The only estate income is the farmland, which is nothing, and the stables, they prop the day to day up, but that's it.

"With investment, it could be carved up as flats or a hotel with riding opportunities. There's so much, but they want it to continue as a relic of the past. Meaningless to everyone else. Pull around to the right, the garages are there."

Matt scowled and drove around the expansive house. To the back, the house was brick and the haphazard additions over time could be seen behind the façade.

He helped her out, and she led him to the back door.

"I don't know if to ring the bell or not. This is the servants' entrance. No one uses the front anymore." She rang the bell and opened the door at the same time.

At the kitchen table her father, Oliver, and his parents sat.

The heat from the range was familiar, and the smell of the place took her back. But this wasn't home, and it wasn't a fond remembrance.

Oliver stood, and no one looked at her, but at the giant at her side. She was beyond grateful for him right then.

"Father."

He looked at his child and stood, she went to him and was surprised that he embraced her, only briefly and barely touching, but he held her.

"This is Matthew Denbridge. My father, Rupert Morris-DeWorthy. Oliver Stillwell, and his parents, Robert and Audrey."

"And who are you to our Willow?" Oliver asked.

Matt didn't answer straight away but held the man's stare with cold derision. After a minute of tension, he took a deep breath and turned to her father. "I am sorry for your loss. I thought it prudent to bring your daughter back here as fast as possible and support her during this time. She is well-loved in Chadford, and her friends are very protective of her. I couldn't not come with her."

The older man, thin, drawn, and who looked nothing like his child nodded and murmured his thanks.

"Well, I'm sure you're exhausted, sweetheart, we should get you upstairs and let your friend get on his way." Oliver stepped closer, his face scrutinising Matt's.

Matt was immovable as stone. "You're mistaken Stillwell, Willow has asked me to stay with her. I'm happy to oblige."

"What are you?" Oliver murmured, leaning in.

The atmosphere changed. "The man who's standing right in your way."

Willow looked up at Matt, feeling everyone look at her as she cleared her throat. "We ate on the way, and other than a cup of tea, I want to go to bed. Ready?"

"Of course. Lead the way." He managed both cases as she held onto his arm. The huge stairwell and grand hallway had water damage, and paintings were missing that had long hung on the walls.

Willow sighed at the bottom of the bare stone stairs.

"Right." Matt put everything down as Oliver appeared. "Come on." He swept her up into his arms and carried her up. She could have kissed him. It was wrong to feel that happy she was in his arms, but she did and didn't care.

Oliver glared at them as she caught him at the bottom of the stairs. For the first time, she wasn't worried. But something was off.

"What is it?"

"I pass for white, most of the time, but I'm tanned still from the summer. Sometimes people like Stillwell see it. What are you? Is what he said." His mouth set.

She guided him to her bedroom. "Do you want to talk about it?"

Matt put her down, and she put the light on.

He sighed. "Not really. I am privileged and get an easier time than most people because I pass as white and straight. When I first met Darby, we got drunk at a Munch, and she helped me figure some of it out. Do you know how many times I've been called a terrorist? A lot. Or people think they can make racist jokes in front of me because they don't know. Sometimes it's hard to know how people will be." He scowled and put his hands on his hips. "But people like Oliver can only hate, they see division to retain power and control. It's predictable and tedious." He smiled sadly. "I'll get our bags."

She wondered about all the things going on under the surface of him, watching the empty spot where he stood. With a sigh, she turned. Her room was as she left it. She hated it. Large and square with worn green carpet, and an old bed. The fireplace was blocked up, and she had the least attractive furniture. It was big enough for couch under one window, and she'd spent much of her time there.

When he put the bags down, she put her arms around his waist.

"Okay?"

"I like all the parts of you. Sorry Oliver is a dick and that you deal with it."

"It's okay." He put his arms around her, squeezed, and rubbed her back. "How are you doing?"

"I never thought I'd come back." She took off her coat and clicked on the electric heater. "We'll have to find you a room."

"Is that what you want?"

"What does that mean?"

"Sit." He spoke quietly and shut the door. "I want you to think about what I'm going to say to you, I don't want you to react, not yet."

"All right."

"I think Oliver Stillwell is a dangerous man."

Willow bit the inside of her cheek.

"If you're right and he cut Peter into a deal to keep you here for years, do you think he's going to let you go now your mother's gone. Why did he let you go before?"

She thought about it. "Some of it's patchy. The fall was bad. I broke my leg and two ribs. I was covered in bruises. I could have died."

"That wasn't his intention, without you he gets nothing."

"No. I was arguing with Peter, I wanted him to stay, but he wouldn't. I'd already become suspicious of him but..."

"He kept pulling you back."

"He knew how to."

"I know this isn't the right time to do this, but you need to think. Without you marrying, what will happen?"

"Dad will sell, he'll have no choice."

"Stillwell will do anything to get you to stay. Bear it in mind."

"What's going on?" Willow sat back, drained and tired.

"You're not safe alone."

"You think they'd do something now?"

"When you're vulnerable and grieving, and the estate's future is in question?"

Willow felt sick again. It had been her fear with Oliver; that he'd get impatient. "You want to stay with me, so he thinks we're together. It's why you came."

"Partly. I get you don't want us, and this isn't the time. I'll never push the issue with you, as far as I'm concerned, it's over with. But I do care very much about you, and I will not allow that piece of shit to get to you."

"He's not a villain."

"He is, Willow." Matt set his mouth, jaw twitching. "Bathroom?"

She nodded to the door in the room, and he went in. "You have to jiggle the flush."

He came back as Willow tried to work out why he was so worried about Oliver. Then understanding hit her around the face, and she sat up. "He asked Peter to hurt me, to make me stay. They knew I was getting restless and unhappy. I'd been better, stronger. He didn't expect it to be so bad."

Matt said nothing but knelt in front of her. "I won't let anything happen to you. I promise." He cupped her face.

"Oh god, I knew. I knew, but I couldn't put it together. I didn't see it." Willow's mouth opened wide, and she covered it.

"I swear, you're safe with me. Look at me."

Willow swallowed thickly, everything turning over, her stomach full of dread and bile, and met his eye. Safe.

Torn between leaning on him for everything and her distrust of men dictating her life, she wanted to go home. Back to Jane and Darby and hang out with the girls and chat shit. She managed a nod.

Matt unpacked, and Willow went to the bathroom, her body ached, and head swam. The adrenaline ebbed, and she let the sensation pass, understanding the implications. Seeing it. Knowing the truth of it and who she was to people who should have cared for her.

"Are you going to drink this milk you wanted?"

"No, it's for the tea," she said absently and switched on the minifridge in the corner of the room. There was still tea, coffee and a travel kettle where she left it.

Matt made them a cup, and she put the telly on. He helped her change, her body finally giving up, and exhausted she got into bed.

Matt went into the bathroom and changed, coming out in lounge bottoms and a t-shirt and turned the heater off before getting into bed.

"It's cold," he said, shivering under the sheets.

"Always. You get used to it."

He smiled and brushed a wave of hair back. "Wanna hug?"

She made a noise of want, and he nestled into her his chest, safe and tied to something other than herself, and it was wonderful.

Matt kept a lid on his anger. Josh's email made his blood boil. The long report of weeks of work culminated in one salient point. Oliver Stillwell might look harmless, but he was a greedy, manipulative shit who needed a good kicking. But with Willow curled into him with those cute little pyjamas, he felt all right. As it should be.

He missed her, his heart pinched with it, and taking a deep breath, inhaled her scent and was beyond grateful she had accepted his help.

He kissed the top of her head as if it was the most natural thing to do. "Willow."

"Hmm?"

He bit back the things he wanted to say and drank the last of his tea. She was too raw. The TV programme cast blue light over everything, the darkness encroaching, and Matt regained composure. "Time to sleep, baby."

Half-asleep already, she snuggled deeper in, and he rested his head back. It was perfect.

Picking up his phone, he read through the email again, determined to do whatever it cost to keep her safe.

By Stefanie Simpson

FUTURE PRESENT

Willow woke early as the dawn crept underneath the curtains. Disorientated, she wondered why she was sweating and on a boat.

She was not on a boat, but become attached to Matt. Sound asleep, she listened to his deep inhale and exhale, and the steady thump of his heart.

Willow smiled luxuriating in the moment. Then she remembered. Heart attack. It was quick.

Tears filled her vision, and she let them come, silent and heavy, the only sounds she made were her sharp breaths.

Matt shifted under her, she must be crushing him, and when she tried to pull out of his hold, he snuggled her closer.

"Where are you going?"

"Nowhere." She buried her face into his chest, and he ran his fingers through her hair.

"I'm here, you're safe."

When her tears stopped, Matt got up and made them a coffee, and they snuggled back up together. Willow couldn't stop looking at him.

"What?"

"I can't believe you're here." Scrunching her mouth up, she reached out and held his hand. "I shouldn't have pushed you away."

Matt closed his eyes, tension ebbing. "I shouldn't have given you space, but I think you needed it."

Willow closed her eyes briefly. "I know you said you were done with us, and I respect that. I wanted you to know that if I could go back, I'd do it differently."

Matt's mouth opened, but he frowned. Blinking, he shifted. "What would you have done differently?"

"Replied to that text for a start."

"Uh-huh."

Matt put his mug down, and hers, and then reached over her, so their faces nearly touched and picked up her phone from the bedside table. "Here you go."

He sat back and drank his coffee. Willow smiled and tapped out a message. *I'd like to see you again.*

When his phone pinged, he looked surprised. "A message from that gorgeous woman I like, how gratifying."

Willow grinned.

Matt's smile fell. "I don't want you to feel obligated or anything, grief is funny, and it can mess with decisions."

"You already feel part of my life, and I don't feel obligated, more that it's already begun. I want this. Us. But I am still pissed off at you."

"That's fair. Josh is still working, and believe me, you'll be glad of it."

"Why?"

"I can handle Oliver. I don't know what the other guy is up to."

"Peter is a shitbag. He won't turn up here."

Matt gave her a disbelieving look.

"He won't."

The look intensified.

Willow blinked. "We could kiss and take my mind off it."

"No. Time to get up."

"I never used to get up. I stayed here because it was always a pain to go up and down the stairs. I lived in this room for nearly ten years. I hate it. And you know what's weird, I don't feel anything. It's like a distant relative has died. I was upset yesterday, but now, I feel like I've had my cry out, and now I'm done."

"My dad died when I was five. I remember snippets, it's mostly vague."

"I'm sorry. I didn't know."

Matt shrugged, his shapely bottom lip jutting out. "Now isn't the time, but when I was a teen, I felt it. It hit me. Other things were going on, but it came later. My point is, it might not be all now. Don't underestimate the effect it might have on you. You might not be able to feel much at the moment."

Willow stretched. "We should get up."

Matt leant over and pecked her forehead. She loved the touch, the rough of stubble and those firm but soft and full lips

"Is it weird we've not kissed?"

Matt smiled at her and bit the inside of his lip. If she reached for him, he'd pull away. He'd have to make a move, she knew it, but the tension was killing her.

"If we do this, it must be a certain way." Matt got up, and Willow slumped down, disappointed. "With the wrong person, I'm one hundred percent sure that I'm toxic as fuck. To the right person, bliss. It's tricky because a physical relationship means something to me. I've learnt this about myself. I get very invested when sex becomes involved. At the same time, you won't know if it's something you want until we do."

"Can I ask you something?" Willow got up and sorted some clothes out.

Matt lifted his brows.

"What about Tabbie?"

He sighed, falling onto the settee. He ran his fingers through his hair, making it stand up on end and made a disgruntled noise. "I thought that we were having a relationship. She's a good sub but very practised. It's like she saw some porn and decided that's how all subs should be. It's not a prescription. I hate this idea that it's one thing, it's not. It's whatever people decide it to be in their dynamic.

"There is so much misunderstanding and shaming about my sexuality, and yes, it's an important part of my identity, which is complicated. Pansexual and dominant. It's not for everyone. Tabbie used me." He shrugged and picked at a corner of a cushion. "I altered for her. But I hated it."

"What?"

"She's an exhibitionist. She loves working the demos, and public work. I did it a couple of times, but it wasn't..." He took a deep breath. "When I told her no, she dropped me."

"I don't get it."

"Aftercare matters. It's the loving comfort and care that happens after play. There's a rush and physical demand during scenes. Chemicals release, you walk a fine line, and as the top, I have a serious responsibility. It also makes me vulnerable in a different way. I care for the sub, but the sub must do likewise, I need reassurance too, I need to know I did well and that they're okay.

"Tabbie ghosted out on me after the last scene, sent me a few cryptic texts. She let me believe I hurt her. It was horrible. For weeks she let me think the worst things about myself." His voice was thick with emotion. "Then she was oh it was fine. She punished me because I didn't want to fuck her publicly. At the time I cared for her, we had a bond, so I let her convince me to start again, and then the same thing happened.

"It's a form of abuse, and it's something we don't talk about much. I've not had a partner since."

Two furious spots of colour appeared on his cheeks. Before he got up, Willow went to him and knelt between his legs, grabbing his hands and putting them to her face. She wanted to be his, she wanted to give him that comfort and care. She hated seeing him vulnerable, and she understood.

"I promise I'll never do that to you. I swear it. I might not like the pain, I don't know, but I want to be your sub. I don't know the words to say."

The vulnerability in his eyes didn't go, but his jaw hardened, and he leant forward, gripped her face, lifting it up and back, he slowly closed the gap until their breaths mingled. His lips parted with a slight smile, and he kissed her.

Gentle and light, he met her lips until her mouth opened and he licked at her tongue. He let her face go, and Willow moaned. Her hands wrapped around his calves, she rested her head on his thigh.

In the cool morning, they stared at each other until Willow shivered, and Matt looked away, breaking the spell.

Willow wanted to crawl onto his lap and hold onto the moment. It was precious and beautiful. The misery that waited for her outside the door was unwanted, and with dread, she stood.

"You shower first." Matt kissed the inside of her wrist as he said it, and for a moment her mind went blank. "I'm a big fan of these pyjamas." He tugged her top, and she looked down and blushed.

Matt made a noise as she went into the bathroom.

She clambered into the powder blue bath and leant against the wall under the dismal shower. Forgoing her hair, she washed as quickly as possible. She didn't want to ruin anything by falling over.

When they were both ready — after several long looks at each other, coupled with knowing smiles — all happiness fell away as they went out. Willow leant heavily on Matt's arm, and he bent his knees and picked her up, and she leant over his shoulder as he took her downstairs.

They were the only ones in the kitchen, and after breakfast, Willow gave him a brief tour. They went out to the stables and found Oliver talking to her father.

The morning bustle, the sight of the horses, and the smell took her back. A handsome grey mare in the yard ambled over and nuzzled Willow.

"There you are, old friend." She let Matt's arm go and rubbed her muzzle.

Matt ran his hand down the mare's neck when she snuffled him. "She's beautiful."

"She was mine. Gerwain was my first horse when I was young, this is Petra, my second. I didn't get to ride her much, but I'd come and see her when possible. Didn't I, girl?" The horse pressed her face into Willow and Willow held on.

"You'll stink of horse." Oliver's voice set her teeth on edge.

"Why are you here?"

Oliver raised his eyebrows in a dismissive look. "We should talk."

"No."

Oliver sneered, raising his brows at her and laughed, taking a step nearer.

"Put your hand on her, and I'll break it," Matt said it in a bored tone, but his eyes glittered in the sun, and Oliver looked from Willow to him and back again.

"And what do you mean by barrelling in here and throwing your weight around like an uncultured lout, you know nothing of our family. Willow has obligations."

"No, she doesn't." Matt's raised voice and seething eyes turned a few heads, and her father joined them.

He looked like an old man to Willow; weary fragile eyes, and slightly dishevelled thin hair. "Let's have this conversation inside, please."

"Of course, father." The pull of who she was and who she could be balled in her stomach where the numb unease turned over.

They all went back in and settled in the kitchen. Matt insisting on helping her father with the tea, his hands shook, and he seemed bewildered.

Willow's hands sweated, Oliver's eyes fixed on her, and she knew Matt was right to be cautious.

Matt felt sorry for Mr Morris-DeWorthy. Memory of grief edged into his mind and he thought about his own father. He glanced back at Willow, wavering between his want of her and desire to put Stillwell in his place.

He put his hands on the countertop. "I never know where anything is, my wife was always in charge of these things."

Matt took over.

"If you're tired Willow, you can go up." Oliver looked at her as he stirred his tea. Matt wanted to throat punch him.

"If you're going to talk about me, I will be present for it."

"You've gone and got yourself some attitude in Chadford, is it from your friend here?"

"Thank you, that's the first compliment you've ever paid me." Willow sneered.

"Enough!" Mr Morris thumped his fist on the table. "Willow, you have a duty to your family. It's time to come home."

"No. This is not my home. I will not be kept here against my will again. I will not be talked over and manipulated. I don't care about the estate or position. And I will certainly not be forced to marry a man who encouraged Peter Cloughton to injure me so that I would stay."

She looked into Oliver's eyes as she said it. Matt watched his reactions, shock and disbelief, swiftly masked by indignation.

"I never-"

"Shut your mouth, Stillwell." Everyone turned to Matt, his dangerous voice echoing around before looking back at Willow's father. "I am sorry for your loss, but during my relationship with Willow, she explained in detail the circumstances of her life, and I have to say I'm disgusted. So, you'll excuse my abruptness."

"You know nothing about our lives," Oliver barked, red-faced.

Matt kept his tone calm. "I know about Willow's life. I know, for a fact, that you paid Cloughton to coerce and get Willow to stay and make sure she didn't leave."

Oliver's venom seeped into his words. "Who are you to think you can come here and-"

"I run a respected security firm. We also carry out protection and investigative services. So, for example, someone comes to us with a stalker, or there's an ex or a troll. We investigate them. I know everything."

Oliver went pale. Willow scowled and looked at everyone else.

"What I am unsure of is her family's culpability." Matt looked from Oliver to Rupert.

Willow huffed. "I'm sat right here, thanks."

"Apologies."

Willow sipped her tea. "I will not be staying after the funeral."

"You selfish girl, you promised your mother you'd marry me."

"I said what I had to. I never wanted to marry you. How's Fiona?"

Her father stood. "Oliver, I appreciate your help, but I'd like to talk to my daughter without her being antagonised, and I think you should go check on your parents."

The silence was heavy, and a draught cut the air. Oliver pushed his blond hair out of his face and sneered at Matt before leaving. Matt knew it wouldn't be that easy to get rid of him.

When Mr Morris sat down, he looked broken. "We had funeral plans in place. I have to wait for the death certificate, and then I can arrange the date. I don't know how long it will be."

"I understand." Willow's voice was sad.

"I know we've not always been close, and we weren't the most attentive of parents, but I don't understand what you think is going on."

Matt kept his breathing steady. "Willow, may I explain?"

She nodded.

"Money and power and the future of the estate. Willow was not willingly kept in the house. Oliver used her illness against her, and Peter to keep her here. Willow was always close to him as a child?"

Mr Morris frowned, turning his cup.

"Nobody helped her. She didn't leave for fun, she escaped. I'm surprised she was allowed to leave."

"We never kept her here. We were frustrated for her and didn't know what to do." He turned to Willow. "I swear, I didn't know. But if you leave, I'll have no one."

Blinking back her tears, Willow tipped her head back. "I can't stay here father. I don't feel safe. Peter did push me, I was never sure, but he did."

"Oliver asked him to make sure she didn't leave. Peter told Oliver every time she was restless or talked of leaving."

"I can't believe it."

"Oliver wants to get into politics, I find it very easy to believe." Matt's contempt rose, but he steadied his breath when Willow held his hand.

"Matt and I are together. I'm not leaving him. Sell the estate. Let it go. You can move closer to me, somewhere modest." Willow shrugged.

"I can't. It's been in our family for over two hundred years. It's our family history."

"It's also falling apart. Trying to get me to marry Oliver is archaic. I'm not doing it, it's far too late for that. I know everything is raw right now but think about it."

He drank his tea and tapped his finger on the table, and after a moment of quiet, he spoke to Matt. "So, you're seeing Willow."

"I am."

"You seem a capable chap."

"Thank you. I like to think so."

"Who is your family?"

Matt kept his head raised. "My father was from Iran, came here as a young man, died young, my mother is white and working class."

Rupert's eyes narrowed a touch. "That irritates Oliver, class means a lot to his family. The aspirational middle are always gauche in that regard." He frowned. "We aren't nearly as formal as we used to be by any means. It was usually about money rather than pedigree. Do you have money?"

"Yes, I've done quite well."

Rupert turned his cup. "Willow, do not take offence, but why are you seeing her?"

"She is beautiful and interesting. We get on very well. It is in my nature to care. I want to protect her. She is strong and resilient. She's had to be. I admire her qualities, and it makes me proud that she trusts me enough to allow me into her life."

She squeezed his hand.

"Well, that's a fine speech." He frowned and looked at his daughter. "I never liked Peter. I was surprised when it was him you were seeing. We'd suspected there was someone. He called us in the evening when waiting for the ambulance."

"Evening? The day is hazy, but it was lunch because we'd eaten, I remember that. He came to the house with lunch for us, and I hadn't seen him for weeks."

"It was tea time when he called us."

Matt scowled and let go of her hand. He held his fury back, clenching and unclenching his fists. He didn't want to upset her any more than required.

"Tell me." Her quiet voice trembled.

Matt closed his eyes at those words. "I didn't want you to think I was manipulating the situation. You know why."

"Tell. Me."

"Peter called Oliver just after one. Oliver came to the house at two, left twenty minutes later. Peter called the ambulance just before four."

No one spoke for a minute.

"You'll never feel safe here, will you?" Rupert slouched back in his chair.

Willow shook her head at her father's question, and Matt saw the sorrow that passed between father and daughter and felt guilt. He'd give anything to see his father again, and she was giving up an opportunity of a better relationship partly for him.

Matt needed air.

CONFLICT MANAGEMENT

Caroline DeWorthy was a peculiar woman and Rupert's sister. She had a loud, abrupt disposition that endeared her to no one.

She arrived at one o'clock.

Matt left Willow in bed, asleep, and went for a walk. He shoved his hands into his pockets and turned up his coat collar and meandered the footpath that the stable hand pointed him to and breathed in the clean air. The need for Willow was becoming overwhelming and they'd barely begun, but she was in his blood already. The image of her on her knees before him, those soft brown eyes and her luminous blush would haunt him forever.

His lust building to a fire, he needed the cold air and strong winds of autumn. After a few hours, the cold finally drove him back. Hungry and worried, he made it back for lunch and the arrival of Aunt Caroline.

About fifty, she'd had work done tastefully, well dressed and attractive, but the moment she spoke, he wanted to grab Willow and go home.

"So," she said, gripping his hand in an odd handshake, sneering as she spoke, "you're the bit of rough Willow's with." She looked him up and down.

"Willow is my partner." Matt made himself as cold as possible.

She smiled, or he supposed that was what she was doing as her mouth went up at the corners. "Why? She's a vulnerable child with no capacity of her own. Why are you interested in her, what's in it for you?"

Matt leant in, his face a mask of contempt and whispered. "I don't give a fuck who you are, you talk about her that way again, and I will ruin your life."

She leant back. "Good. My brother is a weak little shit, and his wife, well, one shouldn't speak ill of the dead and all that. Drank like a fish. Willow needs people on her side, and if you're not, I can end you. Where is she?"

Matt raised his brows.

"In her room I suppose. Bring my bags, will you." The woman sauntered off, and Matt turned around. No one else had appeared to greet the woman. He unzipped his coat and straightened his hair before picking up her vulgar designer suitcase.

She was knocking on Willow's door, and Matt hurried to her.

"In there," she barked and pointed across the hallway.

Matt dropped her bags and stood in front of her, barring the door as Willow opened it.

"Aunt Caroline, I'm glad you're here."

Matt turned to Willow with an incredulous face. Willow gave him a subtle nod, and Caroline barged past him. He followed.

"You can wait outside, I need to talk to the girl."

Matt shook his head and folded his arms.

"It's fine, he can stay."

"You don't need more men, Wills." Caroline closed the bedroom door, and Matt mouthed 'Wills' at Willow.

"Matt isn't Oliver."

Caroline threw herself down on the settee. "Well?"

"Matt is my boyfriend."

"Oh no, no, I'm not having it."

"Matt isn't Peter either. Matt is helping me."

"Really? Hmm." She looked Matt up and down.

She reminded him of a Domme he knew some years back. He took a deep breath, took off his coat and boots and put the kettle on. When they had a drink, he perched on the end of the bed.

"Willow is important to me, and this situation she's in can't stand. I'm staying with her to keep an eye on Oliver, and I have someone trailing Peter. I'm a stable and relatively successful businessman, I know this is about money, but we had a frank conversation with your brother this morning, and everything will be fine."

She sipped her coffee. "If you say so. But understand me, I'll rip your dick off if you fuck with her. I've not travelled nonstop since I found out, organising work and people the whole time, only to find Willow in as bad a situation as she was in before. If I'd have known, I wouldn't have come until the funeral."

"Aunt Caroline was very supportive of getting me out. She helped. She is the CEO of a company and doesn't have much free time," Willow explained.

"No, well, I'm getting on though. Might be time to work less. Enjoy life more. Now your mother is dead, I might see my brother."

"Mother was a bitch," Willow shrugged at Matt.

"Families are strange." Matt sipped his coffee.

"That they are."

Matt explained about Peter and Oliver. Caroline's grim anger deepened.

"I'll fucking kill them both. I'm sorry Willow that it took me so long to believe you."

"I understand."

Matt's phone rang, and seeing it was Josh, he excused himself. In the cool of the landing, he shivered as he answered.

"Peter is in Harringly." Josh's gravelly voice crackled.

"Shit."

"He's with Oliver right now. I'm watching them."

Rage filtered through Matt. "Text me where."

He went back into the room and put his boots and coat back on.

"What's wrong?" Willow asked.

"Nothing."

"Liar."

He glared at Willow, teeth grinding. "It's fine."

"Tell me. We agreed no secrets, trust and all that."

Stretching out his aching jaw, he took a breath. "Peter is meeting with Oliver right now."

Willow paled and sat down. "Why?"

Caroline and Matt stared at each other but didn't answer.

"We'll all go. Time to be done with this." Willow put her boots on, her mind blank.

"Fine. But," he lifted Willow's chin, "do what I say."

"Yes," she whispered.

"So brave," Matt kissed her forehead and hugged her. "Come on." Willow was unsteady and Matt — entering his caveman mode — hoisted her over his shoulder and took her downstairs. They took his car and drove out to the King and Soldier pub and hotel on the edge of the village.

Willow held onto Caroline as the three went in, and there they were, large as life, Peter Cloughton and Oliver Stillwell.

The pub was quiet. Oliver sat back, coffee in front of him, and Peter drank larger. Cloughton looked like he'd lived wildly, and was paying for it now, age catching him with sallow skin, shaved head and stubble. He turned to them, and his eyes went wide.

Oliver's head turned in slow motion, he sneered and then everything went to shit.

Willow shook the whole time. Aunt Caroline had always been a distant woman, almost abstract. The way her mother talked about her made Willow distrust her, but when she visited last Christmas, they'd had a long talk about everything that happened, and though there was tension on all fronts, it had been one of the best Willow had with her on her side.

She was glad to have her there as they went into the pub. Willow never expected to see Peter again, and the strength that Matt and Caroline gave her was the only reason she managed to walk in there.

Matt, tense and still, took up the whole space of the bar. The barman looked at everyone. Peter looked at everyone, Caroline looked at everyone, and then Oliver pushed his chair out, the sound of wood scraping on wood echoed, and he stood, doing up the buttons on his favourite tweed jacket.

Oliver was about to speak, but his mouth merely opened, and Peter pushed out of his chair with a grin on his face.

"You look good, sweetheart." His eyes slid up and down Willow. She knew it wouldn't matter what she said to him, he'd always be the same manipulative slime. She couldn't believe she'd ever fallen for it.

"She's not your sweetheart." Matt's voice made the hair on her neck stand up, and Willow relished Peter's doubt.

"Now, now, I don't know what you think is going on here, but-"

"No buts, Oliver," Matt said, "I know perfectly well. We all do. I know what happened and when and how. I know what money changed hands, I know what you had Peter do, and I know why. But here's my hot take." Matt took Oliver's chair and sat on it. Crossing his legs, he levelled a droll look at

Oliver. "As you're the one with the control in this situation, I'll speak to you. Here's what's going to happen. This ends. Willow will never marry you, ever, it's not going to happen. She will never touch that bag of shit again," he nodded at Peter, "and neither of you will come near her.

"I'd happily let her explain all this to you, but as you're repugnant, fragile and violent shitsacks of toxic bullshit, I won't tolerate the risk, and you won't listen for the same reasons. So, I will state this bluntly in terms you can understand; you won't get her money, you won't get her. Willow is mine." Matt's eyes had a wild look, and though his voice was calm, there was a feral mood to him that screamed danger.

It was so quiet, Willow daren't draw breath until Caroline spoke. "Well, seeing as we've got that out the way." Her loud voice made everyone jump, and the barman cried out.

Peter smiled. "Fuck you, Willow knows what we had was special, maybe it's you that's manipulated her, you-" As Peter spoke, he stepped around Matt and headed for her, Matt's hand darted out and grabbed his arm. Twisting it as he stood, he made Peter look at him with a cry.

"Finish that sentence."

Peter grunted and tried to wrench his arm away.

Matt smirked, keeping Peter in place while struggling.

He spat in Matt's face. "She's not yours, I had her first."

Matt's fist met Peter's face before Willow blinked and Matt lay him out flat on the floor. Matt looked at Peter for all of five seconds and then turned to Oliver who stepped back.

"Listen carefully to what I'm going to say."

Oliver nodded.

"Willow is not a thing for you to use. She's a person and can do what the fuck she wants. There is no obligation to you or anyone else. Willow, tell the man what it is that you want." Matt didn't take his eyes off Oliver.

She cleared her throat and made herself stop twisting her fingers over the handle of her cane. "I don't want you to contact me, I don't want you interfering with my life. I don't want you trying to influence my father about the future. I want you to stay out of my life. Mostly, you need to accept that I will never give you what you want and that using Peter to get it not only nearly killed me but had the opposite effect.

"I might be disabled, I might not have the physical strength or cognitive resilience to fight you like I wished I could, but that doesn't mean I didn't. It doesn't mean you had any real power." Her voice clogged with long-held resentment and anger, tears filling her eyes, and she damned them. "I always resisted you and would have never married you. I loathe you for being a shallow snob, and I hate you for what you did. Him?" She pointed her cane at Peter. "I loathe because he was once my friend, and he used me, and hurt me. You though have privilege and power that most only dream about, and what do you do? Ruin my life. Contrive to make me stay, and have that clunge monkey," there was a hiss of breath from a few of the people in the pub, "coerce me into a relationship and assault me."

Peter sat up, stretching his jaw out, a bruise already forming.

"I'll have your thug arrested, Willow."

"No, you won't. I'll go into great detail about what you've done, and I have the proof. Don't push this, accept that you'll not get what you want, put your toys back in the pram, and fuck off out my life."

Matt took her hand.

"Now, if you'll excuse us, my mother is dead, and my father needs me."

Caroline and Matt supported Willow as they left, and her strength waned. The adrenaline ebbed, and her body tingled.

She slumped into the car seat. They sat there for a moment as the sky filled with cloud, rain in the air.

"Well, that went well." Caroline's voice made both Matt and Willow jump, and Matt turned to her in the back. Shaking his head, he sighed and started the car. Caroline went on. "No, I'm serious. The right people were in that pub, and doing it publicly means that it's fact now. It's out there. Oliver can't do a thing."

"You're right," Willow said, her voice quiet and she rubbed her hands, the pins and needles sharp.

"You okay?" Matt asked, glancing at her as he navigated the narrow lanes.

She looked up, the trees heavy with dying leaves, their yellows and reds fluttering in the wind. "Yes. I think I am."

Matt was worried. It had gone about as well as he hoped in the pub. The fact that Josh lurked unnoticed in the shadows the whole time made him smile. He was so good at his job. It was good to know if it had turned nastier, he was there.

Yet still, he knew that as much as Oliver might be forced to let it go for fear of a public wringing — more than he was getting already — Peter wouldn't. There was a vicious streak in him that lay under his good looks, his attitude showed him that, but he understood why Willow had been infatuated.

Picturing the man in a smile and turning on charisma, Matt believed he could charm the birds. The hint of rugged danger in the mix was a lethal combination and punching him in that pretty jaw was the most satisfying thing he'd done in a while.

Usually it wasn't something that bothered him, and he mostly passed, but that look, the unease of others when they saw he was not white, and brown enough to be Middle-Eastern, the touch of fear and hesitancy, especially in the summer when he caught the sun. He prided himself on his calmness, on the way he handled it, but Peter rubbed him the wrong way.

By Stefanie Simpson

LIMBO

Willow's father sat in front of the large fireplace where a low fire smoked with a whisky in hand, and he stared into the meagre flames with his legs outstretched.

Rain started to patter when they returned to the house, and though Willow was exhausted, she wanted to see him.

She sat in the large comfortable settee opposite him, and he looked at her. He seemed so much older than when she left, but then, she wondered when was the last time she really looked at him?

Matt said he needed to do some work and left to fetch his laptop and find a quiet place, and Caroline showed him to the study.

"Fire's low." Willow watched her father.

"Hmm? Oh." He set his heavy crystal glass down and built it up, poking it until the flames grew and Willow could feel the heat on her.

"Do you want to talk about it?"

Scratching his thinning hair and shook his head, mouth turning down. "No." He drank his whisky.

"I'm sorry."

His watery eyes, milky rings in his irises reflecting the fire cut into her. Willow always hated that look, but it was just his face. "For what?"

"Being a disappointment."

"No, don't be." He looked at the fire. "It was your mother who wanted Oliver in the family. She had an iron fist."

"I know."

"I'm the one who's sorry. We let you down."

"It's all right, I understand."

"Do you?" His thin face crumpled into a frown and he sat forward, coming around from his thoughts, he softened. "I don't want to be alone here. But I won't make you stay. I'll think about selling."

They spent a companionable quiet few hours by the fire. They didn't speak or need to. Willow let the reality of her mother being gone settle. Her father alone in the world. Oliver — hopefully — out of her life. Harringly didn't seem so bad. What Matt had done for her couldn't be expressed in words, it was a feeling she carried with her, and she didn't understand what it was.

Time for it to settle. There was time.

Until there wasn't.

A few days passed. Listless ones caught in the waiting of things. When the death certificate was finally given, the funeral was arranged.

Matt was attentive and sweet but spent his days working in the study, or on long walks, and Willow watched him amble out into the fields beyond the gardens from the bedroom window. Though nights were spent safe in his hold, lost to his lips and touch.

After the vicar left, Willow sat at the window in the library, and Caroline brought a tea tray.

She watched for Matt, and finally, she saw him return from his walk along the rose garden path, bare of colour and thorny, and he looked up and saw her.

He came in, windswept and smelling of the outdoors. Taking the offered cup, he warmed himself by the fire.

"The funeral is Thursday," Caroline said.

Matt frowned and flexed his jaw, it pulsed with the action, and he scowled into the fire. When he did it, her stomach dipped.

"What's wrong?" she hated that her voice was quiet.

Matt looked at her, and she knew. He was leaving. Willow bit the inside of her cheek.

"I have to go, there are things that I have to see to. I have a large and important contract I need to take care of. Liana, the singer?"

"She's a client?" Willow said in surprise.

"We do her personal security. She's on tour, and there are a few issues with the schedule. I hope to be back in time for the funeral."

"Of course, you've taken so much time out already, that's understandable." She smiled.

"I need to pack."

They stared at each other, and she made herself still. She wouldn't cry. She had to trust she was safe; trust him.

Caroline's voice made them look at her. "Why don't you help Willow upstairs then while you pack."

Willow ground the cane into the carpet and made her way to the stairs.

"Are you upset?"

She hated that his voice was kind. "No."

Matt swept her up and carried her. "Lies." He kissed her cheek.

"You've been amazing, and you've done so much. I'm grateful."

"Grateful?" Matt's jaw flexed again, and she couldn't look away from it. When he set her down, he turned her to the wall, pressed her against it, and spoke low into her mouth. "If I could, right now I'd strip you naked and tease you until you told me every secret and thought in your head. You are mine Willow Rose Morris DeWorthy. Mine." He growled out the last word and bared his teeth.

Her skin prickled, the danger of him should have scared her, but she wanted to beg him to all those things with her. Matt stepped back, and she slumped. Her legs turned to jelly, and Matt swept her up again with a grunt.

"This is killing me, being with you and not able to begin. I don't want to leave you, not now."

"I do understand." Her shaky voice made him scowl down at her.

"Did I frighten you?"

"Not frighten."

He made a noise of assent and set her down in her room. "Will you manage?"

"I'm sure I will."

Matt packed and left a t-shirt for her to sleep in as she was holding it in a death grip. She meant to hand it to him but couldn't seem to.

Holding her gaze, he shook his head and leant forward, his warm lips on hers made her flutter inside, and he held her tightly before sweeping his tongue into her mouth. His hands moved all over her, squeezing her bottom, and all Willow could do was hold on.

Both panting when he leant away, he lifted her chin, licking his lips. "If anything happens, you call me. If I can't get to you, someone will. Josh is still here, he'll watch out for you."

Willow smiled gently. "How is it in such a short space of time I've become dependent on you when I was looking for my independence?"

Matt let her go and stood back. "I'm sorry you feel that way." Confusion marred his gorgeous face.

"That's not what I meant, I'm not sorry for it at all. It makes being apart from you scary."

"Is that what I've done?"

"Maybe, but isn't that what happens?"

Matt went to pick up his bag, and Willow panicked.

"Don't go, not when I've said the wrong thing, please."

"Wrong thing? Anything you feel is valid and if I make you feel that you're not your own person against your wishes then-"

"That's not what I said. I feel safe with you, cared for. I don't feel as vulnerable or weak. It's a good thing. But we're so new, and I'm sorry, please, don't be angry with me."

He hugged her, but only kissed her cheek and left.

Willow widened her eyes and blinked rapidly, but her lips trembled, and she cried.

Matt sent Josh a message and drove north. It was a long drive to Manchester. It would be tight to sort everything out and get back for the funeral, but he'd do his best.

He had time to think as he cruised up the motorway. Her words sat uneasily in his stomach. When he stopped at a service station, he called her.

"Hey. I miss you already."

"I miss you too." The smile in her voice made him relax, but she sounded weak, and he ached.

They chatted, and he hung up. It would be fine.

In Manchester, the cause of the problems became clear as the diva threw a vase at him when he opened the suite door, the two security guards following him.

She glared, and her rigid body shook.

Matt calmly put his hands up. "I'd like an explanation as to why you've attempted to assault me." He took a chair, and much as he did in the pub with Oliver, he set it out and sat on it.

"They won't leave me alone, none of you will. I want some fucking privacy." She screeched and neared him.

"Sit. Down." The sharp tone of his voice brooked no argument, and she sat on the bed. "You've had two personal assaults within six months. One of whom was stalking you. This is not a light matter. The reason they got to you was that your security team were lax in their duties. My men have strict instructions, and you should be grateful that they're willing to put up with you.

"The tour isn't forever. You cannot swan off on your own, you've more sense than that, surely. So, I'll make you a deal. Stop throwing things, grow up, display a modicum of reasonable behaviour and I'll recommend an excellent resort for you to visit when you're done. This place is amazing. I worked a job there for an actor, fantastic, you'll love it." Matt leant forward with his elbows on his knees, not looking away from her. "Then you can do what you want, put yourself in all sorts of danger, I don't care, but while my reputation and business is riding on you, you'll do as I fucking say."

Her face went blank, her eyes staring far away. Like she'd given up.

With a sigh, he sat back again, crossing his legs. "What's really going on?"

There was a flash of contempt. "Like you don't know."

"I don't, but I want to."

She closed her eyes. "Am I supposed to believe you have my interests above your employer?"

"You're my employer."

She sneered. "I didn't pick you."

No, Trent, her manager did. Matt tilted his head. "I swear, you're my priority. What do you need?"

She rubbed her hands together, almost squirming in discomfort.

"Tell me."

She looked at him. "Don't leave me in a room alone with Trent or anyone."

"Done. In exchange, behave to my guys." Matt was immovable.

"Fine."

"Thank you."

"As long as you stay."

Matt wanted to throw something himself. "I can stay for a short while, but I have other business to attend to as well." He checked his watch. "You need to be already on your way."

Matt dumped his bag in the room with the other guys, changed into his work shirt and trousers, and escorted her to the car, and they drove to the arena. He looked off to the side of the stage as she sound checked with a pit of dread in his stomach that he was not getting to that funeral.

Willow watched the leaves fall in a strong wind, they swirled up into the air, a draught rushing in from the window at the same time and she sighed. This was why she didn't want a man, and now she sort of had one, and he was somewhere else, and all she thought about was him.

Rolling her eyes at herself, she tried to read but gave up.

Caroline helped her up and down the stairs, and it took so long that she had to have a lie down afterwards. Matt had been gone two days as she settled in the library, and she checked her phone every minute.

He messaged her a lot. Selfies, his gorgeous face with one brow raised, mouth serious. She loved that expression. He sent one in a big grin, the other security guys behind him with Liana on the stage performing in the background.

He sent her one of him in bed, his chest on show. She wanted to nestle into it, the perfect amount of hair there. She loved the feel of it against her skin.

Willow reciprocated of course and even managed to get a decent pic where he could almost see all of her tits. He sent her a message demanding more, and when she refused, he said he'd spank her.

She only replied with a kiss emoji.

Matt was a distraction though. Her mother's death felt distant, as though she were watching it, but not experiencing it. The messages on her phone lightened her heart and let her forget. If she could go five seconds without checking her phone, that would be good. Loser.

"How are you this morning?" her father asked.

"Fine, you?"

Rupert looked absent, as though he'd forgotten something. He sat in his chair, and Willow started to worry for him. Caroline joined them and encouraged her father to get some air. She bundled him up, and Caroline gave Willow a pointed look before going.

That day, the housekeeper that Caroline had organised arrived, and the preparations for a houseful of funeral attendees got underway. She contracted a cleaning company and rooms that hadn't been used in decades were brought out of mothballs.

The chaos was nice. The house was always too quiet and full of empty air. It was meant to be full of people. She kept to the library messaged Matt a few times. When she hadn't heard anything from him that evening, waiting up to hear from him, she went to sleep with a heavy heart.

BLEAK TIMES

M att's voice made her want to sob. "I'm sorry."

Willow didn't even look at the time, but it was barely light. "I was worried." She'd not heard from him the previous night.

"I know, I'm a shit, but things are difficult here." He huffed. "Now we're going north, Willow, she's insisting that I travel with them."

"Okay."

"It's not okay. I promised you."

"Matt, I'm not an unreasonable person. I'm disappointed, and I miss you so much, but this is important, I know. It's fine."

Willow let him go, crushed. He'd already taken so much time out of his schedule for her. The chaos of the house passed her in a blur, and as the funeral approached, she realised she'd have to face all the family she hadn't seen in forever, the village, and Oliver Stillwell.

Keeping in touch with Jane and Darby helped, and then there was Kim. Willow went to uni with her, she was a fireball, who emotionally supported her throughout gathering the courage to leave Harringly in the first place.

The weather grew bitter, the first real cold snap, and there was a frost that morning. Willow looked out to the low mist on the hills beyond, the greyness perfectly fitting. It was barely light, and she hadn't slept. Matt rang, but right then she didn't want to speak to him, she'd cry, and she couldn't. The best way to get through the day was feeling nothing. Not so much because her mother was dead, but for all the unsaid things; the resentments long standing. All the things she would never get to say or address.

Willow got ready and smoothed out the dress when she put it on. In her jewellery box, she looked at the gold chain with the small heart on it.

Peter had given it to her years before, and she'd always worn it, thinking that it was a symbol of his affection. She'd been so foolish falling for his lies. She'd wanted to be loved so much that she was greedy for whatever crumbs he threw her way, and now there was nothing but regret.

She dropped it into her pocket, intent on returning it to Oliver — not Peter — because it must have been him who bought it for Peter to give to her.

Instead, she put on a long silver chain with a small onyx stone that she'd bought when out with Jane.

Willow slipped on her jacket and went down. Her ankle boots were low enough to be on her feet all day, and she went one step at a time, forcing herself onward.

She managed the stairs, going slowly, and a youngish man bounded up to greet her.

"Hi, Willow?"

Piles of people had descended, and she guessed he was a cousin or something.

"Anthony." He had a calm toothy grin and pushed his glasses up his face.

Ah, yes, third cousin. "You were at grandmother's birthday party when we were children. We played in the gallery and got told off for running up and down it."

He grinned. "That's right. I cried."

She laughed as he shook his head.

"I'm on Willow duty." He pushed his glasses up his face again, stuck his elbow out, and they went down slowly.

"Ah, there you are."

Both Anthony and Willow winced as Aunt Caroline screeched across the great hall. She held her arms out, and Willow hugged her when they reached the bottom.

Anthony vanished. Caroline was a scary prospect.

"Now then, Time to pretend you cared."

"How very droll, Aunt Caroline."

Caroline smirked. "Everyone's in the drawing room."

"Good grief, really?"

The drawing room was damp, water damaged, the curtains were virtually in tatters, and the faded, ornate furniture wouldn't last much longer. A few people milled about with coffees, and Caroline fetched Willow one. She did her best in small talk, and her phone buzzed in her pocket. When she drank the insipid liquid, she made her excuses and checked her phone as she left.

Oliver. Willow puffed out a breath and ignored it.

"Hiding already?" Anthony joined her in the cool, dim hall away from everyone else.

"Yes."

"Same, I don't even know why I'm here."

"The estate and death brings everyone out the woodwork. I should be with my father."

"I heard about the Stillwell thing."

"What did you hear?" Willow asked, uneasy about what was being said about her.

"He was a dickhead."

"At least it's the truth."

"Well, Caroline cornered me and tasked me with making sure he keeps his distance. Though I'm probably as useful as a soggy string bean."

Willow smiled. "Well, thank you, any interference is appreciated. Come on. Once more and all that."

Her father looked lost, and she sat next to him when he made room for her on the settee. His hand trembled as he gripped hers. She'd never known him to be affectionate like that, and her heart pinched. The truth was as much as she hated being in the house, she didn't want to leave him.

"Are you all right dear?" he asked with a small smile.

"Yes, but are you?"

"It's very strange." He gave her a tight smile and then everyone began to murmur. They were shuffled out as the crowd gathered in quiet. Willow felt all eyes on her as she went with her father, the hearse and limo waiting for them. Willow wanted to talk to Matt and wished she'd taken the call.

People filled the car and off they went. The church, cold and bitter, reminded her of her youth, and memories of Christmas services, harvest festival, Easter Sunday's when her mother was on her good behaviour, touting Willow to everyone like a good parent.

Willow's bitterness was surprising. She'd thought she'd accepted everything, but her anger ran deep. A well of it sat so far in the past, she'd never shake it.

With her arm wound through her father's, she shut down, lost in her thoughts. Mouthing the hymns, and murmuring prayers she didn't mean, her mother's face stared up from the programme she held onto, creasing it in her fist.

When it was time to leave, she struggled to her feet. Her head swam, and all the stress and strain caught up with her.

She sat back down again. "I don't know if I can do the burial."

"You can."

That voice brought tears to her eyes as Matt crouched in front of her. He held her and kissed her forehead. Willow shuddered a breath as she grasped his shirt. The secure strength cocooning her, she relaxed into him.

"You're not really here."

"I am."

"How are you here? How?" She cried, not for her mother, but that he'd come.

"It's all right. I'm here now," he whispered into her ear as held her tight. Willow held back the sobs in her throat.

Caroline took her dad and herded everyone outside.

"I can carry you."

"No. Just help me walk."

"Okay, have a sweet, I doubt you've eaten." He thumbed away the tears that fell.

He offered her a bag, and she took a few chewy sweets and shoved them in. "Let's do it."

With a nod, he helped her up, and she leant against him, surprised and relieved.

Matt held onto her for dear life. The past few days had been bizarre.

It began with a strange exchange after a concert.

Trent tried to get into Liana's room, and Matt stopped him, Trent sneering as he did. "I pay you, not her, you only need to do what you're paid to."

Matt didn't back down.

She opened the door, he barged past, and she came out a few minutes later, dead-eyed. They piled into a car with a few hangers-on, and Matt stuck to Liana like glue.

Their driver drove cautiously in bad weather, and the rubbery squeak of window wipers working hard cut the tension under inane chatter. Trent, in the front, looked through the rear view at Matt, who was in the middle of the backseat, Liana on one side, and on the other, a woman he didn't know who was virtually salivating at him.

The stranger reached over, leaning over to kiss him, snaking her hand up his thigh. "I love exotic men. How about we go have some fun?"

Matt, repulsed, took her by the shoulders and lightly pushed her back, careful of his own strength. "No, and I'll happily dump you out the door if you attempt to keep groping me."

She huffed.

Whatever game was going on, Matt had no time for, and his thoughts led him to understand one of the things he liked most about Willow was her distinct lack of game playing. She had the self-confidence of a soggy slice of bread, but no games. Liana was rigid, staring out the window beside him.

When they reached the hotel, and everyone went their separate ways, Matt escorted Liana in her suite, making sure they were alone. Her posture sagged as her hands shook.

He put the kettle on and made her a honey tea with a sigh. "Liana, you're not okay, and clearly in the middle of something. I've done this job for a long time. To start, it was one other guy doing VIP bar security with me. I networked managers, agents, promoters, so I've seen stars and celebrities come and go. And honestly? It fucks people up. My advice: look for something real beyond this. Take some time away. People will pressure you to do something because it's what expected, but don't do it to the detriment of your life." Matt scowled at the carpet. Those were the words he should say to Willow.

"I'm not sure if I can extricate myself. Trent is gaining control over me. It never used to be this way, but the tour is never-ending. I'm dreading the US leg." Liana took the tea from Matt, unable to look at him.

"My partner's mother just died. I'm supposed to be with her right now, but I'm not, I'm here, attempting to protect the most important contract I have, fending off unwanted sexual advances from strangers, and watching Trent."

"I'm so sorry, and you're right. Go, be with them, I'll be okay. You're a good guy. Your team will keep me safe."

Matt only had four hours sleep before leaving for the funeral. When he'd called her early, she'd ignored it, and it irked him.

He missed the service, but arriving at the end, relief in his bones, he zeroed in on her. It scared him, his need to be with her.

The image of her on her knees before him, cheek on his thigh was burnt on his eyelids; it meant everything to him. The light scent of her hair as he held her, the feel of her body clinging to his hold settled him and put everything right.

Matt helped her out to the graveside. Oliver Stillwell's scowl seared him. In the distance, he saw Josh. Leaning on a tree, hair hanging forward, and face covered by a scarf.

The air cooled, and in the frigid mist, the mood settled. Matt held onto Willow's waist as she trembled, sagging into him. He knew her legs were going to give, and he held her up until people moved off, and Stillwell hovered until Matt gave him a look that could turn lesser people into sludge.

Turning Willow away from the crowd, he half-picked her up.

"Talk to me."

"In my pocket is a chain, I need to give it to Oliver, and I need to lie down."

He led her over, and she passed him the chain, letting it drop to the ground, and as her breath misted in the cold, she let that delicate anchor go.

In a second, Matt swept her up and walked around the back of the church to the carpark, away from everyone else. He set her in his car and went to find her father. The man shook his hand, and Matt took her back to the house.

Her eyes were closed, and face pinched in pain. Desperate to take it away, he took a moment. This was her reality, one he couldn't affect. Taking her upstairs before anyone arrived, he set her on the bed and helped her out of her coat.

"Thank you." Her voice was slurred and croaky.

"I'm sorry I was late. Rest now."

Helping her out of her boots and dress, he pulled his t-shirt over her head and wriggled off her tights, shimmying on a pair of pyjama bottoms.

"Food?"

She nodded.

"On it." He kissed her quickly and went down as people were arriving.

"You came back then?" Caroline cornered him as he stacked up a plate for Willow.

"Yes." He added a few sandwiches for himself.

"I think she was worried you wouldn't." Her voice was quiet, and the change in her made him lean in. "She's fragile."

"I know."

"So fragile that she might feel influenced to stay. I need to leave myself, and it'll be her father and her. I can't protect her here for much longer." She made her own plate up, and they moved down the line of people. "Her mother always had the power. She said what when how. Without her here, things will be difficult. It leaves them both vulnerable. I've spoken to my brother, and he's lost."

"What are you suggesting?"

"Get them to close this relic up, get him to leave with Willow or me. Sell this place."

It was a good idea. "I'll see what I can do."

"Between the two of us, we might make some headway. The Stillwells are only biding their time."

Matt made his way back to Willow, and her steady breathing as she slept made his heart clench as he rejoined her.

She was the sweetest person. He set the plate down and ate his sandwiches as he watched her, mulling over what to do. She woke and had her rumpled grumpy face, which made him smile.

"Hello, beautiful."

She grunted and picked up the coffee by the bed. "Thank you. For everything."

"How are you doing?"

"Relieved."

"What do you want to do now?"

"I don't know. I want to go home, but I don't know what to do about father, I can't leave him alone."

Matt considered his words. "Bring him back to Chadford. Find him a place. He can be closer to you. It's a bit selfish on my part. I don't want to be apart, but seeing him, I wonder if it would be for the best for the two of you."

"It's a nice idea. I'll talk to him tomorrow. How long do I have you for?"

"Two days. Meera has virtually taken over, but there's a lot to catch up on, I'm behind."

"Then," she said eating her food, "come and hold me?"

Matt grinned and went to her.

Willow slept on and off, and at five, she gave up.

Lying in the dim morning, the chill creeping under the duvet, she turned over, and Matt shifted with a snore.

She watched him and snuck closer.

"What are you doing?" he mumbled.

"Can't sleep."

"Come here."

She nestled into his chest, running her hand over his pec, feeling his trimmed chest hair, and the masculine power of him.

He hummed and rolled her onto her back with only the t-shirt she wore between them. In the dimness, she made out stubble and his dark, glittering eyes. His mouth hovered close to hers, and their lips met in a whisper of a kiss.

"You have the most luscious mouth." His lips brushed hers as he said it, making her hold her breath. Matt shifted his weight, and brought his arm up into her hair, closing his fist around it and making her gasp.

"My lovely Rose, do you like that?"

"Yes."

"Perfect." When his lips met hers again, his weight pressed her down with his dick between them as he overwhelmed her.

She clung on, hands at his waist and she edged his underwear down, feeling his bottom. As firm as it looked, she squeezed.

Matt straightened his arms, so he hovered above her. Licking his lips, he looked down. His eyes were intense, and she wanted him, she wanted to pull him down to her.

He frowned and shook his head, rolling away.

"What's wrong?"

"It's too soon, and everything is too up in the air."

"Okay. Can we still cuddle?"

He sighed and cuddled her. Matt had become a safe place for her. Unlooked for, but completely essential. She held onto him for all she was worth before being tugged back into sleep.

By Stefanie Simpson

RUNNING UP THAT HILL

Willow threw up. Mercifully, she made the bathroom in time and heaved like she hadn't done for several months.

When her fibro decided to mess with her gastric tract, she was bollocked for days, maybe weeks. How well timed.

Stress was also a factor, and life had been stressful. She still had a strange unfeeling emptiness about her mother. Facing it would take time, and though she knew it, it was hard to care and to want to mourn the woman.

Willow came out of the woman's vagina, and she owed her little for that feat.

Matt was working downstairs, and Willow's phone was by the bed. She slumped down onto the floor, pain slicing through her chest like being stabbed with a knitting needle. Unable to take a deep breath, panic nudged, and Willow made herself relax. She let her mind empty, and concentrated on the cool lino underneath her, warming with her body. The draught on her bare legs, the slight smell of Matt's aftershave clinging to her still.

She let her mind drift to him and the moments they shared. Him coming in the shower. How his bum cheeks tensed as he did.

It struck her then how lucky she was to find him. For all her shitty luck health-wise, that a man like Matt would want her, and the possibility of what might be between them lay before her, she smiled. Pain shifted around, and bile rose again.

Lurching over the bowl, she retched her heart out until she was raw and crying. The pain was unbearable. Falling on her side, she clutched at her ribs, letting tears come, hating her body, damning it.

Curling up, cold and unable to move, Willow closed her eyes, shivering as the day darkened.

"Shit, Willow?"

She opened her eyes to Matt's voice, but she couldn't see him. His hands curled around and under her, lifting her up. She screamed, and her throat closed. The movement wrenching the pain through her chest.

Matt set her down in bed and covered her up. He put water to her lips and tidied her hair. She blinked and focused her blurry eyes.

"I'm sorry. I'm not taking very good care of you."

Willow opened her mouth to speak, but nothing came out and too exhausted to even try, she closed her eyes.

She hoped she could hold onto his affection, being that ill didn't make for an attractive human, she knew that, but, please, she didn't want to lose him.

Odd dreams of fear and pain kept waking her, leaving her stomach an angry riot and ribs killing her.

Matt sat her up, putting his laptop down, and put water to her lips, before urging her to take more painkillers.

Running his thumb down her cheek, he smiled. "Want some soup?"

When he was gone, Willow looked at the space he'd occupied. This wasn't fair on him. None of it was. It wasn't fair on her either, but it was her reality. It shouldn't have to be his.

He came back with hot fresh soup on a tray, and a sandwich for himself, he settled back and carried on working.

"Matt."

"Hmm?"

"What are you doing here?" her weak voice barely made a whisper.

Matt paused, sandwich an inch from his mouth. "Rotas. What are you doing?" he murmured.

"Wondering why you're here. What would make a man like you want a nightmare that requires so much care? Like, why? And I'm not looking for reassurance or compliments, I'm serious. I don't get it."

"Man like me?" He put his food down.

"Big, strong and able. Fit. Successful. Busy. I'm sure you have people desperate to be with you. Me though. Me." Willow narrowed her eyes in confusion and shook her head.

"You are very beautiful and sweet. Reserved but so much lurks underneath. I can see it. The desire to wheedle every secret from you keeps me up at night." Matt set aside his work and shifted, facing her. "The desire to do all the filthy things I want to you is like a slow burn of need that's making me twitchy. I don't know how you don't get this yet. I want you, I need to care and give of myself, and you're perfect for me. I'm sorry you suffer, I fucking hate it, but it's not about your illness. It's about you. I want you." He clenched his jaw, making it twitch.

Willow didn't move for a moment, he sounded so angry, and as she stared in silence, he picked up his lunch and shoved the sandwich in his mouth.

"I'm sorry." Blinking back her tears, she ate.

He sagged. "No, I'm sorry. Don't push me away. I know what you're going to try and do. I'm not having it."

"I'm not doing anything."

"You're going to tell me to leave. You'll stay with your father. I'll lose you." With a grim face, he got back on with his work.

Willow watched. He was right. It was her impulse to push him away, and not turn to him. "I don't want to end up using you."

Matt stopped typing. "I get it. We need to make a plan."

"I don't know where to start."

"Finish your soup before it gets cold, that's a start."

Matt stood looking down on the estate. He'd walked a few miles, the trees nearly bare, and ground thick with leaves as the sky darkened. The house could have been beautiful, but it was a decayed relic of the past.

The first spots of rain in the air propelled him back.

He had to go home, and it needled at him. He wondered if trying to hold onto the possibility of he and Willow was too much.

A man, tall with wavy red hair and glasses stood next to an old range rover in the drive as he returned to the house.

"You must be Matt. I was at the funeral."

"The third cousin, right?" Shaking hands, Matt looked him up and down.

"Anthony. Caroline and my mother are second cousins. They're fairly close, though no one sees anyone much anymore." They wandered in, out of the drizzle. The kitchen was warm, and Anthony made them tea. "In the old days, there was a party here once a month. We'd all descend — Willow and

I were young, I'm older — and all the kids would have a sleepover while the adults all got drunk and partied.

"We were pirates or adventurers. I remember Peter. He'd always join us. I think it must have been very lonely for them both on the estate. Until Willow went away to school, then he was different. I doubt he remembers me, not many people do."

Anthony found some cake from the tonnes of leftover food still in the kitchen from the funeral.

"Willow barely remembers me, but she was very young."

"Why are you here?" Matt seared him with his best intimidating look.

Anthony gave him a warm toothy grin. "Willow is a very lucky woman. My interest in Willow is purely about Peter." He sat back. "Don't worry, I'm as gay as it gets. Auntie Caroline called me, well, mother, and then me, but we're all worried. You are — we all agree — the best thing for her, but as you're leaving, and Caroline is also going, and the fact that Uncle Rupert can't find a spoon in the cutlery draw on his own, means that they'll both be vulnerable. My late aunt, for all her faults, which were many, had the ability to shepherd uncle Rupert." Anthony ate his cake.

"And?" Matt asked impatiently.

Tonguing cake from his teeth, Anthony sat back. "Willow was about five, I was ten, and Peter was nine. There were twelve kids here, from babies up to teens. It was rowdy, and Mrs Dorel, the housekeeper, gave up and let us run riot. I remember it was summer, and we'd gone out to the woods. Willow and I were climbing a tree. There's this old oak, it's massive, and has these low branches, which meant we could climb it. I remember helping her up. We played to see who could get the highest. A silly game. Peter played too, but he wanted to win. Willow got pretty high, and he pushed her. It's funny," he sat forward, a frown marring his freckled forehead, "I thought it was an accident, but it wasn't. Even as a boy, he couldn't stand us, and Willow was an easy target because she liked him. He had a quiet spiteful streak even then. He'd be horrible to her, and she'd still fawn over him and make excuses. It took more than twenty years for her to see it. But I think if he got her alone, he'd manipulate her again. I don't know how much she's managed to let go. Her whole life. Not just a few years, she's known him forever. Some people can hold another in their power, it's the way he is with her."

Matt slowly nodded, taking it in.

"Well, now here I am, at my leisure, come to help."

"How do I know I can trust you?"

Anthony laughed. "I'd be more interested in you than my cousin. And that behaviour is generally frowned upon these days. Though, most people are related in some way if you look hard enough."

Matt huffed a laugh. Anthony's eyes sparkled behind his glasses. He wasn't his type, but there was something about the man.

"What do you plan to do, exactly?"

"Someone being here is enough to keep him at bay, and I saw your man at the funeral, the one who lurked at the back with the nice hair, well I assume he's yours."

Matt sipped his tea. "He's keeping an eye on Peter."

"I can handle Oliver. He loathes me." Anthony levelled a dry look at Matt.

"Why?"

"I'm gay."

"Fair enough. Maybe I should tell him I'm pan." After a shared look, Matt went on. "I want to get Willow home, she doesn't want to be here, but her father is alone."

"I work in real estate. My portfolio is decent. Chadford is interesting. The prices are low but steadily rising. Might be a good investment for the future."

"Definitely. How do you want to do this?"

"I'll look online, send my partner to take a look. Buy somewhere. In the meantime, I can find a flat to rent for him. We can get him down there. I'll talk to him. I think he's open to the idea of leaving this place."

"Good. I feel a lot better about going now." Matt ate his cake.

Matt packed, with Willow quietly watching. He didn't want to leave her. "I wish you were coming with me."

"Me too," she whispered as he sat next to her.

Lifting her chin, he paused for a moment before kissing her softly, her hands went around him, and she held him closer. He lay them down, kissing her hard, hands roving over the lush curves of her body. He wanted her so much, his dick throbbed.

"Fuck." He rested his forehead on hers. "Don't stay away too long. I need you. I want you so much."

"I need to make some decisions."

Matt frowned, lifting his head. "About?"

"My future."

A cold feeling went down his spine. "And?"

Willow looked at him, her silence made him feel sick.

"Don't stay here."

"Do you know what this place will need doing to it so we can sell it? Packing dad up and finding somewhere could take months. I know Anthony is here to help, but it's naïve to think it'll be easy."

"Your choice is to stay here in a rotting house for the rest of your life?"

"I never said that. I didn't. Matt, if it weren't for you, I'd probably stay here."

"You're not safe."

"I know. If Peter wants to get to me, he will, no matter where I am. I have a lot of mental unpacking to do, all tied in with this place, with my mother. I need time to work it out. My brain isn't that quick on those things, it takes time for me. It's not about you or us. I want this, I meant what I said. But there are other things here."

Matt stood up, grinding his teeth. "I understand." The hard-checked disappointment and fear cut his chest. "I don't want to lose you."

"You won't."

Matt knew the lie. He knew the empty hope of two people parting with promises. He'd lived it before. Thinking of Kai, of all the promises of one day when they were ready, and they'd moved on long ago.

Swallowing the doubt in his mind, he kissed Willow's forehead and left. He didn't look back, he didn't listen to the crying that followed him down the landing as the draught caught the air.

He said goodbye to Rupert, absently pottering in the library, and shook hands with Anthony.

Matt felt foul as he drove away, everything telling him to go back and carry her off like the dom he was in his heart.

Gripping the steering wheel, he held it like a buoy, losing her was his worst nightmare, but he was leaving, and she was torn between duty and want. Sweat gathered as he navigated the winding lanes.

He didn't doubt her affection, but she was so inexperienced, had been betrayed and manipulated at every turn.

At a junction, he slammed his hand on the wheel. His throat closed, and he turned to head onto the A-road that would take him to the motorway and away from the one thing he wanted.

When he reached his sterile flat, he missed the haphazard piles of stuff lying about. His life was too clean and ordered. The light scented chaos of Willow brought balance to him.

He showered and readied to go into the office and sent Willow a text. *I miss you already.* He added a ridiculous amount of emojis and didn't care.

She replied immediately with even more emojis, and he laughed, feeling better.

Willow felt like punching something if she had the energy to do it. Her father, once he made his mind up about something was beyond stubborn.

"Why, why hold onto this place?"

"Your mother wouldn't want me to sell it."

"Mother is dead," Willow said it sharply, and her voice echoed around the kitchen.

Anthony cleared his throat. They'd had a very long tour and conversation with an estate agent. "Uncle Rupert, being pragmatic might be prudent. Your wife was nothing if not pragmatic. Aunt Marianne arranged an unwanted marriage for your only child knowing that they were grasping unpleasant souls to hang onto this place, but beyond that, she knew it was unsustainable.

"She knew it. You were rarely here, how many months out of the year were you with Willow? It's time to let the past go and move on. Most families gave it up decades ago. You've done well to hang onto it for so long. But now? What's the point?"

Willow reached for her father's hand. "It's time. I'm not staying here, I'm sorry."

"I'm not leaving. This is my home, it's was my parents' and theirs and theirs before that. It's yours too." Her father thumped the table.

Willow pulled back and set her hands in her lap. "It's not. Not for a long time."

Her father stood and left. Anthony tapped his finger on the table. "I'm not sure he'll come around."

"He's a bit lost. I can't stay much longer, I have a job, friends, and this place isn't good for me."

"Then go. If he doesn't want your help, you can't force it on him."

"I know, but he's my father. He has no one."

"Maybe, but all the years he failed you, left you alone. Your family..." he shook his head. "They let the Stillwell's run your life, they chose for you. In my opinion, you owe him nothing."

"What kind of person am I if I turn my back on him?"

"You don't have to turn your back. Leave, and tell him if he wants his child in his life, to come and find you. But you're done. Sometimes we do the selfish thing, and in the long term, it's what's best for everyone. Staying will only facilitate his petulance."

"That's a bit harsh."

"They brought Oliver into your life and insisted you marry him."

"Fair point."

Willow waited a week. A few tense conversations with her father and it seemed like the penny was dropping.

"You're not really going back?"

Anthony helped her pack, and her father in the doorway.

"Yes, I have a job." Hopefully.

"What am I supposed to do?"

"Sell this place, move nearer to Aunt Caroline or me. I'm not staying."

Anthony took her bags down, and her father seemed so lost. He sat on the settee in her room.

"I need somewhere I can get up and down the stairs. I need a bathroom that won't kill me when I try to get in and out of it. I need people around me that don't make me feel like a burden and failure. All those things and so many more are here. I'm afraid that Peter or Oliver will come back. Can't you understand?"

He scratched his forehead. "Fine."

Anthony helped her downstairs.

"Thank you for this."

"How's Matt? He seems nice." Anthony leant in as he asked.

"Nice? That's not a word I'd use."

"Can I say devastatingly attractive?"

Willow laughed as she settled in the car. "Yes. I'm so lucky."

Puffing out a breath, he started the car.

"Bit wary since he left, but I'm trying to hold onto how it felt when he was here."

"What are you afraid of?"

"Look at him, he's gorgeous."

"I did."

Willow gurgled a laugh. "I've spent nearly all my time since he left in bed recovering. It's not like we can go out a lot."

"Maybe he's a homebody. Maybe he's done the dating and shagging and whatnot and wants a relationship."

"You sound like you've been there."

"I have."

"I wonder if it's because I've been lied to so much over the years. It's hard to trust anyone's motives."

"Considering everything, that's fair."

The drive was quiet, and Willow was pensive.

RELEASE

J ane hugged Willow when they got home and welcomed Anthony in.

"We missed you!" Jane scowled, "you look like shit."

"Thanks, I feel it. I really want to go to bed."

"Go on. Don't forget to text Matt, I hear he's unbearable."

"Is he?" Willow said goodbye to Anthony when he set her things down. "You're always welcome to stay."

"Thank you, I'm going to get off. I'll speak to you soon." He kissed her cheek and set off.

Firing off a message to Matt to tell him she was home, Willow crawled into bed and relaxed. Chadford was her home, and she was thankful for it.

Willow woke to the shrill sound of her phone ringing. She didn't know where she was or what day it was, just that the noise was loud enough to wake the dead. Maybe she was dead.

"There you are."

Willow hummed at the sound of Matt's voice and grinned as his petulant tone. "How are you?"

"Relieved you're home and busy. More importantly, how are you?"

"I think I've slept too much." Willow yawned and snuggled into her pillow.

"I have some bad news."

"Oh?"

"I have to go and manage a job, I'm just heading out to my car. I'll be gone until the weekend, maybe even next week.

Willow heard the distance in his voice and wanted to reassure him. He was as insecure as she was. She chewed the inside of her cheek, she desperately wanted to see him. "I understand. I've waited this long, I can't wait a few days more."

She stretched in the silence when he ended the call and sat up, letting the world right itself before testing her legs.

Kim, the friend who'd helped her leave Chadford, texted her that day and called straight away when asked. They'd caught up when she was back at Harringly.

"Aren't you at work?" Willow asked before she said anything.

"No, I'm off this week, just a couple of training days where every man gets to talk to me like a fucking child in that way that they think I can't speak English. Fuckers. How're things?"

"Don't know, Matt's going away this weekend."

"Shit. How are you holding up?"

"Better than I thought. This guy, Kim, he's incredible."

"Men falling over you like bees to honey."

"Or flies to shit."

They both laughed.

"Wills, we need a catch-up. I have some time off, would anyone mind if I came down and stayed on Saturday? I could distract you from Matt being away with shenanigans."

"Oh no. You'll never guess."

"What?"

"The women I live with, Darby and Jane, are gay."

"Really? They a couple?"

"Nope. I'm pretty much the only straight person, other than Suzy and another couple."

"I'll be there in the morning. Set me up." Kim laughed.

"Wait," Darby said as they ate that night, "this is the person who helped you escape? Escape is the word you'd use?"

Willow picked at her dinner that evening as they sat at the table and chatted. "Yes."

Jane and Darby looked at each other.

"I hope you don't mind?"

"No, not at all. What's she like?"

"She's about four-foot-eleven. She's gay. Filipino. Hair to her arse. Swears a lot."

Jane's eyes went wide. "Sounds adorable."

"She is. She's an electrician."

"Why are we only hearing about this now?"

Willow looked up from her plate. "I didn't want to do that thing of, oh you're a lesbian, so obviously you want to meet my lesbian friend. You're not rare unicorns, plenty of lesbians to go around."

Darby laughed. "Jane has a thing for petite women and long hair."

Jane cleared her throat. "Thank you, Darby."

"Well, this should be fun." Willow laughed too.

Jane put her knife and fork down and drank her wine.

"If you're up to it, we could all go out," Jane said as her cheeks reddened. "Shame it's not Kink."

"Let's not scare her away. Besides, I'm always working those nights. We could take her up Town Hill." Jane shoved some pasta in her mouth.

Willow sent Matt a selfie when she went to bed, and he didn't reply. She pushed back her disappointment.

Willow stood on the driveway as Kim parked that weekend. The tiny woman hopped down out of her car and screamed Willow's name.

They hugged for ages.

"You look good. Better." Kim beamed and grabbed her bag.

Jane appeared in the doorway.

"Kim, this is Jane."

The two women shook hands, holding it too long until Kim laughed and cleared her throat.

"Right, where are you putting me?"

"There's the box room, it has a foldout bed."

"That'll do." Though she was small, she was toned, and her muscles were on show as she hauled the heavy bag upstairs. Jane followed her up. She turned briefly and bit her lip as she looked at Willow.

Containing her glee, she went into the kitchen and put the kettle on.

Later, they'd somehow migrated to Jane's room. It was comfortable and tidy, and there were black and white photos along one wall from demos. Women artfully tied and displayed; they were beautiful.

Kim couldn't take her eyes away from them as they sat about discussing the plans for the evening.

The front door slammed, and Darby came upstairs, holding hands with Alie. She was almost ethereal with her deep umber skin, pretty face and cropped hair. With a warm smile, she sat next to Willow, who was lying on the bed, and everyone chatted.

Willow let it wash over her as she debated whether to join them or not. "I think I'm going to have to pass."

"Why?"

"I'm tired."

Kim scowled at her friend. "I did not drive over a hundred miles for you to flake on me. You can sleep all day tomorrow. Do you remember when we first met in halls?"

"Oh no."

Jane perked up. "What's this?" She paused going through her makeup bag from her spot on the floor.

Kim laughed, and Willow shook her head.

"We were neighbours in halls, and on freshers' week, our block went out on the piss. I was studying fucking media." Kim rolled her eyes. "And this bitch was music, we were the only creative types, the rest were all fucking sports or sciences. So, we went wild. Got shitfaced, danced on every table going. Do you remember that time I mooned that copper? I mean, I only wanted her to put the cuffs on me. I got arrested, and the moral of that story is that tequila is evil."

Willow laughed. "She gave you a look, like don't make me arrest you, and you were all like, arrest me, arrest me."

"I was lucky I only got a caution. The things we did."

Willow shook her head.

Darby craned her neck around to Willow. "Wait, you're not the perfect angel you pretend to be?"

"I never said that. Just because I can't do something, it doesn't mean I don't want to."

"Willow used to sing at people to make them fuck off."

"Bit of Mozart in their faces." She shrugged.

"Go on," Jane said.

"Oh no, it's been ages, I doubt I could do it anymore."

"I miss your voice." Kim wiggled her brows.

With a sigh, Willow sat up and straightened her back. She made a few noises, testing her voice, it wasn't as strong. "I don't have the strength anymore. It'll be crap."

She did a few scales and stretched her neck. She swept her legs up and knelt, smoothing her hair back.

Before, when alone, she'd still sing, reluctant to let it go. It took so much, she could only sing in short bursts. She no longer had the power in her lungs or chest.

Singing the opening bars to 'Un Bel Di Verdremo' softer and lighter than she would have once made it sad. But she heard the orchestra behind her and felt the stage under her.

Her heart leapt at the memory. She had loved it more than anything. Her hands reached out as her eyes closed; the notes a memory, knowing the part. She swelled and quietened at the deeper notes. The violin coming behind her. A small wistful smile as she sang. Her brows rising at the high notes, finding the passion and volume again. Tears filled her eyes, her arms imploring, body rigid with control.

Her words coming quickly before the long high note. It fell away, and she still heard the music, and she laughed.

Opening her eyes. Jane had tears running down her face, Alie was on her feet, Darby was slack-jawed, and Kim had an enigmatic smile about her.

"It wasn't that bad, was it? My voice broke a little, but I said it wasn't that strong anymore, what?"

"That was beautiful. You're like an angel."

Lit by a string of fairy lights, Willow started laughing.

"Seriously, you come alive, I've never seen anything so beautiful." Jane wiped her eyes.

"All right, it wasn't that good." Willow coughed.

"It really fucking was," Darby said.

"Well. Thank you. Now I need a nap." Willow lay back down.

After dinner, she was shovelled into a short purple skater dress that went off her shoulders. It was Jane's, and they were deciding what shoes to wear. Kim had a perfect pair of wedges. Everyone looked at her as she held them up.

"What?"

Willow reached over, her hair in curlers, with more makeup on that she'd ever worn, and snatched one.

Holding out her leg she squeezed her toes in. "Look at this. It's like I'm the cocking stepsister here, trying Cindi's glass slipper."

Everyone laughed, and Kim snatched it back.

"Seriously, how small are your feet?"

"I'm lucky if I can get adult sizes, and you know what, kid's shoes are shit."

Willow went with a pair of ballet pumps, not ideal, but it was all she could manage. With her hair in waves, and everyone ready, they called a taxi. Willow spoke to Matt a few times, but he was busy, and grumpy. She nearly sent him a selfie of her all dressed up but didn't want to bother him.

They went to The Crossways Hat. The best description of it was quirky. But the music was good. Downstairs was a bar, and main floor, and upstairs were two smaller rooms. That night was alternative night. Indie in the main room. A rock room and the third was more commercial. They headed in. Willow, conscious of her cane but unafraid to use it like a deadly weapon, took Darby's arm.

"Why this place?" she shouted.

"Dunno, it used to be gay night, then they changed it, but we all kept coming out of protest. No one cares anymore." She shrugged, and they found a table.

It was early, and not too busy. Willow loved the fact they were prepared to have an early one because of her, though she felt bad.

From her bag, she fetched out some earplugs and put them in, not giving a fuck. She sipped her vodka and coke, knowing it made her a bit hyper. She'd pay for it tomorrow. Fuck it.

A few familiar faces joined them. Willow hung back as they fawned over Kim. Not that she blamed them, Kim was wonderful. Willow was content to watch.

At one point, she was dragged off to the ladies. The noise pulsed in her vision and floor undulated. Willow wanted to go to bed. The muffled sounds of people were lost on her, and she was happy enough not to pay too much attention.

"Are you okay?" Darby held her eye, and Willow nodded.

In the ladies, she took out an earplug. "Sorry, the noise levels tend to mess me up."

"It's understandable. How you doing?"

"I'm okay."

Darby turned back to the mirror as people chatted. "Heard from Matt?"

Willow frowned "No, he's busy with work." Slumping against the side, she turned her cane on the spot.

"Is he?" She smirked as put sheer lip gloss on before leading her back out.

Willow stopped in her tracks. Matt was by their table with a bottle of lager in his hand, laughing.

She looked down uncertain what to do. He looked happy, flirting and teasing with Mel, it shouldn't, but it cut her. He didn't tell her he was back, and maybe he didn't want to be with her after all. Matt looked over and saw her. All mirth gone. That was her; joy killer.

He marched over. Uh-oh.

She found herself alone, Matt staring down at her in blue light, muffled bass closing in. She lowered her head, skin goosing.

Matt lifted her chin, making her face him. "Aren't you happy to see me?"

"I... why didn't you tell me you were back?"

He grinned, warm and beautiful, the dark stubble on his face nearly a beard. "I wanted to surprise you." He leant right in, nearly brushing her lips. "Now, answer me, aren't you happy to see me?"

"Yes," she said as she breathed in.

Matt walked her back and virtually pinned her against the wall. Leaning close, he spoke, "Sorry I've not been attentive, I've been trying to focus on work, but all I can think about is you."

Her gaze didn't waver, and though she appeared calm, her heart pounded.

His smile dimmed. "I've wanted to see you, but I thought you needed time or space so I didn't crowd you."

"I'm not doctor bloody who. You could have asked." She sounded irritated, but she wasn't, she just wanted him to hold her. "But if you think I need space, I can leave."

He cupped her face, pressing his body against her, crowding in with his heat and delicious body. "I am sorry. You're right. Don't leave, please. I missed you."

Willow sighed. "Fine."

Matt grinned and bit his lip before making himself serious again. "Are you being a brat? Teasing me?" His lips were too close and not close enough.

He laughed at her arch look and raised chin. Matt kissed her, holding her tight, letting everyone know she was his, and she was. Warm, soft mouth, scratchy beard, and the solid strength swept her up, her surprise and annoyance forgotten.

Dazed, she wiped the lippy off his lips and made sure hers wasn't a mess when he put her down.

He took her hand in his, and she let herself be taken back. Finding a seat, he sat and patted his knee. Willow gave him an unimpressed look, but no one paid them any attention. He narrowed his eyes, waiting and impatient.

She mouthed no, and he mouthed yes.

Willow huffed and went to Matt, he grabbed her waist and turned her, making her sit down on his thigh.

"Good girl."

"Oh please." She turned so she faced him, leaning in she put her hand on his chest and rested her cheek on his as she said into his ear, "I hope you don't expect me to call you daddy."

Matt chuckled and held her closer.

"No. I'm too heavy to sit like this." She looked around at everyone, who were ignoring them, as they sat in the darkened corner.

"You're perfect. I'm a big boy, I can take it."

Heat rippled through her, and the frisson in her belly made her want. She forgot for a moment who she was.

She relaxed against him, and his hum purred in his chest.

"I thought you'd changed your mind." She ran her hand over the back of his neck.

"When I left, I had the feeling you wanted to me to back off. I don't want to be that guy who won't back off. I was balancing my tendencies against what's appropriate. I'm sorry, my Rose."

She lowered her gaze, and he squeezed her thigh.

"Fuck, you feel good. You look incredible by the way."

The words fell out of her mouth before she knew what she was saying. "Take me home."

"No. But I do want to test you."

"How?"

"Obey me."

"What do you want me to do?" Her heart kicked up.

Matt's hand caressing her leg, and his heat, his everything, made her moan.

"I want you to stay very still, and quiet while I feel you."

She glanced at everyone, but most people weren't looking at them. Mel winked before moving off, and Willow took a breath.

Matt ran his hand up and down her thigh. "If I ask you to do something, I want you to do it."

"Such as?"

He took his hand away.

"Okay, I'll do it. Within reason."

"Ah, there's the thing. You have to trust that I won't do anything that would put you at risk."

"Isn't there always risk? I'm not sure I can."

"You're right, but it's quantified, and if you're not able, then your limit or it's my fault, I haven't earnt your trust yet, but I will if you'll let me. I want to teach you, Willow, if you're ready."

Always afraid and torn. Matt wasn't Oliver or Peter. His desire and need for control was one of love and generous care. The allure of what he wanted from her hovered within grasp. She could have something good.

Instead of going around in circles again, she dove in. "I'm ready."

"How much have you had to drink?"

"A glass of fizz earlier and that vodka."

"No more then."

"Yes."

He smiled and brushed his stubbly jaw against her cheek. "Sir."

"Sir?" She laughed, head thrown back.

He squeezed her thigh. "I'm not joking."

Willow's mirth vanished, and she stared. His serious face and tone made her wet. "Sorry, Sir." She half-smiled as she said it, and Matt growled. Actual growling. Her lips trembled.

"Are you laughing?"

"No, Sir." She offered a solemn look.

"Good." The twinkle in his eye reflected the lights. His breath touched her lips, and his eyes fixed on her mouth. His lips quirked up at one corner, and an eyebrow moved.

Willow licked her lips, aware of his hard, muscular body under her. Strong thighs and safe arms held her firmly. "What's your command?"

There was relief in his face as he squeezed her closer. In the dark, as others moved off to dance, he stared into her eyes. Shielded by the table, Matt looked about.

"Put your hand up your dress."

She blinked and cleared her throat. He kept looking around as she did.

"What are you wearing?"

"Solid shaping pants."

Matt laughed, leaning into her shoulder. "Can you get your finger under them? Don't look away. Just at me." He leant back and held her gaze.

Willow did. She was uncomfortable, and her back ached, but fucking hell, she had to do it. Her eyes fluttered as she shifted, eyes on him.

Matt went still and quiet. "Are you wet?"

"Yes."

"Good. Do you want to come?"

"Yes."

"Tough. You can't. Keep your finger there. Keep looking at me. How does it feel to have your finger in your pussy in public?"

She couldn't answer. Her body wanted, needing release.

"You are a good girl. Take your finger out."

She did, pursing her lips together, suppressing desire.

Matt was so close, his lips brushed hers. "Suck it."

Slowly, she put her finger to her lips, catching his mouth, and the tangy taste ran her over her tongue.

He pulled his lips into his mouth, eyelids fluttering. "Time to go home."

Willow nodded.

OH, BUT LUST

Willow said goodbye, still tasting herself. She staggered as Matt took her arm and they navigated their way out.

In the cool evening, she took out the earplugs and blinked awake. It was too hot in there. Taking a deep breath, she relished the sweat drying on her skin.

"How are you?"

"Matt, I need, I mean, I don't know."

"We're not going much further tonight." He led them up to the taxi rank.

"I wanted to see, for you to know."

"If it was possible? Yes, yes, it is, and you're going to leave me unfulfilled?"

He grinned. "But think how good it will be when we are together."

She moaned, and they headed out to Downly.

He held her hand the whole way, and she couldn't stop thinking about what she'd done. That everyone must have known.

"You with me?"

"Hmm?"

He urged her out the car and inside.

"I'm going to kiss you. Let's sit down first though." With a grin, he picked her up and carried her upstairs. And once in her room, kicked the door shut.

Setting her on the bed, he sat next to her. Matt's lips parted and made no move, but let the tension build again.

Running his knuckle across her cheek, he moved closer, and she loved every drawn-out moment. With his breath on her face, she squeezed his arm, desperate.

He speared his fingers through her hair, bringing her close, and when their lips met, heat filled her. Hot, soft lips were firm against hers, the rough of his stubble scratched as he moved against her mouth.

Matt elicited desire she never knew was in her. His tongue stroked and teased as his arms enclosed her. Safe and excited, all at once.

When he moaned into her mouth, she felt up his back to his neck, wanting more, afraid to ask for it. Matt was holding back, she knew it. He was careful with her.

Matt broke the kiss and looked at her. "Your lips are perfect."

She leant in to kiss him again, but he moved back.

"Ask me."

"Please kiss me, Sir." Willow flushed. "Please don't hold back."

"You don't know what you're asking."

"Show me."

His expression darkened, and he held the back of her head, keeping her in place. Leaning over her, Matt waited for a beat before closing his eyes and kissing her. His tongue deep in her mouth lips hard against hers. He pinned her to him, overwhelming her, and after a moment of fear, she let herself go.

Limp in his hold, she managed to keep up her tongue, but nothing else. She didn't have to worry about what she should do, how she should do it. He'd take it, he'd guide with desire.

When he pulled back, they were both panting.

"More."

Matt half-smiled, half-sneered. "You're too demanding." He lay her back and settled to the side of her.

"Will you stay with me?"

"Yes. But no more than this," he said, running his hand down her neck, over the skin above her dress, and his teasing his finger across the neckline. She watched him concentrate on her and shivered as he crossed a sensitive spot under her collarbone.

He kissed it, and her skin goosed. He laughed at her reaction. "You test my control."

"Do I?" Willow's voice was husky. "I think I'd do anything you wanted right now."

Matt went still and then eased her dress up, running his hand up. "Open."

Willow opened her legs. It was a vulnerable moment, and she held onto it, drawing it out, opening them slowly.

He knelt up in between and ran his hands up and down her thighs. She wanted. Needed. As she never had before. She felt sexy, but was she? Not assimilated feeling, but real experience?

"Where are you?" Matt stilled his hands at the tops of her thighs.

Willow squirmed.

"No, my Rose, tell me what you're thinking." He ran his hands back down and lifted her legs up into the air, pushing them back.

She kept breathing as she watched him see how flexible she was. He was smiling.

Pressing her mouth into a line, she resisted.

He let her go. "What?"

Willow shook her head.

"Hey," he lay back down with her, dipping a light kiss on her forehead. "What's wrong? We can stop."

"No. I don't want to stop. At all. But I'm nervous that I'll disappoint you. I've never thought of myself as sexy, but you make me feel like I am. I don't want to shatter that illusion."

"You are sexy, so very sexy. I can adjust to your needs, as long as you want me in charge, I'm happy."

"Yes."

"I love that word, along with please."

"Please," she whispered.

A wicked grin emerged on his face and half-lying on her, he took her mouth in a greedy kiss. With one hand holding her wrists above her head, his weight pinned them there, his other hand roved all over her.

She let him, relaxing under his touch, more aroused than she'd ever been.

When he cupped her, she moaned, finally his large, strong hand where she wanted it. Resisting the urge to grind against him, she trembled.

Matt let her go and pushed her dress up, pulling it off her. He yanked his t-shirt off and undid his jeans. She panted as she watched. Getting up, he undressed, and she couldn't take her eyes from his cock under his moulded underwear. It really was something to see.

Matt made short work of her bra and knickers, and she was completely naked under his gaze.

"I'm not going to fuck you, but you'll come. Yes?"

"Yes please," she panted, not caring how desperate she sounded.

Still holding her knickers, he straddled her chest, and she did appreciate seeing him that close. Matt kissed the inside of her wrist before tying her knickers around them, not too tight, in fact, she could have wriggled out of them if she wanted to. She didn't; she wanted to it to be tighter. To be trapped. To be his.

"Tell me," he whispered as he lay back down. Sucking her bottom lip, he pressed against her.

"I like it."

She watched him kiss down to her breast, not wanting to miss anything he did. He didn't go for her nipple but carried on down.

Willow was self-conscious of her body. She'd watched it abstractly change over the years. Losing muscle mass, the softening of it, and she didn't hate it, it was more she didn't feel at home.

Fibro had disconnected her physicality. She floated around detached from her pain, from the daily struggle of fighting against herself.

"Where's your mind?"

"You talk a lot."

"You think a lot. It's important that we communicate." He looked up before running his tongue along her flesh.

"I don't like my body. It's complicated. Not just self-image. I have so much pain." Then it struck her. She could choose her own pain. That was the difference. It was something she was used to. This pain was a choice. "Will you hurt me?"

"A request?"

"Just a question." Willow sucked a breath as he moved up and sucked the underside of her boob.

"I'm wary of it. But if you wish to, we can try it."

"Why are you wary?"

Matt sighed and rested his face against her chest. "Because you have a lot of pain already."

He went back to kissing her chest and stomach and then down. Oh fuck, he kept going down, her breath came quickly as he ran his tongue down under her belly button.

"I think I've teased you for long enough. You know what I look like when I come, I think it's my turn."

He held her thighs wide apart, fingers digging in, and hovered so close with his breath on her clit.

Matt waited for her to relax, and she did. Their eyes locked as he put his lips on her, and he made a noise like he was eating the best steak in the world.

Then he went at her ferociously. She cried out and lifted her hips, and he let her go until she begged him for more. Licking his lips, eyes heavy, he licked and sucked her slowly, letting sensation build.

Her thighs tensed, and she tried to resist the orgasm, but it was so intense, she couldn't. Willow closed her eyes, body bucking, toes curled as she came.

Matt held firm, eyes locked on her, and when she came down with his tongue pressed against her clit, he was still watching her.

Willow panted and tried not to press against his tongue. He sat up, licking his lips.

"Do you want me to return the favour?"

"Yes." He shook his head. "I hadn't planned on this."

"Matt, please, I want you. Please."

"Don't think you can use that word to get whatever you want."

"Will you punish me?"

"By not giving you what you want."

Her response was a moan.

"Hold the headboard."

She did, her wrists still bound. Matt got up and took his underwear off. She couldn't take her eyes off his cock. She'd never thought of them as nice, but he was beautiful.

He straddled her shoulders, one knee by her head, and the other under her arm, and careful of her, he ran his hand down her cheek. "You sure?"

She smirked and opened her mouth. Matt smoothed her hair as he took her invite. His eyes fluttered as he moaned.

Then there was only his body close up. She couldn't take much of him, and he didn't push her but moved in and out of her mouth in shallow thrusts.

Saliva pooled, and he bunched his hand in her hair.

Leaning back, he looked at her, and she smiled around him, licking at him. He made a deep noise, and she kept doing it.

"Willow, that's good, like that," he said through gritted teeth.

He wanted to fuck her mouth, but his restraint was touching. He was nothing like she expected. Matt pushed deeper, and she took it. He held her head with a firm grip, and Willow relaxed.

Her clit pulsed, and she rubbed her thighs together.

"Open your legs, are you trying to come again?"

She hummed, making him laugh. Matt reached back, still thrusting into her mouth, and put two fingers in her but didn't move them.

Her muscles clamped around them, and it was embarrassing how wet she was.

She opened her eyes as she whimpered. His abs taut with his body twisted, carefully fucking her mouth. Moving her hips against his fingers in time to his thrusts, he looked pained as his mouth fell open.

He was holding back so much. She tasted pre-cum, and Matt swore.

"Fuck, I'm going to come." His hips went faster, and so did hers, tighter and wetter.

Matt hit the back of her throat, and she breathed through it. Her jaw hurt, and she was on the edge, and as he tugged on her hair, she came. As she cried out around him, he stilled and pumped his hips a few more times, filling her mouth with tanginess.

Matt moved with the last spurts and pulling out quickly, removing his fingers, he lay over her, and in a surprise move, he kissed her as she swallowed.

Her face was a mess, but he didn't seem to care, his taste between them as he furiously tongued her. Pausing, he put his fingers in her mouth, then his, slowly licking them. She couldn't stop watching him.

Finally, he propped himself up, taking his weight off her. "That was the best blow job I've ever had."

"Really? I'm not very good."

"Yes, you are. Are you okay? Did I push too hard?" Matt untied her hands as he asked.

"No, but you held back."

"I did, I don't want to hurt you."

"Liar."

Matt laughed. "Okay, fine, but only when you beg me to. Only when you're ready to be punished by me."

"Punished, but aren't I good?" She smiled with big innocent eyes, and Matt bit the inside of his cheek.

"Too good." He kissed her. "Loo?"

She grinned.

Later, all cleaned up, they curled up together, and Matt encased her.

To her, sex had been someone on her and taking their pleasure; it was reality, and anything more was fantasy. Wanting something intangible, and then not getting it. Just a man on top with no consideration for her. Matt was something else. What they shared was so intimate, and though not what she knew as sex, it was exactly that. Her mind opened to the possibilities.

Peter had been okay, and there were times she thought he did enjoy it, but he only took what he wanted. She'd never slept with Oliver. He'd pushed for a physical relationship, and she pushed back. That road was icky and complicated.

Willow shifted tighter into Matt's hold.

Thinking back, the first term of uni held so much promise of escape, of hope, of a different life. But since becoming ill, she'd been suffocated by silence and isolation, but in Matt's arms in a house share in Chadford, she found everything she wanted.

By Stefanie Simpson

IMMERSION

Matt woke and nestled against her soft body in deep sleep. Play and sex were great, but this was what he loved. That simple waking and not being alone.

The pleasure of having her there filled that hole in him. He wasn't designed to be alone, he hated it, and having this sweet woman, who was prepared to try out his desires struck him afresh.

He'd waited for this for so long. Hope had all but evaporated, and unlooked for, there she was. Quiet in the chaos.

Matt smiled and kissed her hair. He loved the smell of it, the heavy waves, and how it fell over her shoulder. Last night went so much further than he planned, but he couldn't seem to help it.

Willow shifted and stretched.

"Hey, my Rose."

She shivered and turned to him. He loved the shy look in her eyes as she nestled into his shoulder. "Hey."

"How do you feel?"

"Good. Knackered, but good."

"I have to go to my mum's today."

"Okay."

"Would you like to come with me?"

Willow went still. "Really?"

"Yes." He leant back and brought her chin up so he could look at her. "Let's get this bit out the way. I like you Willow Rose Morris, and the start we made was everything I want. I want to go further."

She grinned, and cat stretched. "I think I can live with that. As long as you're okay with all my bullshit."

"It's not bullshit. I was worried whether I could help you or not if I'd be too much. I'm okay with it." Matt pecked her lips. "You don't believe me, do you?"

"It's hard. I've been manipulated and made to feel like shit for so long."

"I know. Well, I can prove it to you, in time."

Matt got up and pulled on his underwear and strutted out. He heard Willow laugh as he went downstairs.

Darby, in a bright blue dressing gown with Alie in a fluffy robe, made exclamations of horror at his appearance.

"Matt, Matt, Matt, what the fuck? Cover that shit up in our presence."

He winked and grinned as he started making coffee.

"You seem a hell of a lot happier than you've been in ages."

"Possibly that's because I am."

"Good. Willow okay?"

He grunted a laugh. "Yes. I plan on taking excellent care of my girlfriend, thank you very much."

"Hmm. You left the club early."

Matt took the mugs and went back upstairs without another word.

Willow got up later for a shower, and he followed.

"Um, what?"

He kissed her and walked her into the shower.

"Really?" She leant back.

"Really."

"Okay." Willow sat on the shower seat and stared up at him.

He washed her hair, conditioned it, soaped and rinsed her, all the while he caressed her with gentle love. Her eyes closed as she relaxed and let him take care of her. It was intimate and sweet, and he loved every second of it.

She watched him as he showered, enjoying her eyes on him.

"Nice view?"

"Perfect, though I did enjoy the back of you the last time."

He paused while scrubbing his hair. "You're never letting that go."

"Never." She grinned, leaning back on the tile, eyes on his cock.

Matt luxuriated in her appreciation. The lack of polish and veneer about her, an honest, open reaction without artifice was everything he'd ever wanted in a sub.

He leant down and kissed her sweetly, and she smiled around his mouth. He had to take care, be cautious, but Willow was special to him. Not scaring her away was important.

"How are you feeling?"

"I'm okay. I promise you, if I'm not, I'll say." She shrugged, it made her boobs move, and he glanced down.

"We should get going before I get too tempted."

Willow blushed and stifled a giggle. It was adorable when she did it. Her eyes darted down, it made him want to chase her like a rabbit, and he the fox.

By the time they were ready, it was nearly lunch, and Willow began to feel nervous as the left the house.

"Tell me about your family."

"Just me, mum and gran. Dad passed away when I was a kid."

"You don't talk about it much."

He took a deep breath and face went serious. The ease that he had all morning faded, and she was sorry.

That Matt was fun. "You don't have to tell me about it, I didn't mean to upset you." He didn't say anything, and for some reason, she kept talking. "You're Anglo-Persian?"

He relaxed again and shook his head, turning off the radio. "My dad was a great man. He lived life to the fullest, and I remember laughter and days out. He taught me to drive when I was five."

Willow laughed. "No, how?"

"We drove out to Kettly wood, there's a plane field. It's where the RAF were based in the second world war. Anyway, it's a big flat space. Sat me on his lap and I steered. When I got used to that, he had me change gear, and I had to press my foot on his leg when I want to break or use the clutch.

"We spent hours driving." Matt's grin faded.

"He sounds like a good man."

"He was thirty-two when he died. When I reached that age a few years ago, I had to think about my life. What I wanted. Made some changes."

"How so?"

"Dad came from Iran. Mum and dad weren't married, and we lived with him until he died. She won't talk about him. I think he was her great love. I wish she would, only because I was always so detached from that side of my heritage. I wanted to know where I come from, so I searched for information on him, and I didn't find much, but I know he had a sister. I found her." He grinned. "They live in Canada, she's a grandmother, and I have cousins and family. They're great. I look like him, and she cries every time I see her on a video call. I plan to go one day and visit." He beamed.

"I'm glad."

"In this lifestyle, you have to understand your needs and motivations. You must be self-aware. I learnt about Iran, and its culture, I learnt about sex, and my sexuality aside from sex itself. I came to understand my privilege as a white-passing biracial man, even with the bullshit I get now and again. I'm all those things and more than the sum, like anyone."

She watched him drive in silence.

"There's something else. My mum was devastated when he died. A few years later she had a boyfriend. He wasn't a good man. I understand her, the void dad left was massive, and we were destitute. Seriously, we lived in a two-room flat for a while. She didn't get anything because they weren't married, and although she put his name as the father, there was no will. He was a young man when he came to England alone."

"Are you Muslim?"

"No, mum is CofE and dad was Christian too. Though, I'm not religious."

"What did this boyfriend do?"

Matt gripped the steering wheel. "He was evil, one of those quiet racists who doesn't think they are, but he used to say terrible things to me. To us both. It's how I know ARC. Mum used them. Saved us. It was a long time ago, and it was different then, but it's a good place."

Willow's heart clenched. She let the impulse to blurt anything out pass. "I'm sorry you went through that. You're a good man."

"I think... I think it's some of why I'm this way. Protective. I hate seeing people in distress, or vulnerable. I have to do something."

"It makes sense. The business; you're alpha in charge in the right way. I like it. I've never known anyone quite like you. I'm lucky to."

Matt glanced at her and cleared his throat. "That's um," he grinned. "good to hear."

They turned into a housing estate and onto a narrow drive of a small semi-detached house. Only about ten years old.

He opened the front door and shouted hello, holding Willow's free hand.

"Matt?" A tiny, fragile woman appeared in an apron, bent over, hands gnarled and skin papery. She craned her head up as much as she could, and her face folded into a smile.

Her warm, rheumy eyes were filled with joy as she put her arms around his waist. He bent over and hugged her back.

"Hey, Nana."

"Look at you, always growing." She patted his chest.

"Nana, I've been this height for a while."

"Oh dear, I must be shrinking then." She let him go. "Is this her? Oh, my dear, let me look at you." From a chain around her neck, she put on her glasses, making her eyes larger, and took Willow by the shoulders. "My, my, you are a beauty, aren't you? He's not brought anyone home since the lovely Kai. Oh, they were lovely, but you are a sweetheart, so I hear. Yes, English Rose, they say, now aren't you."

Willow grinned. "Hello-"

"Nana, my name is Elizabeth, but I've been Nana a long time now. Come, come." Nana shuffled off, and Willow looked up at Matt who was looking at her oddly.

"What?"

He shook his head and led her through past the kitchen and into the living room.

His mum, Leslie, was in the conservatory watering plants. Nana sat in her chair and picked up her book and a magnifying glass.

"Mum?"

"Matt, oh," she stopped as she came in. "Well, Willow, it's so good to meet you." Leslie shook Willow's hand, she had a kind face and was very ordinary. She glanced at Matt. Maybe the same nose, but they looked nothing alike. Leslie was pale and very fair with blue eyes.

"I know, no one thinks he's mine. All his dad." She smiled. "I'll make tea."

They settled down, and Matt went to help his mum. He was adorable. Huh, she best not tell him that.

Nana looked up from her book. "How did you meet?"

"Matt rescued me when I wasn't well. I'd just arrived at ARC."

Nana put her magnifying glass down. "ARC? Hmm. He is a rescuer."

"He is. A quality I greatly admire."

"Broken birds don't have to fly."

"Sorry?"

"It's something my gran used to say when I were little. Her husband came back from the great war a changed man. She tried to help him, but he was never the same again. That's what she said of him. Doesn't mean they're not still birds."

Willow smiled. She wasn't a broken, wounded bird. She was stronger than most people, didn't need fixing, and was no inspo-porn story to make others feel better.

For a moment she wavered, was that who she was to him. The broken bird?

Matt and Leslie came back.

"What's up?" he said quietly.

She gave him a tight smile. "Nothing." She sipped her tea.

"Matt tells me you work at ARC?" Leslie asked.

"Yes. Only two days a week, I help with the property service and fundraising. Just admin assistance. It's nice."

"That's good."

The conversation stalled but the smells of cooking distracted everyone, and Nana shuffled up and into the kitchen. Leslie followed with a roll of her eyes.

"So?" Matt turned to her.

"They're nice."

"What is it?"

"Broken bird."

Matt frowned. "No, my Rose, Nana says that a lot. She says it about mum. You're still the bird, and not being fixed doesn't change you from being the bird. Doesn't take your feathers or what you are, only changes the dynamics."

Willow nodded.

He leant in and whispered, "I'm not going to try and fix you, you're fine as you are. Promise me the same thing."

She looked up with a frown. "What does that mean?"

"This isn't the best place to talk about it, later, okay?" He kissed her forehead.

"Now, now, enough of that nonsense." Nana fixed them with a look, and they made their way to the table. Matt carried the plates through as they sat down to eat a nice lunch.

When they left, Nana patted her arm and stared into Willow's eyes. "You know what, you're a sweet girl, I like you." She grinned.

"Thank you, Nana."

Leslie kissed her cheek and then Matt's, and they left. The air was cooler and still full, Willow was tired.

"Want to go home, or we could do something. Mine?" Matt started the car.

"Sounds good. I'd planned to spend time with Kim, but I think she and Jane are getting on well, leaving them to it might be wise."

Willow was surprised that he lived in the centre of Chadford. It was expensive and highly desired, the prices steadily rising due to redevelopment.

Matt lived in a posh flat, in a swanky building. They went into the secure underground parking, and he helped her out the car. She was surprised there was a lift.

"This is nice."

"It's okay."

He was on the tenth floor, and as they walked out, the place still had that new smell.

"How long have you lived here?"

"Six months. I was lucky to get it."

His flat was bigger than expected and nicely decorated. She'd expected cold masculinity, but it felt like a home. Neat and orderly, but comfortable. Everything was new and fashionable.

"Are you tired?" Matt turned to her and lifted her chin.

"I am. Sorry."

"Would you like to lie down for a bit. My bed is very comfortable."

"I have no doubt." She tugged on his t-shirt.

He grunted a noise of pleasure and swept her up into his arms.

"You love that, don't you?"

"Yes. It's possibly in my top five things I love doing."

"Is doing me on that list?"

"Yes." He stilled and held her eye. "It's number one."

She laughed and buried her face in his neck.

"Now, I'm going to let you rest for a bit. Then, if you want to, maybe play?"

"I'd love to."

Matt placed her on the most comfortable bed she'd ever been on. She moaned as she sank into it, soft and giving, but firm underneath.

Matt slipped her ballet pumps off and closed the curtains. She wore a soft jersey maxi dress, and he ran his hands up her legs and pulled it up and off. He hummed in appreciation.

"You want anything?"

"No, a cuddle first?"

He wasted no time toeing his shoes off and climbing next to her, so they snuggled up, and covered them with a snuggly throw.

The dim muted colours of the immaculate room faded as she closed her eyes and inhaled his scent. Her body relaxed, and the pain didn't seem as bad. Happiness was a good drug.

"Oh my god this bed is the best thing ever," Willow mumbled.

"Is it? Better than me?" Matt kissed her shoulder, and she heard the smile in his voice.

"You're the best person ever, this bed is the best object ever."

"Well thank you." Matt squeezed her bum.

Willow hummed and ground against him.

"What's wrong, you need something?"

Willow opened her eyes and shifted, so she looked him in the eye. "I've never been sexual. I've never felt any connection to anyone. Not really."

"Okay."

"Since meeting you, I think about sex. A lot. I think about you a lot. It's strange. I'm... horny." She flushed and rolled her eyes at herself.

"You need rest." Matt's eyes were fixed on her mouth, and they both knew he wanted her too.

"Please."

He moaned, "I love the way you say it. So soft and sweet. You're so lovely." He made a deep throaty noise as he leant in to kiss her, lips greedy and demanding as he squeezed her bottom, making her hips grind against her.

Willow clung on, relishing his desire.

"Fuck, no, wait." Matt rolled her onto her back.

"Rest, my Rose, you need some rest."

Leaning up on his arms, he looked from her eyes to her mouth. Willow watched his look change. Eyes hooded with lust, and an open-mouthed smile, he made a noise somewhere between a moan and a growl. She laughed as he undulated down to her, drawing his bottom lip through his teeth.

"Do that again," she whispered.

Matt threw his head back as he laughed. Willow leant up and licked his neck, the stubble rough on her tongue.

With a grunt, he leant down on his elbows and took her wrists in his hands. His grip caught her breath. Licking at her mouth she opened wide, and he took it, grinding into her, and tongue deep.

He abruptly let her go, and she moaned. Sitting up, he gripped the sheets and steadied his breath.

"You push me, I know you don't mean to, well, a little," he smirked, and she giggled. "I want you. It's hard not to take."

"I want you to. I've never been so excited."

Matt slumped. "Stop, you're killing me. Close your eyes." Standing, his hard-on strained. "An hour. An hour's rest. Then you're mine."

"Yes." The tension heavy, she wondered if her hair was on end from static electricity. With a definite nod, he left the room, and she closed her eyes. He had some serious fortitude. The last peek of him leaving stayed with her, and she imagined all the things they were going to do.

She had no idea.

OPENED EYES

M att watched her from the doorway. She'd been asleep for two hours. Realising it was creepy to watch her, he wondered if he should wake her or not.

He couldn't stop thinking about her in his bed. Where she belonged. Sitting on the edge, he swept her mass of hair out the way, and she hummed. Blinking, she made a cute grumpy face and snuggled into the pillow, inhaling deeply.

"Hey sleepy."

She mumbled something.

"Tea?"

She tasted her mouth a few times and stretched. Scrubbing her face, she turned. "Hey. How long was I asleep?"

"A while. It's four."

"Shit." She sat up, eyes wide, staring off.

"Too much?"

"No, a bit spaced. I never nap that well. This bed."

"Well, I hope you'll be spending quite a lot of time in it. Though, you won't be sleeping."

Matt watched her wake up and blink at him.

"There are things I want to do with you. I want to tell you about them, and for you to be honest."

"Then I'll need coffee," she said it seriously.

Shaking his head, he pecked her lips before going out and putting the kettle on.

"Matt, can I use your bathroom?"

"Of course." He showed her the way and left her to it.

He set their cups on a bedside table and slid out the trunk from the end of the bed and waited for her. They'd played, but he needed to know if she could do it and if it was what she wanted. No more prevaricating.

She came back, looking nervous.

Matt picked up the bedroom chair and placed it by the trunk and sat on it. He settled back, hands on his thighs.

He gestured to the bed with a smile, and she sat making herself comfortable, like a cat settling down. Picking up her coffee she sipped it, watching him.

For a moment, he didn't know where to start with her, but she spoke first.

"I've not had a lot of sex, I mean, you've guessed that much, but I do know we won't get far with you over there."

Matt laughed. With a wry look, he picked his own coffee up and sat back down.

"Right. Last night wasn't planned, and I went very easy on you. In the past, I've always been intense. I'm not always that kind to my subs, but I'm careful. I like to think I'm a good master."

"But?"

"I have to compromise with you, I'm more okay with that than I expected."

"What did you mean at your mum's?"

Matt drank some coffee. "Sometimes the partners I have want to cure me, like having these impulses is wrong, and the love of another will cure it. Once you're in love, it means that your perversion is irrelevant. That the love of another outdoes all else. You see it in books. You see it in the eyes of partners I've had that aren't in the scene."

"So, on one hand, you have subs looking for you to be the trophy master, and vanilla types who think they can cure your needs."

"Exactly. My tastes are flexible because every sub is different, yet there are absolutes for me. I need to dominate. It's my sexual desire."

"I know, and I'm okay with it."

Matt nodded. She was right. He didn't need to justify himself to her, or to anyone. She was here waiting for him.

He put down his cup, and opened the leather trunk, turning it to face him as he sat back down.

"I want to explore your body. To restrain you, play with you. Turn you into a wreck of lust and need so that you beg and plead with me. Until you forget your name."

Willow didn't move.

"Breathe."

She took a deep breath and put her mug down. "Now?"

"Now. I want your mouth, and your pussy, and your arse."

"Arse? You want anal?" She sounded panicked.

"I'd like you to try it, but if it's not for you, that's fine. And this is the point; that you want to try these things and be open to it. This is why it's a difficult line for me to walk. I don't want to manipulate you or be coercive, I don't want you to do things you don't want to, but I want to do these things. Do you understand?"

"Yes, that makes sense. It could be easy to say yes to things because you want them. In a way, I've always done that. Changing my patterns of behaviour were as much a part of changing theirs." She frowned and looked at him. "They were coercive, and they didn't care. You do. You're a dominant, so that question has to be part of how you think. I respect that. It's reassuring. You say this is a choice, and I'm not saying I'll want everything you do, or that it won't be too much. Sometimes when I'm feeling vulnerable, I might not want it at all. But I do want it. I've never thought about anal, but I'll try." She shrugged.

"You sure?"

She nodded hesitantly, and he helped her to the bathroom.

"Now, can you manage this?" He handed her a douche and unwrapped it for her. "It's new."

She reddened and swallowed as he instructed how to use it. "Okay."

He left her in peace, planning out what he wanted.

When she came back, she looked determined. "Until I tap out, I'm yours."

"Yes. You are." Bending to the trunk, he set out a neatly rolled set of black straps and threw them on the bed. "These are bed restraints. I want you to be comfortable. These are Velcro, easy in and out. Ready? That's all I'm going to do to start with."

"Yes. I'm ready, Sir." She settled.

Matt suppressed his shiver. The word made him smile, her doe-eyed sweetness brought out his dominant nature.

"Undress."

She went red at the command. "I'm only wearing my underwear, it's-"

"Off."

She unclasped her bra, and let it fall. He couldn't help but look. Matt found all bodies beautiful. Muscular, skinny, fat, male, female, and everywhere in between. He was fascinated by the breadth of beauty of the human form. He loved how each body was different. Each need and want unique. Willow was everything he wanted. Her full round arse was particularly appealing, and her legs. God, those legs. Full thighs, shaped calves. He had few dislikes with the human body, very skinny legs was one.

Mostly, it was the person that turned him on. Who they were. Tabbie had filled a physical need, but no more. Kai had been his last love and losing them had broken his heart.

Matt wanted more.

He grew impatient, and stood, pulling her down by the back of the knees, so she lay down. She panted as he yanked her knickers off. Pushing her knees apart, he clenched his jaw when he saw her perfect pussy wet.

"Stay."

She obeyed, and he gave her a wicked little smirk. He saw how her hands dug into the duvet. "Yes, Sir."

"You're very good at that."

"Thank you, Sir."

Matt pulled the duvet out from under her and attached the restraints to the bed legs.

"To start, I want you on your front. Okay?" Matt bent over and grabbed her chin. "Say it."

"Yes, please, Sir."

"Perfect." He kissed her.

Licking his lips, he stood back and piled the pillows in the centre of the bed. He pointed, and she moved to her hands and knees and crawled onto the pile.

They spent a few minutes getting her comfortable, and it was such a beautiful sight to see her bottom sticking up in the air, those tits hanging over the pillows, and her flushed face turning crimson as he wrapped the Velcro around each ankle.

Still kneeling, her legs were wide, and he could barely wait to be inside her.

He studied her face as he wrapped and shortened the length of the straps, so her arms were pulled out. Her face landed on the mattress, and she moaned, panting.

"Too much? Take a minute." He swept her hair to the side before soothing her back.

Willow slowed her breathing, opening her eyes at his touch. "It's okay." She moved, "No, it's good."

He hummed. Looking down at her, watching her struggle to test the restraints, an intense desire shuddered through him. His mouth fell open, and he tensed, seeking control.

"Look at me." He barely knew his voice, it was so rough.

Willow's skin goosed, and she did, those Bambi eyes unsure.

Leaning down, he kissed her briefly. "I'm going to take good care of you."

"I'm sure."

Matt tutted and kneeled in front of her, legs wide. "Was that sarcasm?"

"No," she giggled. "Nerves."

"Nerves? Are you afraid?"

"Tiny bit."

"Is it bad I like that?" Matt tilted his head to the side.

"I'd expect nothing else."

Matt bit the inside of his cheek. He loved the quiet strength that came out now and again.

"Do you want to carry on?"

"Yes, Sir."

He pulled his t-shirt over his head and went to the trunk, she turned her head to watch. He fetched out lube and a pair of latex gloves, snapping them on, snug and tight. Her eyes went wider, if possible.

"What do you need those for?"

He stood straight in just his jeans and gloves and watched her look him up and down. Her torso expanded, and he practically heard her heart beating.

Matt only raised a brow at her. "Rules, for your safety. Red, I will stop. Say it."

"Red," she whispered.

"No, louder."

"Red," Willow said firmly.

"If you're unsure, you say amber."

"Amber."

"You want more? Keep screaming my name or green."

She laughed again. "Green, Sir."

He bent back to the trunk and picked out a few toys. Gathering everything nearby, he settled on the bed, his legs around the pillows side on to her.

He unboxed a set of three thin plugs and an oddly shaped dildo. "I'm going to put this inside you."

"Yes please." Willow sounded drugged.

Matt ran his hand up her spine, comforting her, feeling her soft, pale skin under the latex a barrier, the feel of which he loved.

Cupping her bottom and squeezing her cheek, and then down her thigh.

"Matt, um, Sir?"

"Yes?" He leant down and kissed the place where her thigh met her bottom, making her moan.

"I feel exposed."

"You are. What's wrong?"

"I'm not, I mean..."

He lay on his side and put his head on the mattress, facing her, so their noses nearly touched. "What's wrong my lovely Rose?"

"I guess I'm a little insecure about my body, especially like this."

"I forget people are sometimes. I love all bodies. Yours is wonderful. You'd have been revered and worshipped in history as an extraordinary beauty, with a pink blush and full figure. I love it."

He sat up again and ran his hand along her side making her twitch. "This line, how your waist isn't tiny, means I'm not going to break you in half. I'd be terrified of snapping you. Your bum, fuck, the curve, how squeezable it is." He demonstrated, and she ground into the pillow. "Ah, ah, no. Stay still."

Matt tapped her bottom, and she yipped and giggled. "Sorry, Sir."

"Forgiven. You are gorgeous, and not just physically. That's always secondary for me because it's the person. Your reactions, your personality. Willow, my Rose, you make me hotter than anyone I've ever been with, do you understand?"

"Yes, Sir."

"Now, let me enjoy your body."

"Please."

Matt warmed lube in his hands and spread it between her cheeks, massaging her bottom, and up to her pussy. She drew a sharp breath in, raising her head as he slid two fingers inside her.

He worked her easily, letting her relax, and enjoying the sounds she made.

"I wonder what noises you'll make when I'm inside you?"

She made no response other than to moan as he massaged back to her anus. Her internal muscles clenched around his fingers as he rubbed the entrance. Her breathing kicked up.

"How are you doing there?"

"Uh, are you going to...?"

"Yes." He waited for her to say something, but she didn't, and he pressed inside. So tight, so hot, and she sucked his finger in with strong muscle. Willow hissed and tensed. Matt stilled and waited.

"Talk to me."

"That hurts."

"Okay. Now breathe and decide if you want me out or not."

Willow did. Impressed that she didn't panic, he stayed still as she assessed how the intrusion felt.

"Amber? Not sure, but okay."

"That's fair, I'm going to go slow."

She swallowed loudly and relaxed, her hands held the restraints as he worked in and out of both entrances.

The sounds she made were music, and he needed to come. Clamping down his jaw, he let it the feeling peak before working her deeper, she struggled but didn't ask him to stop.

Her face pressed into the bed, and she bit the sheet. The desire to be inside her was almost overwhelming.

With both hands occupied, he couldn't do anything about the ache, and he relished it, but it was time for more.

He kept his finger in her bottom but withdrew from her pussy. She opened her eyes, panting, eyes on him.

Picking up the dildo, she strained to get a look at it. "This is what I want to put in you, the bulbous end will rub you in a particular way, and I'm assured it provides a very enjoyable orgasm."

Turning it in his hand, he put it at her entrance, circling it, wetting it, and her hips followed.

"Ah, ah, what did I say?"

"Sorry, Sir."

Matt eased it into her in a single stroke, and she cried out. Matt moved in and out in time with the finger in her bottom. He felt the dildo move on the other side and he moaned with her.

Willow relaxed, and Matt pushed deeper with both his finger and the dildo.

Her legs strained and tensed. "Matt, please."

"What, my darling Rose? What is it?"

"Fuck, I need to come." She writhed.

"Feel good?"

"Yes, please, please."

Her whole body went rigid, jaw clenched, and eyes squeezed shut. Her thighs shook. His impulse was to deny her the orgasm, but this was new to her, and he wanted to feel her come, as desperate as she was. He loved the surprising strength of her body, he hadn't expected her internal muscles to be so strong. She clamped his finger as she rocked back and forth, coming long and hard.

With a deep moan, she stilled. "Oh fuck, Matt."

"Nice?"

"Yes."

"We're not done yet though, okay?"

"Yes, Sir," she said in a delirious mumble.

He laughed and leant down and kissed her while he slowly eased his fingers out her arse. She cried out. Matt picked up the wipes and cleaned her, and his fingers.

"Now, see this?" he picked up the anal plug, beaded and small.

"Hmm, yes." She smiled. "Sir."

"I'm going to put it in your bottom."

"Okay."

"Hey, you with me?" He smoothed her hair and pinched her chin.

"Yes, sorry, that was intense."

He debated calling a halt. "I'm not sure you can give consent."

"I do, please, Matt, I want this, really. I'll be unhappy if you don't."

"Hmm." He sat back up and added more lube before spreading her cheeks and pressing it in. She pushed onto it. He went slowly, allowing each bead to pop in. When she adjusted, he pushed deeper, the resistance slowly lessening as he went further.

When the last ball was pulled in, and the lip sat flush, she arched her back and hissed.

"How's that?"

"Good. Hurts, but I like it." She sounded surprised.

"I want you."

"Yes, please, Sir, I want you too."

Pulling out the dildo from her pussy, he threw it aside and rolled on a condom. Settling behind her, he relished the moment, squeezing her hips, and nudged into her slowly.

The sensation was so sweet, his blood rushed into his cock. Matt moved slowly at first, delighting in her. It felt like he'd waited for years for this moment. It had only been weeks, but he'd always waited for Willow, to find the perfect partner.

She was.

With each thrust, her hips raised up, face pressed down, and taking it slowly, he studied her.

Willow took a deep breath, struggling. She made a soft sound on her exhale, and Matt leant over her, bracing his hand next to her.

"Willow?"

She swallowed loudly. "You're holding back. I thought you want me? To play? To dominate."

"Considering you're tied up and at my mercy..."

She smiled wickedly. Her red lips curving upward, and her heavy lustful eyes strained back to him. "You're being gentle."

"I don't want to hurt you."

"Do you think if you say that enough, it'll be true?" Her eyes flickered, and she hissed, grinding against him.

Matt grunted, annoyed, desperate, needy, and thrust hard into her. "Like that?"

She cried out loudly. "Yes. Like that."

Pushing back up, he shifted, and gripped her hips so hard, he knew he'd leave bruises. He nearly let her go, but she begged him.

"Please, please."

Matt didn't hold back, her tight heat was too alluring, and he fucked her. She screamed and struggled until the pillows dislodged, and he threw them out of the way and took her prone. One arm circling under her hips, and leaning on his elbow, took her hair in the other.

He was fast and hard, and he let go, the ferocious need to fuck unleashed. His balls tightened, and with a hard thrust, he came.

He moved a few times, the intensity so good, and complete relief. Letting his head drop into her hair, he pecked her skin and took a moment.

"Matt?" she whispered.

"Hmm?"

"Can you, sorry, I need out."

Alert, he pulled out and undid her. "Willow?"

She didn't move. Placing his hand on her lower back, he eased the plug out. She tensed, and when out, she shook. Matt carefully cleaned her up and removed the condom.

"Willow, you're safe. I'm sorry."

"Bathroom."

He took her quickly and folded his arms as he waited. Matt tidied the bed and picked her up when she opened the door, and lay her on her back, getting her comfortable. "I'm here. I need you to speak to me."

Taking a deep breath, she opened her eyes. A smile edged at her open mouth, and she reached up to his lips, touching them.

Matt frowned, holding her fingers and kissed her fingertips, feeling a slight tremor in them. He held her hand to his cheek.

"I love this bit. The affection and comfort. The sweetness." He kissed her hand. "Talk to me, please."

"It was more than I expected, intense. Good."

"Willow, you don't have to lie, you're safe with me, I wouldn't be angry or anything. You need to be honest with me."

She licked her lips. "I'm thirsty."

A pit of dread and disappointment sat in him. He poured a glass of water from the filter jug in the cool of the kitchen, taking a moment before going back to her. She was snuggled under the duvet and looked too sweet for words.

She inched up, took the glass and gulped it down. "That's better. What's wrong?"

Matt gave her a smile. "I can um, take you home, if you want, I don't mind."

"What? You want me to go?"

"No. I don't." Emotion burnt the back of his eyes, and he made them wide as he blinked.

"Then what is it, what did I do wrong? I'll go if you want, I thought..." She put the glass down, looking lost.

"Willow, it's all right, but you clearly aren't okay. I'm not going to hold it against you if this isn't what you want."

"I never said this isn't what I want, I never said I didn't like it either. I was thirsty. A bit shocked. Wait," she reached her hand out, and he took it. "Come back, hold me."

Releasing his breath, he got back into bed, and they snuggled down together.

"I missed this so much." She kissed his chest.

Matt relaxed his whole body.

Willow nestled her face into his neck, and he held her tight. "You are incredible. Overwhelming. I was so overwhelmed. It hurt a bit, I've never been... hmm, is had the right word, because it felt like I'd been properly taken." She laughed.

"Sorry."

"Look, I'm not that fragile. Weak, yeah, but you didn't break me. I'm still kind of aroused though."

Matt set her back, studying her. His emotions were so all over the place, he'd not read her carefully enough. Face flush, lips red, the sparkle in her gaze as she looked at his lips, fuck, she looked so good.

Matt kissed her in need. Pressing her under him. She moaned as her legs curled around his, her hands holding on. His lips took from her, and she struggled to keep up. His tongue stroking hers, and he needed her again. Needed to be inside her.

"Willow, I'm going to fuck you," he whispered into her mouth. Her nod wasn't enough. "Say it."

"Yes."

With a grunt, he leant back and rolled on another condom. Matt shifted her down the bed by her legs. "This is as vanilla as I get."

"I don't mind, do whatever you want."

"Open."

She obeyed without hesitation, he looked at her; wet and perfect. Matt climbed up between her legs, looking down on her.

"Willow," Matt clenched his teeth, desperate to devour her, to use her body, and for him, it was an act of love, but to her, it might be brutal.

She met his look, nipples hardening, her chest rising and falling quickly as she widened her legs and reached back to hold the headboard. "Show me. Let go."

She didn't know what she asked. How could she? Matt shook his head, but Willow let go of the headboard and sat up. She reached down and grasped his cock and kissed his chest, humming against him.

"I want it."

Matt clamped his jaw and ground his teeth for a moment. "Good girls don't demand."

"Then I'm not good."

"Bad girls get fucked and punished."

"Do they, Sir?" She ran her tongue across his nipple.

Matt grabbed her hands and moved, pressing her down. He watched her pupils get even wider as he slid into her. It was a beautiful sensation.

Matt made her his.

SPACE

Matt was a god. A touch dramatic, yes, but it's what Willow thought. She never imagined it would be that good. That she would feel sexual and powerful under his control.

Being tied up had aroused her so much, once was not enough. His reaction to her after was oddly sweet, and that such ferocious power lay under it did things to her that she didn't expect.

She'd been shocked by her own response.

Willow wanted his strength, wanted his power and wanted to drive him wild. Her body pulsed with desire, and her heart shook her chest.

Matt slid inside her all the way.

He was perfect, he didn't split her in two, but filled her, and it made her contract around him. He stayed perfectly still until she squirmed and whispered to him.

"Please."

He took her hands, crossing them over her head and held them tight.

Matt smirked at her as she panted and begged.

He pulled out slowly and thrust hard, and her eyes went wide. He did it again, and then he fucked her relentlessly. Every breath a grunt, every thrust hard, Willow tried to keep up with him at first, but she couldn't. All she could do was keep breathing as he overtook her body.

Matt abruptly stopped and withdrew, she cried loudest at that, and bereft of his body, she felt small. Matt licked into her open mouth as she clawed for breath.

"Are you a good girl yet?"

Willow moaned, and Matt held her face.

"Look at me and answer."

"No."

Matt laughed as he took her thighs and held them up, resting her legs on his shoulders. "Watch me."

She did, her heavy eyes fixed on his body as he pushed back in. The angle was intense.

He smirked at the noise she made. "Hold on to something."

She held the headboard as he took her, muscles flexing, body rigid.

He rubbed somewhere sensitive, and the feeling was almost too much, the pain-pleasure of it, the sight of him, even the tension in his mouth as he went, all of it was so arousing that she came before she even knew she was coming. The feeling was so intense, it hurt. Her body moved of its own volition, and she couldn't keep her eyes open. Matt rode her out, faster and harder. He kept going, and Willow almost sobbed, but she didn't let go, she held on.

Minutes — but it could have been hours — later, Matt stilled, flexing into her a few times, and growled his breath as he held her legs.

Willow opened her eyes. He looked delirious. Drawing his lips into his mouth, he came around and said her name. It sounded fragile, and her heart pinched. She wanted to cry. She couldn't move, and Matt set her feet down and pulled out. Once divested of the condom, he moved her arms from the headboard, and carefully held her.

Kissing her forehead, he looked down on her, but neither of them spoke.

Willow's emotions hit her all at once. Her impulse was to say she loved him. The words on her tongue, yet it wasn't enough, it didn't say everything. Instead, she smiled, completely adoring him, touched by the worry in his face.

"I'm yours," there was barely any sound in her voice.

Matt breathed out, face pinched, and he rested his face in her hair, holding her, soothing her with his hand down her back. "And I'm yours."

Willow woke, and she ached. Her muscles protested at moving, but she desperately needed a piss. They'd been too busy cuddling and comforting each other for her to get up and go, and now her bladder wasn't having it.

Extracting herself from Matt was a struggle. He radiated heat, and she was sweating.

He shifted and mumbled, sitting up. "What?"

"You're cute grumpy, but I need a wee."

"Shit, failing in my duty of care already. I should have made sure you went before. Come on." With a kiss to her forehead, he helped her up, and they went to the bathroom. "It's six, want to shower? We did fall asleep early."

"We did, a shower would be nice."

"How do you feel?" Matt asked as they got in after she'd seen to herself.

"Sore, everything hurts, but it's hard to explain; like it's nice. A reminder. I can still feel you. It's not like other pain. It's been on my mind a lot. Pain."

"Because you're in it?"

"No, well yes, but I mean thinking about dealing with it, and the pain you might give me is a choice. I'm used to pain — as much as anyone can be — it's unpleasant and debilitating, but it's also transient and adaptive. It changes, it rolls, and I spend so much time responding to it, catching up. Pain you might give me is asked for, it is control that I have. I know it doesn't make a lot of sense, and I'm figuring it out-"

"No, it makes total sense."

Matt manoeuvred her to a wall and took slow, delicate care of her body as he washed her. He made her breakfast later and took her home. She was exhausted, and not seeing anyone when they got in, he helped her to bed.

Willow felt heavy and tired, but when he was gone, she was empty.

"What are you doing?"

"Moderating the forum." Jane didn't look away from the laptop screen as she worked.

"What forum?" Willow made some food, her bed hair was spectacular, but she didn't care, and in her comfy pyjamas covered in pandas, she sat down at the table with Jane.

"We have a website. It's how this thing started. Darby and I wanted a place where we could discuss BDSM that was inclusive. So we set this thing up, and all the wonderful weirdos came out the woodwork. From there, we set up a meeting at Passion House, and then because someone knows someone, Kink at Passion House was set up. You know a lot of these spaces are white cis orientated, there's safety for them in that privilege, so we wanted to subvert that and make sure it was for everyone.

"It's evolving, we tried different things, but we didn't want it to end up being too much and want it to be more inclusive. So here me and Darby are, accidental organisers of a sex demo business." Jane shrugged. "But it ties into Tabbie's shop, we make commission, we have other demonstration artists appear, and I found a burlesque performer, so we might even put on a show. It's taken on a life of its own."

"You make money off the ticket sales?"

"We do, and let me tell you, those tickets — the VIP ones that we make money off — are pricey and there's a waiting list now, legally it's tricky, but we navigate it. We started out doing four a year, but we're bi-monthly now."

"Wow."

"So, are you coming along?"

"To the next one?"

"Yep. Matt's not doing the security for the first time. Darby is demonstrating with Tabbie, and she'll be performing," Jane peered over her glasses at Willow and then went back to her laptop, "so be warned."

"You don't like her."

"No, I think she saw him as an exotic danger and couldn't see who he was underneath, a sensitive sweetheart, and she punished him for it." Jane turned her mouth down in distaste.

"Does she realise what she did?"

"I don't know. I think she's too selfish to understand. Filip is a better fit for her because he's less kind. Matt wants to worship and delight, Filip wants to devour."

"Matt's good at the devour part."

Jane choked on air and laughed.

Willow could look at that website, but she didn't. Whatever Matt said or did in the past was irrelevant. Who he was now and with her was what mattered.

"I need to go shopping."

"What for?"

"Something to wear, and maybe some," Willow cleared her throat, "well..."

"Sexy things?"

"I'm the frumpiest human ever, and I know Matt's not that bothered, but I want to feel sexy."

"Ooh, I know the place. We should all go. Suzy too while Kim's here."

"Where is Kim, I've not seen her."

"She's asleep." Jane couldn't hide the dirty grin and gave into it.

"I'm so happy for you."

"I'm annoyed you kept her a secret. She's a joy."

"Okay. Shopping it is."

Later, everyone met in a restaurant near Berkley Tower. A crisp, bright day with low sun was balmy compared to the wet miserable weather they'd had for weeks.

Suzy was already there when they joined her. They settled down and ordered lunch.

Darby didn't waste time, "I'm surprised Matt let you out of his sight."

"I'm supposed to be resting, and he has a contract that's been giving him some grief. He's busy right now."

Willow kept up as best she could with the chatter as all the woman talked in several conversations at once. Kim gave her a sad look, but Willow shook her head.

Afterwards, they went into the boutique nearby and helped Willow pick something out. The gaggle of women all giving advice.

Suzy stayed them. "Guys, stop. What's your budget?"

"I don't have one, it's not important."

"Can I ask you — and feel free to not answer — but you only work two days a week, how can you afford to have no budget."

"Oh, well, I have a trust. I receive a portion of it as an income. No one told me that before." She wondered if it was an oversight on her mother's part or on purpose. Willow would never know, "I had to get a job to make it look like I was earning anything I had." Willow looked over a bra she was holding, "Anyway, at one point they tried to make me sign the money over, I refused. It's all about money."

The women stared.

"What?"

"Willow, that's, that's..." Jane sat down on one of the chairs.

"Fucking evil." Darby almost spat it.

"Yeah, but mother's gone now. I worry about dad, I can't make him sell." She swallowed, and Kim hugged her from behind. "God, you're short."

She laughed, and they shook off the moment.

Willow chose a few items, all well-fitted and supportive, and sexier than she'd ever owned. In the fashionable shop, she couldn't find anything to wear, and they found a shop further in town. Her legs ached, she was dizzy and so tired, she'd have bought anything they told her to.

Willow ended up with a black dress that was too short and showed too much cleavage and yet still looked elegant.

Everyone, shopped out and shattered, went home, Suzy and Alie left, and everyone else went to Blackthorn Villa.

They sat in the living room with tea and cake and watched telly.

It was a good day.

Matt was antsy. He'd secured two more contracts, and had interviewed people to take on, and was knee deep in paperwork and references with his mind wandering.

He'd not seen Willow since Sunday. They'd talked, and he knew she'd spent all Monday in bed, so he left her in peace. That he needed her so intensely worried him. The desire to be with her made him fidgety and short tempered.

"What's up your arse?"

"Nothing," he snapped at Meera, who merely gave the 'the look'. That expression that said watch yourself was expertly doled out, and Matt knew he was in trouble. He rubbed his face. "Sorry."

"Apology accepted. Ah, you're in love." She pointed at him.

"I'm not."

She pursed her lips and tilted her head before sitting back folding her arms. "Uh-huh."

"It's too early for that, it's new, and... fragile."

"I see."

Matt gave her a foul look and got back to work. Checking the time, he knew Willow would be about to get off work.

"Oh good grief, go, I can finish up."

Hesitating, he grinned and kissed her cheek. She swatted him away with a laugh, and Matt peeled out of there.

He knew Suzy usually dropped her home since she had the car scrapped, but Matt needed to see her. He made it to ARC in time and seeing Willow's surprise and smile made his day.

Greeting her with a searing kiss and lifting her off the ground, she laughed and held tight. He did love being with her. Meera's words came back to him. He did, he loved her already.

His breath caught, and he held her tighter.

"Matt."

"Sorry." He set her down with a grin.

"What's up?"

Kissing her hair, they walked back to his car after a raised brow from Suzy, and he quietly stuck his finger up, and she laughed as she said goodbye.

"Seriously, you have a weird look on your face."

"I missed you." He started the car. "You must be knackered, take away?"

"Jane's cooking, why don't you join us?"

"Home cooked food? I'm in."

Willow watched him as they drove.

"Question?"

"How do you stay in shape? I mean," she pointed up and down him.

"I go to the gym three times a week. I used to run, but my knees aren't what they used to be. I'm getting old. But," he manoeuvred through the evening traffic, the day already faded, "I like working out and the discipline."

"Does wonders for your image?"

He laughed. "Don't be cheeky."

"Or?"

A frisson of joy went through him, she wanted to push? Fine. "I already told you what bad girls get."

Willow frowned.

"What's up?"

"I want to ask you a personal question, but I don't want you to think I'm asking it for the wrong reason or I'm being inappropriately nosy."

"Okay. Ask."

"You say good girl to me, what would you say if I weren't a woman? I'm not fishing, just curious."

He laughed. "With a guy, it's boy, but it depends on their pronouns, plus it's what feels right. Kai was the only enby I've been with. You want to know? Jane told you about the website? You could trawl through it. Any questions you have might get answered on there."

"I don't want to look."

"Why?"

"In case I read anything I'd rather not."

They drove in silence for a while. "Sub, I called them sub. There's nothing on there I'm ashamed of. I have no secrets."

"Everyone has secrets."

"I'll tell you anything about me."

"Worst thing you've ever done?"

"I said some horrible things to my mum when I was a teenager about my stepdad, about her. A lot of anger there. Resentment about my identity. I went off the deep end a bit. I nicked things because we had no money. I'm not proud of it."

"What changed?"

"ARC. We got out after he beat me up. I had a BDSM porn mag, I was already thinking of that stuff, and he kicked the shit out of me for it. Called me a pervert, the works. He was never explicitly racist with name-calling, but it was little things. Jokes he'd make, language he used."

"How do you rationalise things like that?"

"With time. I let a lot of things go, I'm wary sometimes, a bit paranoid. I consider people's motives and reactions."

Willow didn't say anything else, and he glanced at her, tears spilling over as she screwed her mouth up.

"It's okay, it got better. They put us in a secure house, he was arrested and went to prison. ARC helped mum get a job, we got a house.

"When I was about eighteen, I was at a party, and this girl was being hassled. It pushed me over the edge, and I lost my shit. Broke some kid's nose. My friend, Hass took me aside to calm me down and clean me up, I was a mess, and we ended up kissing.

"I knew I liked women, hell, loved them, but accepting I liked guys too was a big deal. For me, the term pan fits better. Took me some time to understand gender and realise it was the sub aspect that attracted me regardless of gender. Human, kinky, and willing, and I'm good to go."

He pulled onto the drive.

"You're wonderful." Her voice was quiet.

"Yeah, yeah."

She unclipped her seatbelt leant over to him. "Wonderful." She pressed her lips to him, and he let her, unmoving, a small bemused smile spread as she did.

Her face hovered close to his and unclipping his belt, kissed her back, holding her and seared her with a kiss.

Setting her back, he held back the want to do things to her, and helped her inside, willing his boner to go.

The house smelt of delicious garlicky carbs and was surprised to see Jane and Darby with Kim and Alie.

"Matt." They said it in unison, and he resisted the urge to take a step back.

Dinner was a squeeze but fun, and after helping to clean up, he excused himself and Willow and took her upstairs.

Her eyes started to close and pale face pinched with pain. Helping her to bed, he undressed and snuggled down with her.

"I'm sorry we can't do anything." She slurred as he picked up her book.

"No, it's enough to be near you." He kissed her head, and she relaxed as he read. They were on the third book of EE Queen's series.

Matt read for a while and stopped for a moment to see how she was. Her eyes were on him, and she looked so soft in the shadowed lamplight.

"What?"

"You look really cute in your glasses."

Matt put the book down and took them off. "Don't ever call me cute."

"Okay, distinguished."

"Old." He pinned her underneath him, making her laugh. The feel of her body shaking with joy under him was the sweetest.

He looked at her mouth. "You're tired, I should let you rest."

"You sound unconvinced."

"Hmm."

Willow reached up to kiss him, but he leant back. He kissed her cheek, then her neck, pushing her head up.

He worked down her skin with languid ease, sucking and tasting her.

When he reached the neckline of her nightie, which tantalised him, he pulled it down, exposing her breast, he worked down it but frustrated, he took it off, letting her flop back down into the bed, making her laugh in a plume of hair.

He worked everywhere until he reached her thighs.

"Wait."

He blinked up as he was parting her legs in order to have dessert. "Yes?"

"I want to try other things."

"What other things?" He nipped the inside of her thigh before brushing his jaw across her soft skin. When her breath hitched, and she arched her back, Matt did it again. "What do you want, Willow?"

"Whatever you want to do with me. What's your desire?"

He squeezed her thighs. He loved how her body showed him everything. Her nipples peaked, already darkening. Her breath quick, how she squirmed for his touch. Matt raised himself up, and she looked at him.

Her lips parted as he hardened his jaw, his look becoming cold and mean. Yet the words hovered. Showing her his deeper truth was harder than he thought.

"Do you want to hurt me?"

He took a deep breath.

"Spank me? Make me beg for you to stop."

He hissed.

"Do it."

He nearly shook his head, but Willow grabbed his t-shirt, twisting it in her hand. "Matt, there will be times I am unable to give you what you need. There are times when I am and want it. This is one of those times. I'm tired, but okay. You should take those opportunities if you want them. If you don't, okay, but you're looking at me like a tasty cake."

"You'll say red if you need to. For any reason."

"I promise."

Matt moved quickly, heart thudding. He grabbed the tie from her robe, tying her hands behind her back.

"Shit."

"What?"

"We can't, I don't have condoms with me."

She made a noise and leant her head forward. "If it's any consolation, I go and have my IUD fitted next week."

"Why wouldn't you tell me that?"

"I just did. Besides, we can do other things, can't we?"

"Do you think talking back to me will help you?"

"I hope not."

"You're testing my patience."

Willow smirked, her eyes knowing, and it was the perfect pushback. He bared his teeth and set her over his lap, front down. She gasped and let herself be moved about. Matt squeezed each perfect round cheek and tapped her lightly.

"It's going to hurt."

"How much?"

He slapped her bottom where cheek joined thigh, and she screamed. As she wriggled, he held her tied hands in place against her back.

"That much. What do you call me?"

"Sorry, Sir."

"Better."

Matt ran his hand over her body, between her legs, finding her wet.

"I'm going to spank you properly, and it will hurt."

"Yes, Sir."

He struck her bottom, alternating cheeks with the flat of his hand, he watched the skin grow pink as she struggled, and waited for her to call a halt.

At ten strikes, he stopped the tops of the legs and bottom, bright red. Willow panted her breath with shock on her face.

"Rose, Look at me."

Her eyes darted to him, and she laughed. Matt pursed his lips. Matt put two fingers inside her, and that laugh turned into a startled gasp.

Letting go of her hands, he smoothed her hair and began stroking inside of her.

When she squirmed, he kept her still, never looking away from her face, his fingers always moving, finding the perfect angle. He wasn't gentle as he fucked her with his fingers.

Her thighs tensed and seeing she was about to come, withdrew.

"Fuck, no, please, I'm close."

"I know."

Matt kept her still and waited for the urgency to pass.

"Knees." He shifted them both, so she was on her knees on the floor, and taking off his underwear, sat on the edge of the bed.

She opened her mouth. He didn't have to ask her, but she didn't artfully do it; annoyance, frustration, and lust sat there in her look. Her mouth was sweet and warm, and her tongue moved around perfectly. He didn't care she couldn't take much, that he was in her mouth was enough.

Keeping his thrusts shallow, he held her head to support her.

Matt's balls tightened, and he managed to pull out. Willow sat back, lips red.

He leant down and tipped her chin up, kissing her sweetly.

"Do you want more of my cock?"

"Please, Sir."

He pecked her lips, savouring them, before guiding her back to him. She surprised him by taking a more, he let her try, she gagged but kept going. He held her head again and guided her, holding back, but it didn't take long for him to come. Her perfect mouth was too good to resist. Her trust and ability to give brought him to climax with a cry, his head arching back as the sharp pulse in his cock rushed. Picking her up, he set her on the bed in front of him with her back against his chest. Her arms pressed into him and her head rested back.

Matt spread her legs over his. "Look at me."

Willow craned her head back, lips parted, looking dazed. Matt pressed his two fingers into her, rested his thumb on her clit, and her eyes fluttered. With one hand he teased her skin, her nipples, anywhere he could reach.

He'd set her legs over his, and when she bent her knees, he went still, and crossed his ankles over hers, pinning her legs.

She made desperate incoherent noises as he worked his fingers in and out. He got hard again, his dick pressing into that perfect softness at the top of her bottom.

Her thighs shook, her body twitching, and she held her breath.

"Breathe, relax."

"Can't, I need to."

"Need to what? Hmm? Rose, tell me." Matt slowed his strokes and relished the smooth perfection of his fingers inside her.

Her answer was short tense breaths.

"Answer."

"Come. Please." Her choppy voice pleased him, and he nuzzled her hair and kissed it.

Pressing his thumb on her clit but not moving it made her hips twitch.

"Stop seeking it. It'll happen."

Willow keened, her desperate unabashed need was lovely.

Two more slow strokes were enough to send her over the edge. She had no control of her body as she came. Matt's arm went around her, cupping one breast. The fingers inside her still working steadily as she contracted tightly around him.

Pinned to his body, completely at his command was the best rush. He throbbed himself, as her orgasm didn't seem to want to end. He hummed as she finally stilled, her legs twitching, and resisted his continued stroking.

"Enough." She bucked.

It was so exquisite. He kissed her shoulder but didn't stop.

"Fuck, Matt," her teeth clenched, and she struggled. "I can't. It's too much."

She needed to say it. She needed to know he would stop. Willow needed to find the line for herself and have courage.

Struggling more, resisting him, she came again. Screaming, he couldn't understand what she was saying. As she lifted her hips, legs rigid, and body shaking, she said the word.

"Red." A growl, but the word.

Matt stopped immediately and let her go. Leaning her over, he untied her and laid her down.

He was so close himself, it hurt.

Willow pressed her legs together, eyes closed, clutching the duvet. Matt resisted putting his hand on his cock. His body pulsed. Opening her eyes a few minutes later, her eyes shot malice but smiled slowly.

He leant forward and ran his hand through her hair. "Fun?"

"The best. Thank you."

He grinned, and his dick twitched. Willow glanced down at it.

"I'll go and take care of it."

"You don't have to go."

Matt put his finger in her mouth, and she sucked her taste off him. Her tongue swirled around. Willow was a contradiction, so delicate and sweet, but so resilient with a thread of strength and will.

He ran his finger down her front, her eyes sleepily watching, and gathered all the wetness from the tops of her thighs and coated himself in it.

Settling close, he kissed her lightly stroking his cock with her watching.

"Are you okay with this?"

Willow reached out, clearly exhausted, and put her hand around his. Her gentle touch and light tremor made him ache. Matt set her hand under his own and kissed down to her neck. She stretched it to him as she fisted his cock hard and quick. The rush as he came on her stomach was intimate and vulnerable as he buried his face in her neck.

After a few moments, he sat up almost embarrassed and didn't know why. She grinned. Matt cleaned her up and helped her to the bathroom, and she was asleep in minutes when they curled up together in bed.

Matt didn't sleep and lay there thinking. Willow was exceptional. Everything he wanted, and he wasn't mistaken or over eager. He loved her. In the darkness, he made out her face, the sound of her breath, and with it, he was terrified.

BEST LEFT UNSAID

Willow shifted as the titles of the next episode of the show she was watching played. Matt messaged her. He was doing that a lot since Monday.

What are your plans this weekend?

Willow smiled wryly. *I have a date with the girls. A night out.*

Kink?

Yes. He'd not mentioned it to her, so she was cautious. *I assumed you didn't want me to go with you. No big deal.*

Willow Rose DeWorthy-Morris. I will spank you for that.

Promise? She giggled knowing he was serious.

He didn't reply for a while, and Willow tried to watch the show but was too distracted to pay much attention.

Would you be so kind as to accompany me on Saturday evening as my date?

I'd be delighted.

Willow couldn't stop smiling to herself, excited and nervous.

On Saturday Darby got all her equipment ready, and Jane flitted about. Willow stayed in bed until the afternoon when she dragged herself out of bed for a shower.

Darby appeared in a latex dress. Her hair elaborately styled in an up-do looked almost fifties.

"You look incredible."

Darby fluttered her gold eyelids. "Thank you. Time to get you ready, kitten." She set Willow in the chair at the dressing table and rolled her hair.

"Thank you for helping me."

Darby glanced at Willow. "You're welcome. It's good to see Matt happy."

"Alie is nice."

Darby bit her lip. "She is. We knew each other years ago, so I was a bit unsure at first. Going back. We've both been through a lot and changed."

"Does she mind, about the demo stuff?"

"No. She loves the photography I do. It's like a persona." Darby moved onto Willow's makeup. "It's part of me, it's not all of me. It was an outlet at first. Now it's like a job. Why?"

"Just interested. This world is... new I guess. I'm figuring it out."

"You like it?"

"With Matt? Yes. Generally? I'm not that sure."

"Kink is an eyeopener. You'll see some weird shit. But, and this is important, if you are ever uncomfortable, you must tell Matt."

"What will I see?"

"There's a dancefloor, like any other club. Then there's a gallery bar, where we are. It's quiet, then beyond are the demo rooms, which are private. There's usually people having sex. For others to watch."

Willow flushed.

"Then there's us. Tabbie will be tied up and suspended by me, and then Filip and her will demonstrate. It's intense stuff. We're looking to change it up next time. Don't worry. Matt will guard you like a bear. No one will touch you, that's not what it's like in there."

"How do you control that?"

"Matt. He's not working, but the team is. There is a heavy security presence. We have policies, and measures in place. No camera phones, coded wristbands. It's a small gig, expensive. We've only had a few incidents, and they were handled. Those people banned."

"With Matt in charge, I'm not surprised."

Darby laughed. "Right. Sexy outfit."

Jane came in. "Ooh, just in time." She wore leather trousers and knee length boots with a corset. Her figure curved beautifully. Her hair pinned up, makeup heavy, with new clear-framed glasses set on her face.

"Wow."

"Thank you, it's so much effort to dress up." She pulled a face.

The cami suspender was an all in one that went past her bottom. Supportive, it just about contained her tits. Tight and corseted with sheer panels down the front and back, Willow let Jane lace her up.

"Matt is going to have fun getting you out of this."

Willow gurgled a laugh.

"Nervous?" Darby asked as she opened the pack of stockings.

Willow widened her eyes, and Darby smiled, scrunching her nose up. The stockings were plain topped and a heavy denier, but they'd definitely be on show.

"Do you think this is too much?"

Jane and Darby laughed. "You're going to have more clothes on than most to be honest."

Willow put her hand to her stomach at Jane's words, and then Jane tightened the laces even more.

"Too tight. I need to breathe."

Jane made a disappointed noise and loosened it.

The sturdy metal garters were fiddly, and Darby did them up. "There."

Her dress covered the underwear, but the stockings were visible. Willow put on her heeled ankle boots, toning down the look.

"It's perfectly you."

Darby agreed, and with her cane in hand, they made their way downstairs.

"Right, we have to go, are you sure you want to wait for Matt?"

"That is my instruction."

"You look beautiful. Don't let him have his way when he sees you because he'll want to."

Willow laughed while they gathered their gear.

"Wait," Darby said, grabbing a camera. She posed Willow in a chair, hands on her cane, her legs parted, and Darby coaxed an enigmatic submissive expression from her.

After taking several shots, and happy, they left.

Willow waved them off, not even seeing the photos as they whirled away, and was left to wait in the quiet when they'd gone. Princess made herself known, and Willow shooed her off, not wanting cat hair all over her.

She watched at the window for him, turning her phone in her hand. She'd borrowed a little clutch and kept checking her makeup. Then she took a few selfies, hardly recognising herself in them.

Matt arrived early, mercifully, and Willow made herself relax and stay calm as she opened the door. He didn't speak or move. He gawped. Mouth open, eyes taking her in.

"Too much?"

Matt wore well-fitting trousers, a tailored white shirt, and a black waistcoat. He looked hot as fuck. "We should stay in."

"No. I was warned not to 'let you have your way', so I'm not. Do you like it? I feel–"

"You're so beautiful."

She looked up.

"Willow, you don't have to wear or do anything for me, I... think you're perfect as you are. But you look incredible."

"Thank you, it's not for you, I wanted to feel sexy for a change, but I wasn't sure if it was too much."

"No." He moaned as he neared and ran his hand down her front.

"We should go."

Matt didn't kiss her, sparing her dark red lipstick. "I'm going to fuck you later with that dress on."

"And not see what's underneath?"

"Show me."

Matt managed to walk them back to the hall wall, and Willow pressed into it.

He clenched his jaw when she didn't respond. It had grown dark, and with the back of the hall lit, he held a danger to him that made her heart pound.

Matt lifted her skirt slowly, feeling her garters, and when he felt further up, he raised a brow, and Willow smirked. Raising her dress higher, he paused at her waist and swore before putting it back down.

"You're right, we need to go."

He hustled her out, and she laughed. Matt gave her that look, the one that said she'd regret laughing, and he'd save it for later.

She couldn't wait.

Even the spanking had been wonderful, not that she expected to like it. The cold sting, the sharpness of it. How her skin warmed. Willow hated her pain, but it wasn't like anything else she'd experienced.

It made her happy. Such an odd thing. Matt drove them, and he parked in a small carpark at the back of the club.

The evening was cold and drizzly, and Matt ferreted an umbrella out of the car that covered them both. "Listen, I have some rules — I know — but it matters."

"Okay." She nestled closer, clinging onto him.

The pulse of house music rumbled as they went in, Matt punching a code on a keypad, and then a muffled wall of sound hit her. The door clanked closed behind them, leaving them in a dim corridor.

"No booze. I socially drink sometimes and have the odd beer or glass of wine, but I'm not a drinker."

"I know. That's fine." Willow slouched against the wall, hoping it was clean.

A security guard in a Denbridge security t-shirt came down the corridor and past them. He and Matt exchanged greetings, and the guy went out for a cigarette. Matt ushered them further in.

"Matt tell me, please."

"I have an image, and I have this thing about being in public like this. Not that what other people think matters so much, but how I show who I am among my peers. Does that make sense?"

"Yes. You want obedience?"

"It can be taken a certain way, and I don't want you to think that I think all women should be submissive and are less than equal. It's not about that. At all."

"I do understand. It's the power dynamic. Sexual gratification through submission. You're the big scary alpha dom, so it makes sense."

"Are you laughing at me?"

His hard tone made her grin. "No. If I wasn't enjoying what this is, I wouldn't be here. I know you wouldn't make choices for me that I didn't want you to. This is my choice, this is my power to give what you desire. I get it. Lowered eyes, deference. I will look at no other man. Anything else? Speak when spoken to?"

"No. This is your first time, it's a lot to take in. I want you to have a good time, to enjoy it. Suzy and Effie will be here too. She's usually collared."

"Do you want to collar me?"

"Yes. Not yet."

"Why?"

"It means something to me." Matt frowned.

"What?" Adrenaline pounded in her blood. She would be screwed tomorrow, but Willow intended to make the most of this. She leant into Matt, looking at his mouth, not his eyes. "Sir?"

Matt put his arms around her.

"It's a personal thing. I never collared Tabbie, she didn't understand. It's about love. A commitment."

Willow was surprised at the emotion in his voice. "I understand."

Matt took her hand and lead her into a small office. In it were a few guys that he introduced Willow to as he collected a box from which he took a delicate white and gold mask. Willow left her coat and phone there, and Matt led her into the club when she put her earplugs in.

Matt affixed it to her.

"You're not wearing one."

"No, don't like them on my face." With a serious look, his tone became hard.

"Can I take your arm please, Sir?"

Matt blinked and let go of her hand. She held tight to him as they reached a service lift. "I'll spare you the main club, it's a bit much, even this early."

"Are we okay?" Willow shifted the mask on her face, feeling ridiculous. Matt felt like iron under her grip.

"Yes. Sorry. I'm nervous."

"About being with me?"

"No, not like that, people are territorial. You're new. Most of us are rainbows and puppies underneath, but some people are arseholes."

"Just like everywhere then?" Willow grinned up at him before lowering her eyes. "I know you'll protect me."

"You know what to say, don't you?"

Before Willow could say anything else, the lift opened, and they walked down a narrow plain landing and into the gallery bar.

It was half-full, people beginning to arrive, and Willow took it all in. Yes, she was kind of underdressed. People approached, eyes on her as they spoke to Matt. Willow ground her cane into the carpet.

Tabbie wore a silk robe and heels. Her hair and makeup perfect. Jane flittered in behind them and hugged Willow. It seemed it was a marked thing to do, and Darby did the same when she came over.

Willow saw Suzy and Nathan, and she waved. They were joined by Effie and Stuart, and she was in fact collared. Willow observed her deference, much more pronounced than at the barbeque.

A performance. Personas. There was so much play and artifice to demonstrate truth.

"Come."

"Yes, Sir." They left the group of people that Willow hadn't paid attention to and sat at a table with their friends.

Willow sipped the apple juice and soda that Matt bought her and chatted with the others, and she played her part. Matt constantly touched her, reassured her, his strength making her safe.

Later, the crowd swelled, and the atmosphere changed. They moved off in groups to an adjoining bar where a small platform was set up.

The scene was led by Jane and Darby with Tabbie stood on the stage. Seeing Tabbie naked didn't bother Willow, and the precision of Darby's work was beautiful to see. The crowd watched, chatted and were respectful as Tabbie was bound and suspended. There was applause. Tabbie looked happy.

After photos were taken, the crowd shifted.

Matt leant down. "Do you want to watch them fuck?"

"No." Willow didn't need to see it. She didn't need to think that was what Matt had done with her. She didn't mind, but not hot for it.

In the third room, couples were already in play, the security even heavier. "Matt, I'm not sure this is for me."

"Let's go back to the bar."

It was quiet, and they talked, people came and went, and it was clear when the main event was over when people filtered back in.

The table filled up, and Willow was a bit bored. Everyone wanted Matt's attention. Everyone wanted his time, so she observed it. The dynamics, studying people around him, those who were threatened, those who were attracted. He could have anyone there.

A security guy charged through the gallery bar, straight up to Matt, leant down and whispered in his ear. Matt's relaxed yet controlled demeanour fell away, and he looked lethal.

"I'll be right back."

Willow quirked a smile, and he pecked her lips before going.

Not long after, Tabbie rejoined them in the smallest dress that Willow ever saw and preened as she was fawned over and admired.

Effie chatted to Willow, but it was hard to pay attention. She kept thinking of Matt's face as he left and then Tabbie came and sat down and then everything went tits up.

HONESTY AND BULLSHIT

Matt peeled down to the office with Bal on his heels. Seeing Bal there might not have been that big a deal to anyone else, but Matt knew otherwise.

Baljit was Matt's coordinator for all the little and large jobs and managed them on the ground. He was great at it. He was also keeping an eye out for Josh.

Matt hadn't heard from Josh for a week, not that it was unusual, but he usually checked in every few days.

The words, "There's been an incident," made Matt cold.

"Well?"

"Meera talks to Josh every day, it's not her job, but she worries."

Matt nodded sharply. Meera did mother everyone, especially the women on the books, and Josh. "She knew him before he came and worked for us and spent a lot of time with him when he was at Capta rehabilitation hospital after the fire. It's natural."

Bal folded his arms, clearly hesitant to go on.

"Speak."

"She hadn't heard from him. When she doesn't, she asks me to check in only because he has his arse in his hand about something, and she knows he'll answer me. I couldn't reach him either and traced him from his last check-in. He was attacked."

Matt's jaw hurt from grinding his teeth.

"Someone beat the shit out of him. He's in hospital. Meera's on her way there now."

"Where?"

"Kettly Grange Hospital."

"That's only ten miles from Chadford. He's here then."

"Who?"

His heart thudded in his chest, and Matt wanted to kill Cloughton and go get Willow. Digging out his phone from the lock draw of the security desk, he called one of his freelance investigators. He wasn't busy and agreed to check into it.

"How bad is it?" Matt finally asked, his thoughts ordered, and anger reined in.

"A good kicking, a few broken ribs. Whoever it was, took his phone and wallet."

"Shit." Matt opened and closed his fists. Josh had a secure phone, but there was everything on it including Willow's information.

"Radio one of the guys to watch Willow — my partner."

Matt rang the police, in particular, his favourite sergeant. "Wilkes."

"Oh god, it's you. I'm working, Matt."

"There's the possibility of an incident."

"What have you done?"

"Nothing, but one of my guys was attacked. The person might be after my partner."

"All right, give me the information."

Matt sent it over. Not knowing where Peter was filled him with dread. He went back to the floor, determined to get Willow safe and found her gone.

Willow watched Matt go and felt exposed and vulnerable, but with her friends, she was okay. Tabbie sat in Matt's empty seat, appearing to be queen. It was all polite and well-mannered. Matt had been gone twenty minutes, and Willow became agitated.

"Don't worry, he won't leave you long."

Willow sipped her drink. "Excuse me." She stood, straining to appear graceful, and crossed the bar to the toilets. The cool brightness in there woke her up as she took off her mask and took out the earplugs. Everything was bright and harsh. Finding an empty stall, she barely had a minute to manoeuvre before she realised her mistake.

How was she supposed to piss?

Her knickers were under the stockings, and she only managed to wrangle them down so far, but she accomplished it.

Putting herself right, however, took more work.

"Willow?"

She closed her eyes and swore silently. "Yes, Tabbie?"

"I thought I'd come and check on you, just in case."

"Is Matt back?"

"No. It's odd. He doesn't normally leave his sub alone in public."

Willow rolled her eyes as she tried to put her knickers straight. "Must be important."

"Hmm. Maybe. You didn't stick around for the demo."

"I wanted to see Darby work. It's beautiful what she does."

"Too squeamish for the fucking?"

"It's not my kink."

"Matt and I did it."

"Yes. He told me."

"I don't think he liked sharing. Not that I wanted to have sex with others, but men watching us seemed to piss him off."

"I suppose." Willow straightened her stockings so they were level.

"It tore us apart in the end."

Willow puffed out a breath and exited the stall, washed her hands and checked her makeup.

"It's so sweet you made an effort to join in. It's hard to fit into groups like this when it's not your thing, and you're like you are."

Willow reapplied her lippy and swept her hair to the side. "Like me?"

"Differently abled."

Willow clenched and made herself relax. "Okay. I'm disabled. It's nothing to be ashamed of, it's part of my identity. If that makes you uncomfortable, tough. Differently abled is some ableist bullshit. Please don't."

"But why use disabled?"

Willow blinked at her. "Respect my request or leave me alone."

She shrugged and tidied her own makeup. "You want to see?"

"What?" Willow was already walking away.

"Me and Matt?"

Willow went cold. "No thank you."

Tabbie pulled out her phone.

"You're not supposed to have a phone, and honestly, I don't want to see it. I don't mind that you guys did it, but I'd rather not see your demonstration."

"Oh no, this was private. I filmed it for us to enjoy. Has he fucked you up the arse yet? It's his favourite. Hanging me from the ceiling and doing breath-play is his second favourite. He's a brutal fuck. Tit slapping, and — now this is a killer — he's so good at the humiliation. Do you let him call you slut and whore? He loves words like that. I thought you could watch this and get some pointers."

A woman came in, and Tabbie turned back to the mirror. Willow felt lightheaded, but she wasn't going to back down. Not after everything she'd been through.

"Show me."

If Tabbie was surprised, she didn't show it. She tapped opened her phone, and Willow knew she wasn't bluffing.

She pressed play on the video. It was a few years old, Matt's hair was different, he looked leaner, and seeing him naked with Tabbie hurt more than she thought it would. The only thing she noticed was the collar that Tabbie wore.

Willow left, shoving her earplugs back in.

She didn't even look back at the table. Her hands trembled, and everything fell away; a truth she couldn't comprehend about the whole thing being a lie, but Willow was disorientated. She couldn't grasp it as the ground turned over and the world spun.

The heavy muffled bass reverberated in her as she went out and carefully made her slow way down the stairs down to the VIP dancefloor.

Pushing her way through, she spotted the man that went for a cigarette earlier.

"Help me."

With an arm around her shoulders, he took her to the foyer. In the cooler quiet, she pulled out the earplugs.

"Are you okay?"

"Do you know what happened to Matt?"

"He's been called away on a job."

"Has he left?"

"I don't know. I can find out."

Willow wasn't sure what to do. She didn't have her coat or her phone, but she didn't want to see him. She didn't want anything or anyone.

"No, it's okay, I'll be fine now. Thank you for your help."

"You should probably hang on."

"No. I think I've seen enough, thank you." Willow knew this was what Tabbie wanted. She should fight back, and what? Engage in a pathetic bitch fight? Tabbie wanted the drama and the attention. That Matt would choose the disabled mouse over her? Tabbie couldn't process it.

She hobbled out, forgetting what she was wearing, forgetting it was cold, and that it was a long fucking walk to the taxi rank, which she realised a hundred yards from the club. Should she go back?

"You're never alone."

There in the middle of Town Hill, surrounded by dozens of people, Willow had never been more afraid.

That voice had a power over her she couldn't explain. Once, she'd clung it. It gave her comfort and what she thought was love.

Now it made her nauseated and gave her a foul sense of unreality.

She hated Peter Cloughton, and there he was right in front of her.

"What are you doing here, didn't you get the message before?"

"Yeah, well." He offered a soft smile with a deep breath to denote his capriciousness that she loathed.

"Well, what?"

"He's not here, is he?"

Willow went cold. If she had to fight, she would. She had her cane. There was always a police presence in Town Hill, and the van wasn't that far away. Willow shivered in the frigid air, light rain dampening her skin.

"Look at you. You never dressed like that for me." The charm only lasted for a moment, and it fell away. She knew the thing that lay under it.

Willow was tired. Unimaginably, marrow-deep, soul and spirit tired.

Matt's hands on Tabbie. The latex gloves, Tabbie's collar. He'd not collared her. Peter Cloughton here in Chadford.

Her mind clicked slowly.

Why had Matt left her alone?

"Are you going to cry?" He stepped forward, and she stepped back.

Her footing fumbled, and she fell back and onto her arse. She shook her head, delayed panic and fear built.

"Hey." A woman stepped out from the queue for the club, as everyone watched. "Are you okay?"

"She's fine."

The woman ignored Peter and bent down. "Don't I know you from somewhere?" She smiled, eyes fixed on Willow.

She helped Willow to her feet and guided her to the wall under the portico. The bouncer in his heavy coat watched Peter, and Willow's gaze fixed on him too.

His face soured. "Do you think this is over?"

"I do," Willow said calmly.

"I don't."

"That's not up to you."

"We'll see, sweetheart. Time to go." He held his hand out.

"What's the matter with you? Do you think you still have any say or power? Do you think you still matter? You nearly killed me. I walk with a cane now because of you. I have eight pins in my leg because of you. I left my home because of you. You can fuck off and die in a hole of misery that you created, you lying, manipulative sack of dogshit." Willow shook.

There was a collective noise from the crowd.

"Think you're the big fuck now with witnesses?"

"Is that a threat?"

"Nah, you'd know if it was. Give your boyfriend a message for me; tell him to fuck off, and if he sends someone else to follow me, I'll fucking kill him. Him stalking me is fucked up. Oh, and by the way, Oliver says hello."

Peter stepped back as a figure came hurtling out of nowhere and tackled Peter Cloughton to the ground.

Before he managed to fight back, Matt wrestled him onto his front with his arms pinned behind him. Matt leant down and said something into his ear as five police officers descended.

One officer interceded and spoke to everyone. She seemed to know what was going on and Willow had enough.

"I want to get out of here."

The woman who'd helped her put her arm around Willow and helped her to the taxi rank.

"Thank you."

Willow cried all the way home.

By Stefanie Simpson

YOU CAN'T PATCH THIS BITCH

Willow lay on the bed unable to get undressed. Still in her makeup, and in need of a wee, she couldn't move. Sometimes, Willow shut down. It had been a coping mechanism for years. She didn't want to talk, she didn't want to look at anyone, she wanted to be silent and alone.

When she'd broken her leg, in the hospital, she didn't speak for nearly a week. It upset people, frustrated them. Willow didn't care.

She needed to exist and no more.

Humiliation was nothing new, but this was something else.

Without her phone, she didn't know what time it was, but at some point, she fell asleep.

Then she wasn't alone.

"What the fuck Willow?" Jane's angry face blurred, but Willow didn't answer.

She didn't move.

"Willow? Look, Matt was arrested. Matt. Do you know what this could do to him?"

Willow turned her face away.

Jane huffed. "Let's get you undressed."

Willow allowed herself to be handled. Matt was supposed to do this. Undress her. When Jane unlaced the back, all pretence left her. This was not meant for her. This life wasn't hers. Tabbie was right in many ways. She thought Willow was only playing dress up. It was true.

There was relief in it. Willow could love Matt. She could lose herself in his strength and seductive power. He filled the whatever it was she lacked.

Peter had imitated it. But Matt was real.

Her bullshit had him arrested. His ex was determined to sabotage Willow.

Jane helped her into pyjamas, her annoyance lessened by the time she left her, concern in its place.

Willow went back to sleep.

On Sunday afternoon, Darby came in. She wore bright blue fluffy pyjamas with her bonnet firmly keeping her hair in place.

"Brought you a coffee. Jane says you're not speaking. So I'm going to."

Willow took the cup. Darby slipped under the duvet with her and settled with her own mug.

"Something happened other than Peter. I can guess who."

Willow took a sip.

"You need space from the world right now, I see it. I think you're overwhelmed. Peter is manipulative. So is Tabbie."

It was hard to make any sound, but she did. "He collared her. She showed me."

"So?"

"He told me he didn't collar her because it means commitment for him. Tabbie showed me a video, it was supposed to embarrass me, seeing him fuck her. It was gross, but she was collared."

"Oh."

"She's right though. About me. All of it. How is he?"

"Livid."

"That's fair."

"He's been released without charge. Peter was arrested. It's a good job Alie is a solicitor."

"Peter only threatened me."

"He also beat the shit out of the guy Matt had following him."

Willow looked at Darby.

"You look like a panda."

Willow wiped under her eyes, making it worse. "Is he okay?"

"He will be. Matt's angry and confused, but mostly he's hurt."

"Do you know why I like Matt so much? The openness. No games, this is who I am and how I feel. It's so different from every lie I've ever been told. He lied to me. Now whether I want to or not, everything he'll say, I'll question. It took a huge leap on my part to trust anyone enough to try."

Willow blinked hard.

Jane joined them later, and the three lay in Willow's bed with snacks watching telly while Princess came and lay with them.

The door went at seven, and all three of them went still.

"I bet that's Matt," said Jane. "I guess I should get the key back off him."

"Shit." Willow got up to wash her face.

"Well, it's not like he'd let it go." Darby got up and collected their stuff.

Matt was casually standing in her room when Willow came out, a shiver went through her, and her throat closed.

"Hi." He was angry despite his casual air. Voice clipped and eyes focused.

Willow sat on the bed, crossing her legs, and gestured for him to join her. He perched at the foot and tossed down her phone on the bed.

"Your coat is downstairs."

"Thank you."

"So, what the fuck?"

She had to own it. Taking a steady breath to calm herself and swallowed. "How's your employee?"

Matt's jaw twitched. "Fine."

"Okay. You lied to me, and it's not a big lie, I don't think, but I thought you were different. Last night made me realise how ridiculous you and I are. You could have anyone. But me? I have to ask why that is."

Willow glanced up at Matt. His lips were nearly white, they were pressed together so hard. "What fucking lie?"

"You told me you never collared Tabbie."

"I didn't."

"She cornered me alone in the ladies and showed me a video on her phone of you two that she filmed. She wanted to show me that I didn't know the real you. To humiliate me. It's not the video, or what you were doing together. She was collared."

He went blank, blinked once and stood.

When he spoke, after a minute of tense quiet, his voice was quiet and measured. "For the record, I never put that thing on her. She always wore it of her own volition like a fucking fashion accessory. If I say I've not done something, I've not done it. You believed that I collared her? Believed I lied to you? I don't mean anything to you, do I? That you so casually believe I'm a liar and disrespectful is hurtful. What we've shared, the actions I've taken have demonstrated my affection for you. I think they speak for themselves.

"I was arrested trying to protect you, and you just fuck off. I wanted to help you, to give you everything, to love you. Nothing I could do would be enough, would it? The damage to you is too great." His eyes were bright as he shook his head. "But because my ex wore a collar, you assume I'm a liar. I think that says more about you than me. Well, excuse me, Willow, I have to go erase a sex tape of myself that I didn't know existed."

Willow felt like she'd been slapped. "I'm sorry."

Matt paused for a moment, and she wanted to take it all back and apologise, but she didn't have the words, she didn't know how. It was best he hated her and was the easiest way for him to let her go.

"Goodbye." Then he was gone.

Matt stood in Tabbie's flat with revulsion. He didn't hate many people and tried to be friends with his ex-partners, but she was outside of enough, as his mum would say.

She smirked. Fucking smirked.

"You can take that fucking look off your face."

"Oh come on, Matt, she's out of her depth."

"That's not up to you. My life has nothing to do with you because you're not in it. Show me the video."

"Why?"

"You taped it without my consent. You violated my trust and our boundaries. Have you uploaded to the internet?"

"No, of course not."

"Show me, now."

Her eyes flickered, and she picked up her phone. The clip was from two years ago, and the quality wasn't the best. Matt snatched her phone and deleted it. "Is it on your computer, on another phone?"

"Laptop." She pointed at it, and Matt went through it. Three more videos and a handful of photos. He scrubbed them.

"I'm going to say this once to you. Everyone will know about this, they need to be warned about your behaviour. You're not the first arsehole we've had, and they've always been dealt with the same. Not everyone will have a problem with you, but I do. I won't be quiet about it, or ashamed. I'm appalled at you. What did you think you were going to achieve?"

"I... her? Her, Matt. I don't understand it, you are not vanilla."

"That's not your business. And while I'm here, don't think I hold any lingering affection for you. You treated me like shit, and I gave you chances, the benefit of the doubt, tried to communicate with you, but you were flippant. At no point did you care about your impact on me, about the consequences of your actions. You think because this is what I am, it's who I am. I'm more than a dom. Nothing would compel me back to you."

Her mouth flapped before her angry tirade of self-pity started. Turning away, he wouldn't listen and left. Too angry to process everything then, and too hurt to feel it.

What was he going to do?

Willow looked at the computer screen and zoned out. Her hands shook, and she balled her fists.

"How are you holding up?" Suzy asked gently.

"Does everyone know?"

"Yes. Matt confronted her. Deleted the video. I hear that man's been charged with ABH."

"Good."

"Willow, talk to Matt."

"He said it all."

"So that's it?"

"I'm not sure what else to do."

"Apologise?"

Willow hovered over her phone when she got home. She'd thought about it all afternoon. The realisation sunk in. She'd lost him. Hitting her all at once. Willow sat on her bed. Matt was the best thing that ever happened to her.

She should let him go, had to, but guilt needled and ate at her. Suzy was right, so Willow texted him.

Matt, I'm sorry about everything, I was wrong, and that doesn't make it better, but I wanted to say it. I'd like to apologise in person.

Willow watched her phone all night but didn't get a reply. At least she'd tried.

A week. A long drawn out and tedious week. Willow mimicked her life. Got on with it. The longer she didn't speak to Matt, the worse it got. The reality of not being his settled, and with it, the knowledge that she loved him. His absence brought it sharp.

Willow had never been in love, not like with Peter. That wasn't love. Matt had found a way past her defences and set up shop.

Well, the shop was closed but very much there.

It hadn't been a wallop, but a slow incline to it. That she'd done this; ruin what was probably the only chance of real happiness that she'd ever have made it so much worse.

She went to work. She ate. She went through every action as if she were Willow but didn't feel like Willow. Not anymore.

Sitting down to dinner, the three women ate in silence, and Willow couldn't stand it.

"I know you're pissed with me," she ventured.

Darby and Jane looked at each other and then her.

"And I'm sorry if this is difficult. I've been thinking, maybe father was right. Maybe I should go back. I mean, Peter has been arrested, Oliver doesn't have any power over me. Father's alone. I don't want to make any of this awkward for anyone, so I'm giving it some thought."

"You're running away? Giving up on your independence because you fucked up?" Darby levelled a cool look at Willow.

"I've tried to apologise. I know I was wrong, but I'm not going to be that arsehole that pushes and pushes. I'm not like that."

"Take Matt out of the equation. Do you want to be back in Harringly?"

"No. I want to be where I'm wanted."

"You're wanted here."

"I don't think I am. That's my fault."

"It's also Tabbie's doing."

"If I'd paid attention more, realised how I..." Her voice trailed off, and she shook her head. She couldn't say it. Willow would have to contain it. Keep it small and tucked away. "I'm going to bed."

"Okay." Jane smiled with pity in her eyes.

Saturday was icy, and Willow sat by her window not reading the book in her hand and stared out into the pale and rimy garden.

She didn't hear the doorbell, she didn't hear or feel anything, just the gnawing ache in her body and heart.

Jane tapped her door. "Your father is here."

She blinked and stood, not quite believing her.

Rupert was sat at the kitchen table with Darby. She poured him a cup of tea and smiled up at Willow as she joined them.

Princess curled around his legs leaving a trail of hair as her mark, and then promptly sodded off.

"Hello Willow." Rising from the chair, he hugged her. Actually hugged her. When he let her go, holding her shoulders, his strained smile faded, and he frowned. "You don't look happy."

"I'm sorry father, I wasn't expecting you."

He gestured for her to sit, and Darby squeezed Willow's shoulder before leaving.

"I am happy to see you." She poured her own tea from the large pot, dropping it with her usual graceless thud on the wicker mat.

Rupert straightened it for her. "It's been difficult. I had a rather disturbing phone call from your gentleman friend."

Willow suppressed her snort. "Oh?"

"Hmm, he's very concerned about your wellbeing. That much was obvious from the moment you two stepped foot in the house. Anyway. I understand Peter made quite the scene."

"He did."

His brow creased, and he scratched his forehead as he always did when he was worried. "You were right."

"About?"

"The house. I've come to an arrangement that will please you."

"You're selling?"

"Yes. That's why I'm here, partly anyway." He smiled and took her hand. Hers was cold and his warm, still with that tremor. "I'm staying at that big, new, and completely ghastly hotel complex out of Chadford off the motorway, anyway, I'm here for a week, and I'll be looking at some houses that Anthony suggested I look at."

"Really? You're moving here?"

"Well, if I sell the estate, I'd rather not see it. Caroline is always hither and thither, and I'd rather not see her all that much. You're my only child. Time to be better."

Willow blinked rapidly and pulled her lips into her mouth. She swallowed the emotion in her throat. "Only if it's what you want."

He patted her hand and sipped his tea. "Do you want to know who I'm selling to?" There was a mischievous smirk to him.

"Who?"

"The Stillwell's. They offered, I said no, and the price kept going up. There was a whiff of selling, and they wanted it."

Willow sat back.

"Might as well take as much from them as possible. It'll serve them right. The amount of work that needs doing." Rupert shook his head. "Too desperate for status."

"What about the horses?"

"Ah, well. They're getting the stables as a running business, for all the good it will do them, but I want a place with land and stabling. Horses were always my thing. You can have your horse back. She's as patient as a saint for the young riders learning, she loves it. One place has the most potential. Other side of Kettly Wood, wherever that is, out of the city, and on the county border, but only half an hour from Chadford."

Willow didn't know what to say. This was the most they'd talked about important and yet inconsequential things ever. He was completely different.

"You're surprised."

"You could say that."

"It's taken me some time to understand, and with your mother gone I've reassessed many things. I've had a lot of time to think. You'll have your own room. I think the ground floor, and you can come and spend time with the horses."

"That sounds wonderful, dad." Willow couldn't stop the waver in her voice.

"There, there, child, it's all right. So how's your chap?"

"Not my chap anymore. I messed it up."

"I am surprised. I thought he was in love with you."

"Really? I'm not sure. I hurt him and can't fix it."

"Then I'm sorry." He squeezed her hand. "Your housemates are nice."

"They are, I'm very lucky." Willow warily eyed her father.

"I wondered if Caroline was gay."

Willow choked on her tea. Rupert patted her hand and pushed over a napkin.

"Turns out she's bisexual, well so Anthony says." He shrugged. "Anthony's boyfriend is very nice. I think they should get married, but people are very modern these days."

Willow's coughing fit turned into laughter, and once she started, she couldn't stop. Rupert got up and patted her back.

"Didn't you know? Dear me Willow, I thought you were openminded about these sorts of things." She laughed even harder, tears streaming down her face as she shook. With a final cough, she wiped the tears from her eyes.

"I'm glad you're going to be here. I'm thrilled, I am." Then her tears started in earnest, and Rupert held his child while she bawled her eyes out.

REDRESS

M att was having a shitty day, which was topped by the last shitty two weeks.

Having to be at Chadford Central police station, again, wasn't helping matters. Sitting composed and calm, he thought about Josh. He left hospital and vanished. Matt knew he had a cottage somewhere up north, but not where. When they first met, things were bad for him and was suffering and lost. Quietly stalking stalkers and violent men bent on destroying the lives of others gave him a steady purpose. Matt resisted the urge to fold his arms.

"Sorry to keep you waiting." The detective sergeant came in the casual interview room where Matt waited.

D.S. Shah sat adjacent and put her folder down next to her smoothly and deliberately. Matt instinctively relaxed. The last officer he spoke to asked him about his middle name being Shalita and gave him the 'what are you and is that dangerous' look but Shah was more reasonable.

"A complaint was made to us, about you."

Matt frowned and sat forward. "Cloughton."

"No. When it was made, I wasn't convinced. I know the work you do. I know the cases you've had involvement in. I worked in the domestic violence prevention programme. I remember you, Mr Denbridge. I remember the woman whose life you saved when her ex tried to abduct her."

Matt only watched, waiting for the but.

"I know about the work you do with ARC. I know Danni well. So, you see I was surprised at the allegations."

"May I ask, what and why I'm not under caution?"

"That you coerced a woman into a violent relationship. That you abused her as part of a club."

Matt's jaw pressed together, and it flexed. "I see." He hoped it wasn't Tabbie looking for revenge, because so help him, she'd regret it.

"We know about the club night, it's quite famous."

Matt went very still.

"The website, the adult shop. I'm surprised, but it's not a crime if no money changes hands for sex in private, and there's consent, and it's not of interest to us."

"Is this where I'm supposed to justify my actions?"

"No."

Tabbie wouldn't risk it, surely, she had too much to lose. Matt expelled a breath. It was Stillwell who made the complaint. "Oliver Stillwell."

"Why would you say his name, in particular?"

"This is about Willow. Peter Cloughton, the man who attacked my employee, had an arrangement with Stillwell to coerce Willow to stay in her family home and prevent her from leaving. It was about money and control. She came here, and we became friends, and then more, but now it's over. It was consensual and mutual, and Oliver is a hateful man."

D.S. Shah made some notes. "Okay. Thank you, Mr Denbridge."

His whole life might be upended by Stillwell. Matt's reputation and business at risk.

"Are you all right?"

"Stillwell wants to ruin me. You're going to pick apart my life. It'll bring me into question. Stillwell will win, and there's nothing I can do. Anything else?" Matt was weary beyond measure. All he wanted was to turn to Willow, but he swallowed that pain. Matt wondered if Tabbie had anything else hidden away and would she use it against him.

"No. We'll be in touch."

Matt went home after a long conversation with Meera asking her to take on a few things because he needed to get himself together. Then he called Jane.

"I'm sorry, what?"

Matt winced at her tone while he made himself a cup of tea.

"Tabbie could cause trouble if it gets out, it could kill the club. The police know me, and I think the DS was giving me a heads up. They know about Stillwell."

"All right. Leave it with me."

Matt took his tea and went to bed.

Willow was livid. Beyond actual anger. She could barely form words. She and Jane drove in silence to the police station.

As they parked, Willow tried to calm down. "The fucking cheek."

With that, they went inside, and Willow sat down with a surprised looking detective who spoke to Jane.

"I'm right here, you can talk to me."

Shah's mouth opened and closed. "Apologies, you're right."

Willow took a slow breath. "Right, I don't know what is going on, but I understand Matt has been accused of abusing me? Correct?" She didn't wait for Shah to answer, "Let me stop this in its tracks. He didn't. Matt is the kindest and best person I know. He singlehanded stepped up and kept Oliver and Peter away from me. Oliver had Peter push me down a huge set of stairs that broke my leg so that it had to be pinned. I nearly died.

"Oliver Stillwell is an evil, vile monster, and I'll tell you what, how the hell do I make it so he comes nowhere near me. How do I prevent that goblin ruining my life again?"

"If you want to make a formal complaint against Mr Stillwell, you can, you can make a formal statement."

"Check the financial records. Money changed hands between them. You can access my medical records. Matt has dates and times of them meeting."

"We'll speak to him."

"Whatever he's accused of, he did not do it. I love him."

"My understanding was you were no longer in a relationship."

"That's entirely my fault, and nothing to do with Matt."

Shah made notes.

Willow tried to call Matt, but he didn't answer her, and nothing she could do would take it back.

Matt slipped on his thick wool coat, watching the sleet come down outside, it was a dull grey afternoon.

Meera put the Christmas decorations up, and his eye caught the tacky plastic tree, and he puffed out a breath. He needed to get over this shit, but he couldn't let it go.

He knew what Willow had done. Standing up for him, and he was touched by it, though it made the ache worse. The thing about finding exactly who and what you want means it's that much harder to live when it's gone. Yet he was too angry and raw to face it. Matt wasn't sure what he was angry about anymore. He loved her and lost her. She thought he was a liar, and yes he was hurt by that, but was that it?

He tied his scarf around his neck and buttoned up. It was the Blackthorn Villa Christmas party and it was going to be quite the event. He hadn't seen anyone since Kink.

She'd be there.

Perhaps it was time to face her. Get it done with. Matt left the office to do his Christmas shopping. He was cold and grumpy, and despite the weather, the city centre was packed. The late-night shopping crowd fuelled by a brass band and Christmas market stalls made him feel worse. The cheer around him was starting to piss him off.

He turned out of the main wide and crowded street into an old arcade filled with boutique shops. He passed one, only to turn back and stand at the window. Having BDSM brought to the fore had some perks, and its assimilation into fashion was one. The one piece in front of him made him think of Willow.

He went in. Matt came out with several things for himself, but one for her. He paused, ready to turn around and take it back. But he couldn't make himself.

Willow had dinner with her father. The sale was in process, and he'd packed up and put into storage all the things he'd keep and shut the house up.

He'd put an offer in for the modest house he was keen on with the stabling. Hopefully, in the new year, he'd get the two horses he was keeping moved down and get settled.

The hope of a new future for them lessened his grief, and she was getting to know him. Out of all the bad, Willow was happy in that. It wasn't her hope, but it was enough.

What she didn't want right then was to see Matt. She'd hovered over his number, set to delete, but she couldn't do it. Nor his photos. She looked at them far too much. Sometimes she was pathetic and morose, and other times, numb.

An absence of self — it was the same feeling of other she had in her body, detached from reality — but Willow continued to get on with it. It's what people did.

Willow put on some lipstick and a belted jumper dress that fell off one shoulder. Throwing her hair to one side, she went downstairs to catch the start of the party and planned to vanish after a few hours.

Finding a spot in the living room, Willow relaxed back with a mulled wine. The tree looked pretty covered with fairy lights.

She hoped she'd be as unobtrusive as possible, sipping wine in the corner, but her heart beat too hard, and her hands shook. She hoped he wouldn't turn up, yet that part of her hoped he would, just to see him.

People filtered in, the same familiar faces, looking sideways at her. Their hesitation was understandable.

Suzy came and sat with her for a bit until distracted by Nathan. Willow stared at nothing and didn't notice the room empty.

Feeling something was off, she looked about, and Matt stood in the doorway. She swallowed loudly. He didn't smirk or get that needy look that she loved; there was nothing. Her chest contracted, and she was sure her heart was in her knees.

Matt came in and shut the door, and then leant on it. "How are you?"

Willow remembered to breathe again and tried to find her voice, only she couldn't think of anything to say.

"Fair enough." Matt frowned.

"I didn't expect you to..." Willow stuttered and ran out of breath. Her mouth pinched.

"Thank you for talking to the police. It avoided a rather lengthy investigation that could have ruined my career and reputation."

Her head bobbed as she forced her throat to open. "You're welcome. It was the least I could do. You deserve so much better than the bullshit in my life ruining yours."

"And how is all that bullshit?"

"Shitty. I ended up making a formal complaint against Oliver and Peter. It won't get anywhere, but at least he's off your back."

He frowned. "What does that mean for you?"

"Very long and detailed interviews about my relationship with both. My father's been interviewed. A few friends, Kim, Aunt Caroline, Anthony, doctors, everyone, and they'll want to talk to you about me too. Sorry, but I don't think they're investigating your life, which is better."

"Shit."

"Yes, it's not been fun."

"I'm so sorry."

"Don't be, sometimes we get what's coming. Sometimes we don't. I wonder what I ever did to deserve it. Mostly," Willow found her voice, "Mostly, I'm sorry for what I did to you. How I treated you was wrong, and I deeply regret taking my personal insecurities out on you." Willow wanted to tell him that she loved him, but her actions — the shit she lived — meant letting him go. A cruel thing and bitter thing. "But thank you for being you and being in my life. It meant a lot to me, and I hope you find the happiness you deserve one day."

Matt didn't speak, and all the hair on her arms went up on end.

"Okay, well. I've had a long day." She stood up, and leant on her cane, unwilling to look at him.

He still stood in front of the door and didn't look like he wanted to move, his eyes intent on her.

"Please let me pass."

"No."

Willow shut her eyes, holding back her tears.

"We could start again."

That flutter in her heart at being near him, and the sound of hope was too seductive, but Willow resisted her want. "You deserve better."

"No." His hard voice shook her.

She glanced up as a few tears escaped. "Really? You want to put up with my bullshit? You think the crap with Peter and Oliver is over?"

He looked choked, and it surprised Willow. "You've risked a lot to protect my reputation. Did you know that would happen?"

"Yes, well, I figured as much. That doesn't matter, it was the right thing to do. It could have been so much worse for us both."

"I'm very grateful."

Willow wiped her eyes. "Don't be, it was the least I owed you. I'm moving out."

Matt's back stiffened. "You're going back to your father?"

"He's moving to Chadford. Just waiting for the sale to go through."

"I miss you." Matt slumped back, his hands behind him.

"I miss you too, but I should go."

Matt waited a few beats and widened his eyes, but she saw the tears in them. Any anger between them, gone, and she wanted to hold him. Cling to him.

In a quick move, he pushed off the door and opened it.

"Goodbye, Matt."

He didn't say a word and let her go.

RETURN

Willow sobbed her heart out like a baby. She'd barely cried that hard when her mother died. The remembered feel of Matt holding her, of giving so much strength, made it worse. She was bereft.

Bad Christmas music thumped up through the floor, and Jane appeared.

"What happened?"

Willow hiccupped-sobbed. "I love him and let him go. Always thought that line was some fucking bullshit. Turns out it means something."

"Why?"

"This, what's happening. I'm sparing him."

"You're being a dick. He's gutted."

"It's done." With that, Willow started crying afresh, looking at Jane's crooked wire and tinsel halo.

"Did Matt ever hear you sing?"

"No."

"Shame. He'd love that."

"Jane, it's too late. Sometimes you have to do the right thing. This is the right thing, and it hurts, but it's for the best."

"Fucking hell," Jane pointed at Willow, "suck it up."

Willow gawped.

"I mean it Willow, I'm not having it."

"You can't just make us be together."

"Yes I bloody-well can. Now fix your face." Jane pointed at the dressing table.

"I'm tired."

Jane was immovable. Willow made an impolite noise and tidied her makeup.

"You're a bit blotchy, but you'll do."

Downstairs, Jane gave her a vodka and cola, and in the kitchen, Matt leant against the side chatting with Mel.

He briefly looked at her but turned away.

Jane shouted over to Mel. "Did you bring your guitar?" The kitchen collective groaned.

Willow looked about and realised that Tabbie wasn't present. Interesting. She stared at Matt. He stared back. Ushered onto a chair, she gave Jane a pointed look.

"You getting Willow to sing?" Darby asked.

"Wait, wait, I don't sing pop music."

"You have to know some Christmas songs."

"I'm not a pop music person. I just... don't know any."

"Heathen," Darby said.

"Yes."

"How do you not know any songs?"

"I know many pieces of music, thank you, they happen to be classical pieces. They take up memory space, I remember most of them, but not all."

"Willow is incredible." Jane nudged her.

"I'm nowhere near as good as I was."

"Sing something."

Willow drummed her fingers on the table and cleared her throat. She took deep breaths, stretching her lungs and hummed along to the easy tune Mel played, warming up.

"Okay, I have it." It was one she often sang quietly and to herself.

Purcell was always her favourite, and she hummed the opening bars of 'If Love's a Sweet Passion, then Why Does It Torment', closing her eyes. When she sang it, she sang to Matt, a clichéd move, she knew, but she didn't care. For all she'd done, she loved him. He cared for her, and she'd never know anyone like him in her life again.

Willow could hold onto him in that song. Whenever she'd hear it, she'd think of Matt. When she opened her eyes and looked at him, his face was exquisite, reflecting how she felt. The sweetest pain.

When she finished singing, everyone clapped. Her voice no longer held the crystal tone it once did, but she kept her pitch and breath, and she was proud of that.

Matt didn't move for a moment but finally turned away, and the magic was broken, and Willow was alone again.

"That was beautiful, let's do something Christmassy."

"All right..." She burst into 'Deck the Halls' and everyone followed with the fa-la-la-la-la, in a loud, raucous tone, making them all laugh.

They sang it through twice, and her voice gave.

"That's it, I'm out. I'm done in."

As much as they attempted to cajole her, she refused as the group got drunker by the minute.

"Leave her be." Matt cried, and he was met with a chorus of boos.

Willow laughed, catching his eye. He gave her a solemn look but dipped his head with a smile. Swallowing it back, she got up and wobbled down the hall calling goodnight.

As she turned to the stairs, Matt still watched her, and Willow wanted him to come to her. She wanted to take it all back and tell him she loved him.

She didn't.

Matt had never heard anything so perfect. She hummed now and again, or quietly sang under her breath, and he never quite heard her, but that full clear sound tinged with fragility almost broke him.

The need to gather her up, to bend her to his will nearly mastered him. He was not that man. He was not. Respecting her wishes and letting her go was going to kill him.

He poured himself a large drink and pulled a face at the taste.

"You don't normally drink." Mel's tone was light, but he knew the concern underneath.

"I know it's a bad idea, but sometimes..."

"You love her, don't you?"

Matt put the glass down. "I have to go."

After a few hasty goodbyes, he grabbed his coat and left. He'd planned to get a taxi but walked instead. It was a hell of a walk, but he didn't care.

Bitter wind and frost underfoot made it a hard walk, and he relished it. Sparing him from the complications of her life was bullshit, and she knew it. The cold air was sharp in his lungs, and he walked faster, hands in his pockets, collar turned up.

The reality that it was over felt cold and sharp as the evening took what was left of his breath. He should have told her he loved her. Being open always worked better. At nearly eleven, he couldn't go back, so he carried on home.

When he finally reached his flat, it was after midnight, and he crawled under the covers, shivering and closed his eyes, hoping for the sleep he knew wouldn't come.

Willow napped as her father drove them to Anthony's. He and his partner had invited them to stay for Christmas, along with Aunt Caroline.

When she woke, the quiet volume of the radio and the sound of Bach made Willow smile.

"You're very quiet."

"I was asleep."

"You know what I mean."

Willow didn't answer. She'd ordered all her shopping and left a pile of gifts. One of which was for Matt. For all the ache, she couldn't not.

He always wore belts; wide, thick, quality belts. She bought him a handcrafted black leather belt with a small silver BDSM triskele on the buckle.

She almost didn't leave it for him but made herself just before she left.

Jane almost swayed her, almost convinced her to pursue him, yet she hesitated, reluctant to.

It was a nice Christmas, and Jaz — Anthony's partner — was fun, and entirely sweet and generous with wine.

The day after boxing day, they drove back. She'd heard nothing from Matt. Jane promised to give him the gift on Christmas eve, and Willow knew then it was over. It was understandable, she'd said no.

She deleted his number. The finality of it left her sick.

"I worry about you." Her father said when they got back to Chadford, the house empty, other than for Princess mewing in the hallway.

"I'm okay, and not long until a new start."

"Hmm. You should talk to that chap of yours."

"He's not my chap."

Rupert levelled a dry look at his child and kissed her forehead before leaving her to rest. A small box sat on her bed.

She toed her boots off and looked at it. Willow had an early Christmas with Jane and Darby the day before she left, so the gift was odd.

Picking up the box, perfectly tied with red ribbon, she found no label, and opening it, nestled in satin was a silver chain with two linked circles.

Her heart squeezed. Engraved on one circle was 'Love. Obedience. Devotion.' And on the other 'Love. Control. Domination.'

It wasn't a collar, but delicate and pretty. The engraving beautiful. Was he offering her another chance? Had to be. A note was attached with the words: *Your choice.*

She clutched it tight. It sat short on her neck at the right length. Her smile faded in the mirror, and she rifled through a drawer and found the business card he gave her and put his number back in her phone.

She took a picture and sent it to him with a heart.

Words were too much.

Willow undressed and crawled into bed, she clutched her necklace and closed her eyes, and remembered every moment with Matt.

When he looked at the belt, Matt hadn't spotted it straight away, but he laughed. He wasn't vain with his clothes, and though his style was modest and classic, he liked subtle touches of his identity to be there.

It was perfect.

He thought of the necklace. Odd how they both bought the other a gift.

He'd dropped off the box to Jane, and she gave him a knowing look. "Don't," was all he said and went to work.

Christmas was always busy. A full rota, he'd taken on several temporary staff, and there were gigs all through until New Year. The photo gave him hope, but he wouldn't push hard, and as much as he tried to focus on work, he couldn't.

It was the first New Year Kink at Passion House gig, and it was going to be intense. After the shit show in November, he considered working it, but he needed to show his face, and not hide in the control room.

He smiled as he got ready for Kink, thinking of the moment he saw her in that little black dress, knowing what was under it. He never got to see.

Maybe he would, maybe. He smiled to himself and looked at the photo of her wearing the necklace. Her full lips, her smooth skin, and hint of cleavage was all too perfect.

Willow would come to him. Hopefully. Her ridiculous noble gesture didn't cut it. She did what she did because she loved him. That was good enough for him.

Although he was — currently — without Willow, he was easier knowing that Tabbie wouldn't be at Kink performing. He puffed out a breath as he finished dressing, finding the belt a perfect fit.

Ousted from their community, she'd well and truly fucked up. Filip still saw her, but publicly, he'd distanced himself.

Taking a red wristband from the security desk, he didn't bother with a mask. It was a point of pride to show his face. In the busy gallery bar, it was business as usual, and he spoke to everyone he knew.

It was bound to be busy, considering the show they were putting on.

He moved through, nodding to his guys, all on duty, and moved through to the next room where the stage was.

He saw Jane milling about, her usual serious face in place with her mic set, and he smiled, seeing Darby and Alie laughing nearby with Kim, so it seemed that was going well, and then... Matt stopped in his tracks, and Willow looked straight at him.

He'd not expected her to be there, never hoped for it.

There she was, perfect and the sexiest fucking person he'd ever seen. She wore his necklace, body squeezed into that black dress again.

He wanted to go to her and sweep her up. Instead, he spoke to the people he knew and meandered over. She didn't take her eyes off him, and when he finally reached the group, he didn't speak to her until he'd spoken to everyone else. She looked at him, her lips twitched, but she looked down, demure and perfect.

Being so close to her again made the hair on his neck stand up. It was unspoken, the need and comprehension of what was between them.

"Willow."

She swallowed and put her hand to the chain.

"It looks beautiful."

"It is, thank you, I love it."

"Good. And thank you, the belt is perfect."

She beamed and glanced up. "I'm so pleased you like it."

Before he said anything else, the lights flashed, and the audience settled in. Matt stood next to Willow — who was perched on a stool — as the burlesque show got underway. There was a group performance before a BB Lady came on.

He'd heard of them; a London based stage show of eclectic female empowered performers and the woman on stage was famous.

"Do you know who she is?" he leant down and whispered to Willow.

"No, who?"

"E.E. Queen."

"No." All her demure sensibility gone.

Matt didn't think about it but put his arm around her and kissed her forehead, remembering himself, he stood back. "Apologies."

"Are you sorry?"

"This is what you wanted." They both knew it was a question more than a statement.

The music was too loud, the room too crowded.

"I thought it was the right thing. Fuck the right thing."

Matt let his breath go, buying himself a moment so he didn't fuck her right there up the wall.

"Fuck the right thing. How are you?"

"Honestly, tired. Bone tired. But Jane wouldn't let it go and made me come out, considering how much I," she stopped and sobered.

"Rose."

Her lips parted, and he had enough. After a second glancing about, he helped her off the stool, and he led her out. Screw New Year, it was shit anyway.

"I'd like to leave right now. No more messing about doing the noble thing. We belong together," he turned her, bringing her flush to him, and cupped her face. "We said it, do you remember? We said that you were mine, and I was yours. That's real to me."

Fighting tears, she nodded.

"Good."

He led her down the cool corridor, and down the service lift. Her arm wound around his, and it involuntarily flexed, and he almost moaned when she rested her head there. Matt drove them the short distance to his flat.

"Willow, how do you feel?"

"About which bit?"

"Having sex right now?" he asked casually as they went up to his floor.

"Yes, please. I had my coil fitted. It was uncomfortable. I had a complete exam with a clear bill of health. It hurt at first, but I feel a little better. It's helped I think. But the first week was horrible."

"When did you get it?"

"Just after Kink."

"It's been shit for you."

"Yes. We should talk about it."

"Do you need to now?"

"No. Right now, I need you to make me yours again."

Matt opened the front door and shut firmly behind them. "I'm always yours. And you are mine." He emphasised 'are', and Willow's cheeks went pink.

"Ready?"

"Yes."

By Stefanie Simpson

MAY I HAVE SOME MORE

Willow didn't think it would be this easy, but the look he gave her in the hallway made her wonder.

"Rules. I'm going to say things to you. I'm going to do things to you. Because Willow, you've been a bad, bad girl."

Willow bit the inside of her cheek.

"You need to be punished." Matt stepped close, not touching her, and spoke near to her mouth so his lips brushed hers, "you need to be taught who your master is. Who is it? Hmm?"

"You, Sir."

"Yes, that's right. Look at me."

Willow made herself look into his eyes, too close, too intimate as she held her breath.

"But if it's too much, you know the rules. You say red. This is why it's called play. We play this out. Consensually."

"Yes, Sir." Willow made her voice even and firm, and oh god, she wanted him so much.

"Open your mouth."

She did, still looking at him. Running a finger over her lips, he smudged her red lipstick and smirked.

"Come."

He walked backwards and led her into the bedroom. Matt pecked her lips and hovered, brushing his jaw on hers. She missed the smell of him, the feel of his stubble, everything.

"Matt, red, sorry, before we start."

"What's wrong?"

"Nothing, but hold me for a moment."

He grinned and nestled her close, her arms went around his waist, and she buried her face in his chest, her favourite place to be.

He held her head and kissed it. "I missed you," he whispered.

"I missed you too."

"Willow, I need to fuck you."

With those soft, needy words, she fell into a puddle of lust.

Matt lay her on the bed and kneeling next to her, his expression hardened as he looked her over. "You've been a bad girl."

"I'm sorry."

"Are you? Bad girls need to be punished. They need to learn."

"Yes, Sir."

Matt yanked her dress up to her waist. He bit his lips and made a noise. "I've fantasised about this underwear, and you denied me seeing it. Cruel and wicked girl," he murmured as he traced his finger along her gartered thigh.

She would have laughed at his words but for the firm touch of his hand stole her breath.

"Stay."

She did but watched him open the trunk when he dragged it out. He set a roll of shiny black tape next to her and snapped on a pair of gloves.

The image of him with Tabbie flitted into her mind, but she swallowed as she watched him move about.

Matt unbuttoned his shirt and slowly slipped it off, his eyes never leaving hers as he picked up the tape. "This is bondage tape. I've thought about using it on you. In detail. Hands. It won't stick to you, just to itself, okay?"

She lifted her hands out, and he kissed her palm before cutting off a length of tape. He bound it firmly around her wrists.

Matt turned her over with her arms above her head and ran his hands up and down her thighs before squeezing her bottom.

"You can choose. My hand or a paddle."

Paddle?

"Quickly or I choose for you."

"Paddle." Willow buried her face in the duvet.

Matt shifted behind her and moved her to a kneel, but she kept her face buried. Matt slipped down her pretty knickers to her stocking tops and stretched the cami up so it exposed her bottom completely.

He kissed her cheek with a nip before resting the paddle on her skin.

"The beauty of a paddle is that this side is firmer." He tapped the leather side on her skin. "And this one is softer." He ran the suede side across her. "It also has a more even strike than a hand. Shall I show you the difference?"

"Please, Sir."

Matt slapped her bottom hard, and she yelped. The sting warming as he struck the other cheek with the paddle.

"Thank you, Sir."

He made a noise of pleasure as he struck her bottom firmly, alternating cheeks. Willow cried out at each one, her body jolting, the heat of the sting, and the pain made her wet and swear.

"You hurt me Willow," Matt said in a pause.

"I know, I'm sorry." She couldn't help the tears that came, but it wasn't the pain, it was his tone.

Each slap, sharp and hot, made her pulse hammer. She winced and tried to move as her skin became sore.

Matt held her in place.

"Who are you?"

Blinking out of her haze, she moaned and shouted out as he struck her lower onto her thighs. "Your Rose. Yours." She wriggled under his hold, but he held her firmly in place with his free hand holding her hip.

"Stop, please, I'm sorry, I'm so sorry, Matt I love you, and I'm sorry." Willow cried, she couldn't help it, she didn't want to, but couldn't help it.

Matt moved off her in a second and unbound her wrists.

"Willow, come on, Rose, I've got you."

He slid her up and over his body and held her, rocking her gently as she cried.

"I'm sorry, I'm sorry." She wriggled out of his hold. Her skin stinging yet perfect. Chemicals rushed her blood, and she was almost delirious.

He smoothed her hair and wiped her face. His eyes brimmed with tears, and she ached.

"I do love you. Everything you've done for me, everything about who you are. Everything that makes you Matt, I love. I don't deserve it. I've taken and been selfish."

Matt shook his head, and a tear spilt over. She kissed it away. That he didn't say anything made her stomach turn.

"I understand if you don't, I-"

Matt kissed her, squeezing her to him, every touch was need, and she took it. He rested his forehead on hers as they panted.

"Look at me." His rough voice commanded her. "I love you too. With all my heart."

They stared at each other, and a slow smile crept up Willow's face. "Show me."

Matt's wicked smile made hers bigger, and he ran his finger along the delicate necklace. "I love that you're wearing it."

Willow lowered her eyes, and Matt kissed her again.

"Matt, Sir."

"Hmm?"

"I like being restrained."

"Do you?"

"I do. It's like," Willow tilted her head, "I can give in. Let go."

"What about if I rendered you completely immobile because..." he made a noise.

"Yes please."

Matt wasted no time; pulling her dress off, he went still. He took her hair, looping it around his fist, and kissed down her neck to the swell of her breasts. His firm grip all over her body made her squirm.

He hummed into her breast, lightly nipping it. "I'm torn, I want to fuck you with this on, and I want to fuck you trussed up."

"You can do both? It's restricting." Barely able to open her legs with her knickers at her thighs under her stockings, she showed him.

Matt set Willow down over the side of the bed, throwing a pillow for her knees first, and set her there. He bound her wrists up to her elbows, and the tape was smooth against her. Willow felt cared for, safe and encased.

Matt did the same to her ankles over her stockings and up to her knees.

Willow swallowed and ground against the bed.

"No."

She moaned, her bottom sticking out over the edge, she was vulnerable and exposed, and so turned on, she wanted him to hurry up.

With her legs bound together, it was going to be more intense, and her wetness seeped from her. Matt knelt behind and licked her as he squeezed her sensitive bottom and spread her cheeks apart.

Matt ate her pussy from the back until her hips started moving on their own and he pulled back.

"No," he grunted.

"Please."

He struck her bottom a few times, and she begged for more.

"I've never had sex without a condom."

"Really?"

"I want to. With you."

"Please, Sir, yes please."

Keeping her cheeks firmly apart, he pushed into her. He was large, and she called out at it. He went all the way, pressing into her. It was incredible.

He moved slowly at first, letting her adjust, and with a hard, deep thrust that made her raise her head, he took her. She knew he was unable to hold back any longer.

His fingers bit into her flesh as he rode her, she jolted hard making her clit rub on the corner of the bed.

She trembled and came and gave into the painful intensity. Her tight binding, the sweat under it, the rough feel of lace rubbing her as Matt fucked her; all of it was so good.

As it ebbed, she wanted more and begged Matt to come. He laughed and stilled. He let her hips go and slapped her bottom.

"Oh, I'm not quite done with you."

He withdrew, and she moaned. He re-entered her in a hard thrust, she supposed he took off his trousers, but instead there was the cool wet of lube on her skin between her cheeks.

"Oh fuck." That's why he had the gloves on.

He pressed a finger, keeping her cheeks apart with one hand.

"Matt."

"Yes, my perfect Rose?"

"Are you going to fuck my arse?"

"Not today, you're not quite ready. It can take some getting used to." He moved his hips in time with his finger, and Willow clenched.

He swapped his finger for his thumb, pressing it all the way in. She never thought thumbs as particularly large, but it felt huge.

It hurt and stung, but good. Willow arched her back at the feel, almost freeing her boobs, making them rub on the top edge of her cups, and she knew she'd come again.

Matt grunted and fucked her, his hips relentless.

"Willow." The rough of his voice was enough, and she came again, straining against it and jaw clenching.

Matt went wild losing all rhythm in her. She felt the twitch of him as he stilled and came, moving slowly, enjoying his long orgasm. He'd pressed her hard into the bed, and she bit the duvet, muffling her scream.

Matt withdrew slowly and rested a moment against her, littering her shoulder with kisses. Willow grinned in a haze as he unwound the tape and rolled it up, setting it to the side.

He undressed her with delicate care and fetched a flannel, the warm dampness on her skin as he wiped her face and cleaned her up was the sweetest thing. He smiled and kissed her softly, and his voice brought her back to the moment.

"Beautiful Rose."

She giggled.

"I really love you." He shook his head.

"I really love you." She reached for his hand, her body already limp and spent.

"Bathroom?"

"Please."

He carried her, and set her down, waiting outside for her.

Willow couldn't believe her luck, and covering her face, smothered her joy.

WHAT'S NORMAL ANYWAY?

Rupert scowled as he ferreted through a plastic box and found two cups. Willow watched him. They were surrounded by boxes and bags, but neither made a move to deal with any of it.

"You know," he said, plugging the kettle in, "I don't think you should move in here."

Willow was surprised, it's what he'd wanted, and they planned it. He'd settle in first, and then Willow would move in.

"You don't want me here?"

"It's not that." Rupert moved around putting things away as the water heated. "Your mother told me how everything was going to go. She decided what went where, including me. I haven't made decisions about my life for thirty years." He frowned and took his glasses off.

The day darkened, rain pattering the windows, and Willow shivered.

"I'm starting to find my feet. You and your chap should be together. I like him very much. You shouldn't be coddled out here with me, you should be with your friends. You'll be more isolated here, and I don't want that for you. I do want you to come and see me, maybe stay now and again. Your mare is here after all. Go and live your life, Willow."

She blinked, unable to speak, and he patted her shoulder as he set down her cup. The front door opened, and Matt appeared.

His gaze went straight to Willow, and he kissed her forehead. "Right, we've come to settle you in."

"No, no, there's no need."

"We can't let you do all this on your own."

Jane and Darby with Kim and Althea followed Matt in. "Hello, Mr Morris." Jane waved, and they made a start.

Furniture was placed, books and records unpacked. Matt put together Rupert's bed. Within a few hours, the bulk of organising was done. Rupert mostly organised the kitchen as he wanted it while handing out instructions.

They had a curry in the kitchen before Matt gathered Willow up and took her to his. She hugged her father before they all left, and he smoothed her hair back from her face. He smiled at her, and though the light tremor of age lingered, years of taut stress and tension were gone. Warmth sat in his eyes.

Not that the past was forgotten, but she could let it go, and found middle ground with him. She wanted that relationship, she wanted to know if it was possible.

Willow closed her eyes on the drive, the wipers cut along the windscreen as rain hammered down.

"I had a phone call today."

Willow blinked and yawned. "Oh?"

"It was the CPS. They're not prosecuting Stillwell."

"Well, we weren't expecting them to." It was no less disappointing. She stared out the window.

"I've been thinking about what next."

"What next?"

"Us." He pulled into the underground car park and the cool air as they got out woke her up.

Matt took her hand and smiled as they went up.

"Well?"

He let them in and pressed her against the wall, letting her coat drop to the floor. "How do you feel about moving in? With me."

"Have to been talking to dad?"

"He spoke to me. Asked me if I was serious about you. I said yes. He said I should stop wasting time then."

Willow shook her head with a smile. "He's a different man."

Matt hoisted Willow up and took her to bed. "You've not given me an answer. Do you want to think about it?" A small flicker of doubt flickered through his eyes.

Willow held tighter to his neck and kissed him hard.

With a hum, he set her on her feet, hands feeling her, returning her affection. He'd worn her out in the first few weeks to being together. The more they fucked, the more they wanted it.

Matt pulled at her clothes but halted. He licked his lips and closed his eyes, and Willow smirked at his fight for control.

"How do you feel?"

"I'm moderately tired with middling pain."

"I have a gift for you." He stepped away. From the chest of drawers, he took out a gift box, and Willow sat, slipping off her boots as he handed it to her.

"That's so kind."

His eyes glimmered. Willow cleared her throat as she opened it. A thick black leather collar. Blood rushed between her legs, and she slowly looked up, making herself deferent. Her heart pounded when she met his face.

"Yes, Sir."

"Do you like it? If you're not ready, or want to think about it, I'll understand."

"It's perfect." They talked about it, and he'd fished about her tastes.

His chest swelled, and he took it from her, buckling it as she held her hair up. Stiff and restricting, she shuddered in excitement.

"Willow, I love you, and you're mine." He ran his finger along the collar and tugged on the ring.

"Yes Sir, thank you." Willow kept her eyes lowered and relaxed.

"Look at me, my Rose."

She stretched her head up to look at him.

"I want you."

"Yes please, Sir."

Undoing his belt, he slid it off and unbuttoned his shirt. "Open your legs for me."

Willow obeyed. He undressed completely, and she relished his body, every perfect and imperfect bit of it. Kneeling before her, he carefully undressed her, they didn't speak with the sound of their breathing and their hearts loud in her ears. His fingers trembled until she was nude before him.

Gathering her hair, he kissed her in greedy want, leaving her panting and wet when he let go. He clipped a lead to her, wrapping it around his hand.

He pulled it, so she stood. Matt urged her onto the low upholstered chair he'd recently bought.

"Stay."

She lowered her eyes. Matt secured her wrists and ankles in thick leather cuffs and attached a set of straps under the chair, leaving her pinned with her legs spread wide and arm at each side. She couldn't move.

"That's what you bought this for."

He smirked and picked up the lead. She arched with the tug and moaned. He opened his mouth but frowned.

"What's wrong?"

Matt took a breath. "You are the most beautiful person. Like this, you are a dream."

Willow struggled, knowing he loved it, and his cock twitched in front of her.

"I want to spend my life with you. I want us to live together, make whatever family we can, in whatever way makes us happy, as long as we're together."

"Yes. I want that. So much." Tears filled her eyes, and he brushed them away before sliding her hips forward to the edge of the seat.

Kneeling, he eased into her. With his hands roving over her body, teasing her nipples, and the sensitive bits he liked to so much.

He squeezed her hips, jolted into her, building her need, but withdrew and stood. Willow opened her mouth, knowing he wanted to take her mouth.

"Such a good girl for me, aren't you?" With a raised brow and a smirk, he straddled her, holding the chair back with one hand and the lead with the other.

He pushed into her mouth. They'd practised a lot, and she was adept at taking more. Pinned and unable to struggle, she focused on her breath, letting her and his taste fill her senses.

Training was fun. Willow saw she gave him everything until his control fell apart, and he was hers as much as she was his. She'd smile if not for the cock in her mouth. His grip tightened, pulling her to him. She gagged, and he let her go, pinching her chin, he claimed her mouth in a hard kiss. She panted when he let her go in a half-smile.

Caressing his way down her body, he nipped and kissed along her skin, sucking her nipples, nipping the soft flesh of her hips and thighs until she squirmed.

Clenching his jaw with his eyes on her pussy, he massaged the inside of her thighs.

"Please."

"What do you want?"

"To come."

"Hmm." He bunched his lips and tilted his head. He reached behind him to the trunk, and she shook her head.

"No, please, no."

This game was the best game. She loved it. He tugged her collar until she smirked, and he laughed.

"That's how you want to play?"

"Yes please, Sir."

"Then let's see about your mouth."

He grabbed the gag he favoured most. He attached it, widening her mouth, and saliva pooled and fell as she tried to swallow. Matt with lust-heavy eyes, ran two fingers over her lips, drawing her lead closer, and she moaned, fighting the urge to grind. The wet heat between her legs overwhelming her.

"Fuck."

She levelled a knowing look at him.

"For that..."

He rolled a condom on, grabbing the lube. It was time. She'd had plugs in her arse nearly every time, gradually increasing in size. He also grabbed a dildo.

Matt adjusted her legs, so her thighs were strapped to her calves, and spread wide as he re-strapped them to the chair.

"There." He eased the dildo into her pussy.

She arched into it. With a generous amount of lube, he pressed his thumb into her arse, working the lube into her. It hurt, as it always did at first, and he waited for her to relax.

When she nodded, he pulled out his thumb and eased his cock in. She screwed her face up as much as she could, crying out. The sharp stretch, even as he went slowly, made her sweat. He held her bound legs, crying out himself, and pushed deeper. Her eyes went wide, but she focused on her breathing, her discomfort exquisite.

She blinked at the stinging tears, and he waited, so patient with her, so loving with the pain he gave her.

He flushed, and mouth twitched up to the side, and she knew he was close, moving slowly, head arched back, and his powerful body shaking as he held back. He took a breath and levelled a look at her. "With me?"

His rough voice made her clench as she blinked.

"Fuck." His eyes widened. His cock pressed against the dildo, the space tight and hot.

Thrusting in shallow and gentle moves, he held the lead again, his face set, muscles tensing as he went, Willow narrowed her eyes, letting her body go, and taking it. The ache, the sharpness, and overwhelming sensation balanced against the man inside her, who cared and loved her.

Unable to move, she let the squirmy pleasure take over, her nerves tightened, and ecstasy rose from her feet up, radiating out of her in waves, until unable to hold back she came in a shuddering clench. Abandoned to reason or thought, she screamed. No pride or dignity, no constraint bound her, the physical discomfort became pleasure. Her vision mottled and eyes rolled back. Every muscle clenched as Matt lost himself in her.

"Willow." His breathy voice brought her to him, the sole focus of her want, he shut his eyes, almost pained, and he bucked, abs tensed, lurching forward with a roar.

He thrust a few times, head rolling back before setting a drugged focus on her. He eased out, unclipping the gag and Willow stretched her lips. He unbound her, and her limp, tingling body was his.

He cleaned up, and lifted her, taking her to the bathroom. He helped clean her up, holding her.

"Are you okay?" he asked, still catching his breath, forehead against her.

"Yes, my love." Her lips brushed his.

Later, curled up with a cup of tea and a snack, she lay her head on his chest and relished the hard thump of his heart.

Matt stroked her hair. "I never thought I'd be this happy."

"Neither did I."

"Promise me you'll keep me in check."

She propped her head up. "What do you mean?"

"If I push you too far."

"The danger is I'll get lost with you." She kissed his pec. "I guess if you get too big for your boots, I'll remind you about the time you had a wank in my shower."

He burst out laughing, and she relished the rumble in his chest before she settled back into the thump there.

Her favourite sound. She fell asleep to it at night, and as long as it beat, it was hers.

Matt kissed the top of her head. Her limbs ached, body was weak, and she closed her eyes, safe and happy and whole.

The End

No Cure Required

Coming Up:

Neon Hearts

Anthology of Short Stories

Other works:

Demon Beauty

40847364R00155

Printed in Poland
by Amazon Fulfillment
Poland Sp. z o.o., Wrocław